JOHN RAIT

RAZORBILL

EVERY NEVER AFTER

LESLEY LIVINGSTON is a writer and actress living in Toronto. She has a master's degree in English from the University of Toronto, where she specialized in Arthurian literature and Shakespeare. She is the author of an award-winning urban fantasy trilogy for teens that includes the novels *Wondrous Strange* (winner of the Canadian Library Association Young Adult Book Award and Ontario Library Association White Pine Honour Book), *Darklight,* and *Tempestuous.* Visit Lesley online at www.lesleylivingston.com.

# EVERY NEVER AFTER
Lesley Livingston

razor
bill

RAZORBILL
an imprint of Penguin Canada

Published by the Penguin Group
Penguin Group (Canada), 90 Eglinton Avenue East, Suite 700, Toronto, Ontario, Canada
M4P 2Y3

Penguin Group (USA) Inc., 375 Hudson Street, New York, New York 10014, U.S.A.
Penguin Books Ltd, 80 Strand, London WC2R 0RL, England
Penguin Ireland, 25 St Stephen's Green, Dublin 2, Ireland
(a division of Penguin Books Ltd)
Penguin Group (Australia), 707 Collins Street, Melbourne, Victoria 3008, Australia
(a division of Pearson Australia Group Pty Ltd)
Penguin Books India Pvt Ltd, 11 Community Centre, Panchsheel Park,
New Delhi – 110 017, India
Penguin Group (NZ), 67 Apollo Drive, Rosedale, Auckland 0632, New Zealand
(a division of Pearson New Zealand Ltd)
Penguin Books (South Africa) (Pty) Ltd, 24 Sturdee Avenue, Rosebank,
Johannesburg 2196, South Africa

Penguin Books Ltd, Registered Offices: 80 Strand, London WC2R 0RL, England

First published 2013

1 2 3 4 5 6 7 8 9 10 (WEB)

Manufactured in Canada.

Library and Archives Canada Cataloguing in Publication

Livingston, Lesley
Every never after / Lesley Livingston.

ISBN 978-0-14-318208-5

I. Title.

PS8623.I925E94 2013          jC813'.6          C2012-905174-8

Visit the Penguin Canada website at www.penguin.ca

Special and corporate bulk purchase rates available;
please see www.penguin.ca/corporatesales or call 1-800-810-3104, ext. 2477

ALWAYS LEARNING                                                    **PEARSON**

For Cecmonster

# AD 61

S tuart Morholt awoke in a bag.

All things being equal, he probably should have considered that a stroke of extreme good luck. Change one single letter in that word, and he could have just as easily woken up in a *bog*. Or not at all. Neither of those possibilities was even remotely a stretch at that moment. As it was, the bag was bad enough. It was made of coarse, scratchy fibres that irritated the skin of his cheek where his face rubbed against it. It bounced roughly up and down in a motion sickness–inducing fashion and it reeked, overwhelmingly, of fish.

Morholt loathed fish.

He loathed a pair of smarty-pants teenage girls named Clarinet Reid and Allie McAllister even more than he loathed fish. And that hatred was particularly relevant to his present situation because those ridiculous, meddling girls were the two reasons he now found himself bound for destinations unknown and—damn all the luck—probably about to be horribly killed.

When, finally, Morholt was unceremoniously dumped out of his bag, he almost immediately wanted to crawl right back into it. The woman standing before him was wearing what looked like a cloak made entirely of raven feathers. Her cheeks and forehead were covered in the bright blue swirls of Celtic war paint. She reached down a hand and grabbed his face. Morholt's body jerked spasmodically as if he'd been mildly electrocuted.

"Ow! Bloody hell." He grimaced through clenched teeth.

The woman staggered back a foot, her black gaze sharpening as if she'd understood him. Just as *he* understood *her* when she said, in her own, ancient language, "Blood ... indeed. You have power. I can smell it on you."

"I'm surprised you people can smell anything beyond your own rank emissions," Morholt muttered, forgetting for an instant that the woman could understand him.

But she ignored the insult and leaned in, eyes closed. "You smell of blood," she said, breathing deeply through flared nostrils. "And fire ..."

"And fish. Don't forget fish."

"You also smell of gold." Her hand shot out again and she gripped him hard around the throat with fingers like iron bands. "Stolen gold."

"Oh!" Morholt gasped at the pain. "That. Yes ... well—"

"*My* gold."

Stuart Morholt silently cursed the names of Clarinet Reid and Allie McAllister. He figured he ought to get in just one more juicy mental profanity, because he was definitely about to be horribly killed. But the truly infuriating thing was this: not only was he about to die—at the hands of a pack of worthless barbarians at the arse end of a backwater world, no less—but he was about to die *thousands* of years before he was even born.

EXACTLY 1,951 YEARS LATER, Clarinet Reid picked up her cell phone and dialed a number. Cringing at the jarring double ring of the British telephone system and half-hoping there'd be no answer, she wondered frantically how, exactly, she was going to explain the situation. By the time her aunt Maggie picked up, she'd decided she might as well just come right out and say it.

"Mags?" she said.

"What's wrong?" came the immediate response.

"Nothing!" Clare yelped. Then took a deep breath.

*I thought we decided to "just come right out and say it"?* muttered her brain in disgust. *Shut up,* Clare muttered silently back. Except she knew her brain was right. Maggie had to know. Clare would need her help, eventually. And sooner or later her aunt would find out everything anyway. Especially if she turned on BBC news to find out that all of Somerset County had been sucked into a time portal.

"Okay," she continued. "Maybe not ... *nothing.* More like everything. More like Al is trapped in the past, Milo thinks there's a dangerous spatio-temporal vortex opening up all over Glastonbury Tor, Boudicca's blood curse is alive and well, and a very angry goddess is about to unleash a screaming horde of demon warrior women out of a hell pit right in the middle of Somerset." She stopped and took a breath.

"I see," Maggie said dryly. "So just a typical day for you then, is it?"

Clare winced. "Pretty much. And here's the kicker: I still don't know how he managed it, but ... somehow? Stuart Morholt is behind the whole thing."

There was a long pause on the other end of the line. Then Maggie said, "Tell me everything. Start at the beginning."

But Clare just shook her head, tears of frustration that Maggie couldn't see welling in her eyes, and said, "I don't have *time.*"

"Blog Buddies."

Clarinet Reid turned from where she stood at the open door of the van she'd just tossed her luggage into and gazed in bemusement at the slender, raven-haired seventeen-year-old girl standing next to her. "Excuse me?"

"That should be the name of our blog," Allie McAllister said, without pausing to look up from whatever it was she was reading off the screen of the tablet computer she held in her hands. "Y'know. Like 'Bog Bodies' but—"

"You're punning," Clare silenced her with a stern tone. "I thought we agreed. No punning."

"Technically, it's not a pun." Al glanced up, deadpan. "It's word-play."

"No."

"But—"

"We're not going anywhere near a bog this time!" Clare shook her head adamantly. "At least, I don't think we are ..." She turned and called over her shoulder to her aunt, who appeared at the door to her townhouse, lugging duffle bags out to the van. "Yo, Mags. Are there bogs where we're going?"

Maggie shrugged the canvas straps off her shoulders and dumped the bags on the sidewalk at Clare's sneakered feet. "No, dear," she said. "Not anymore. They drained all the marshes and turned it into arable farmland a very long time ago. And anyway, I would have thought you'd already had enough bog-hopping to last a lifetime. Or, perhaps, several."

"Yeah." Clare smiled at Maggie and saw the shadow of concern hiding behind her aunt's serene gaze. She supposed she could hardly blame her; it had been there since the beginning of summer, when Clare had, quite inadvertently, messed about a bit with the space–time continuum by flinging herself to and fro between the present and the far-distant past in a series of events the girls now cryptically referred to in casual conversation as the "Time Monkey Shenanigans."

Clare had found herself smack in the middle of a war: an epic historical struggle between the mighty Roman Empire and a particularly feisty Celtic warrior queen named Boudicca, who'd been bound and determined to withstand that might using any means necessary, which meant calling on some fairly dark forces of magic. Blood magic. And somehow, somewhere along the line, it was *Clare's* blood that got tangled up in the whole mystical mess.

Hence Maggie's concern.

But now that almost an entire month of summer vacation had gone by without so much as a spatio-temporal blip, Maggie had at least loosened up enough to let the girls head out on an excursion of sorts. She'd even been the one to arrange it.

"Okaaay," Al mused, oblivious to Clare's contemplative silence. "How about … Skel-e-mail Remains?"

Clare turned and raised an eyebrow. "What?"

"Y'know. Like 'skel-e-tal remains,'" she said, overemphasizing her pronunciation to make the point. "It's more of a stretch, but …"

"Seriously. *What?*"

"Skeletal remains." Al blinked at Clare. "Bones."

"I *know* what skeletal remains are, Al." Clare sighed indulgently and regarded her best friend since grade three. "I'm just not exactly sure why you're talking about them."

"Because we might actually find some!" Al enthused gruesomely. She tucked the tablet under her arm and mimed holding a skull up in front of her face, à la Hamlet. *"Alas, poor Yorick,"* she intoned dramatically, *"I knew him, Horatio ..."*

"Put that down!" Clare waved away the imaginary noggin. "You don't know where it's been."

Al pretended to toss the skull over her shoulder and grinned. After a moment, Clare grinned, too. The girls were, in fact, almost giddy with excitement. And *that* was something Clare would never in a million years (give or take) have thought herself capable of in similar circumstances only a few weeks earlier. They were going on an archaeological dig. With digging and everything. In *dirt*.

To be fair, the dig was a smallish affair, and they'd only be there for a couple of weeks, tops. The excavation was situated at the foot of the ancient hill of Glastonbury Tor, a British Heritage site as well as the locale for an annual music festival. For years, Glastonbury had discreetly hosted small, unobtrusive digs that were really more along the lines of training exercises for university students with the help of a handful of enthusiastic volunteers like Clare and Al and usually not really all that exciting.

Recently, in one of the fields around the Tor, a farmer had made a discovery of small-to-midish significance to the historical community—by deftly running his tractor over a fragment of what turned out to be an ancient Roman slave chain dated to sometime around the first or second century. The find was deemed interesting enough to round up the usual bunch of pasty-white library lurkers and send them out into the field to soak up some vitamin D. And it proved the perfect opportunity for Clare to test her new-found academic resolve, born out of her time-trippy experiences with the past. And Al was more than willing to tag along.

Maggie had wrangled the gig for the two girls using her museum and university connections, and she'd made a promise, as part of the bargain, that Clare and Al would do a video blog while they were there—a kind of running commentary that the museum would feature as a learning tool in its education outreach program. They hadn't settled on a name for it yet.

Clare had been partial to "Clare and Al's Magical Mystery Tor," but then she'd always had a fondness for the Beatles. Al was leery only because she thought using the words "magical" and "mystery" might be tempting fate.

"Oh. And 'Blog Buddies' *doesn't*?" Clare said suddenly.

"Doesn't what?" Al straightened up from doing a gear check.

Clare realized she'd been continuing a conversation silently in her head and had only just now spoken out loud. "Nothing ..." she murmured.

Al's suggested riff on "Bog Bodies" was cute. But Clare had vivid, haunting memories of the Iceni warriors Boudicca had sacrificed—ritually killed and thrown into a bog—and even more vivid memories of those same warriors coming back to life, busting out of their glass museum cases where they'd been on grim display, all zombie-like and gross and wanting to kill her.

Al had an occasionally morbid sense of humour.

Well, whatever they decided to call it, their video commentary was their ticket to the dig, so Clare wasn't going to be too precious about it. In truth, she'd been a little surprised that Maggie had even agreed to a Glastonbury expedition—let alone arranged for it to happen. It was, after all, the one place where Clare's aunt had experienced her own particularly unsettling paranormal experience back in the eighties. But, not wanting Maggie to rethink her decision, Clare tried, wherever possible, to avoid bringing the matter up.

She remembered distinctly the first time her aunt—the esteemed, analytical, and not really given to flights of unnecessary fancy Dr. Magda Wallace—had ever talked about it. After Clare had confessed to her own bouts of paranormal activity, Maggie had talked about her experience at Glastonbury Tor. The place was supposed to be some sort of magical, mystical hub of arcane energies. A gateway to the Otherworld or a portal to hell. Or even—and this both amused and unsettled Clare—a vortex into the past. But, as Maggie had more recently explained, it was the only dig she could wrangle volunteer positions for that summer and so

Clare had enthusiastically agreed, cancelling out trepidation with excitement. Mostly.

In some ways, she wished the dig had been anywhere *but* Glastonbury Tor. Even somewhere in Norfolk, Boudicca's erstwhile stomping ground. At least she was familiar with the history around those parts. *Intimately* familiar.

*Yeah ... okay. Maybe digging around Good Queen Bonkers's old 'hood isn't such a great idea.*

Let sleeping Druids lie. Surely Boudicca's blood curse wasn't as far-reaching as Somerset. And anyway, Clare and Al had done some reading in preparation for their little excursion and there was virtually no written record of anything catastrophic happening in the immediate Glastonbury area around the turn of the first millennium, which was whenabouts Clare had wound up during the Shenanigans.

They were good to go.

The only thing that put any kind of damper whatsoever on the whole affair was the thought that Clare would be away from Milo for a few weeks. Milo McAllister was Al's cousin. He was also Clare's ... she didn't quite know what. But definitely something. Something tall and blond and over-the-top genius-level smart in a way that somehow didn't make Clare feel dumb. Also, he'd wilfully allowed himself to be temporarily possessed by the spirit of a Druid warrior prince named Connal—all so that he could help Clare find Queen Boudicca's hidden tomb, right a couple of historical wrongs, and save Clare from being trapped forever in the past. And he'd done it in a manner that made it look like it was all in a day's work. Even when Connal's spirit refused to be evicted and they'd had to fight tooth and nail to keep Milo's own soul from being trapped and lost forever.

He'd done it for Clare.

Since that time, Clare and Milo had been almost as inseparable as Milo and Connal had been—although in a much less scary-mystical-rampaging-Druid sort of way. Clare had initially worried that Milo's feelings for her might have been a byproduct of all the

excitement—even though Al had repeatedly, eye-rollingly assured
her that he'd been pretty much crushing on her since he was a kid.
But Milo seemed just as keen on spending as much time together
as possible as she did. And so the thought of being separated from
him for any length of time, so near the end of her summer tenure
in Britain and just when they were on the verge of becoming ...
whatever it was they were on the verge of becoming, was a down-
side. Even though Clare totally understood that Milo had a job to
do in London and he couldn't just up and go gallivanting around
the Somerset countryside on a whim.

Milo made maps. Complex digital maps for the Ordnance
Survey, Britain's venerable mapmaking agency. Somehow, Milo
made mapmaking sexy. Clare couldn't quite wrap her head around
that fact, but as a girl who'd recently discovered that she could
mystically travel into the distant past, Clare was willing to just roll
with things. Most things. It was easier that way.

As she crouched down over the duffle bags to double-check
she'd packed everything, Clare came across the heavy canvas work
gloves her aunt had given her. They were purple and red tartan,
a tiny bird with a red rhinestone eye embroidered on each cuff. A
raven. Maggie had special-ordered a custom-made pair for each of
the girls. Al's were exactly the same as Clare's—except her tartan
was black and grey—and she was just as thrilled that Maggie had
been so thoughtful. Well, in Al's case it might have been thoughtful. In Clare's, it was *care*ful. The merest touch of Clare's bare skin
against an ancient artifact could—and had, on more than one
occasion—send her tumbling through a vortex to wind up back in
the past. Hence the gloves. And long-sleeved T-shirts.

Maggie had witnessed firsthand her niece's astonishing abilities
and knew the potentially dire consequences. But, Clare suspected,
Maggie also recognized that, for the first time in Clare's young
life, Clare was actually engaged—mentally, emotionally, one hundred percent invested in learning about something that didn't
come from a magazine or a mall—and Maggie, in her understated
British sort of way, couldn't be more thrilled. She really seemed to

want this for Clare. And Clare sure as hell wanted it for herself. She *wanted* to do this. And she *could* do this.

Couldn't she?

"What are you frowning about?" Al asked, misinterpreting why Clare was suddenly staring so intently at her gloves. "Glastonbury is a tourist town. There's bound to be at least one nail salon in a five-mile radius of the place."

"Well then *I'll* be fine," Clare snorted and stuffed the gloves back into her gear bag, ignoring the chill that had just crawled up her spine. "But unless you packed your own supply of Midnight Matrix Glossy Black, *your* manicure is toast, pal."

Al's standard mode of couture fell on the techno-ninja side of things—sleek and dark-hued. It had started out in middle school as a kind of silent rebellion against her mother's arty-farty, elegant-whacko bohemian style. Clare was never sure if the rebellion had worked or not—it was so hard to tell what, if anything, Mrs. McAllister noticed about her daughter—but Al had grown into the look and now wore it like a second skin over her own alabaster-pale flesh. And the dark hair made her grey eyes look super cool and mysterious. Clare had been briefly amused, wondering how Al was going to cope with the required sunhat. But then Al had surprised her by doffing a beat-up, black suede cowboy hat with a hand-rolled brim and silver-coin band that somehow not only worked with her streamlined black attire but actually complemented it.

It was a striking contrast to Clare's own low-slung jeans, butterfly-sparkly long-sleeved T-shirt, and Aussie outback–style chapeau perched atop the long, loose waves of her tawny locks, but then she and Al had always seemed like the odd couple—when in reality they were closer than sisters. It was one of the reasons why Clare was, impending Milo-lessness notwithstanding, really glad Maggie had set up the dig gig. She'd had twinges of unease where Al was concerned, simply because Milo was so much a part of the picture now, and—as much as she knew Al adored her cousin—Clare didn't want her to feel any third-wheeliness. Their friendship was way too important to risk that. Clare and Al were like each other's shadow. They knew each other's thoughts. They spoke the same language—

"We're off to Glastonbury!" Al suddenly exclaimed, heaving her gear bag into the van. *"Hic iacet Arturus rex quondam rexque futurus!"*

*Okay ... maybe scratch that last one.*

"Al? Do I have to Heimlich you?" Clare asked.

"No. Why?"

"You kinda sounded like you were choking there."

"Very funny." Al sniffed in mock hurt. "For your information and enlightenment, that was Latin for—"

"'Here lies Arthur, The Once and Future King,'" Clare said airily.

Al gaped at her.

"Oh c'mon. Who *doesn't* know Latin?"

Clare had a tough time keeping a straight face for the few seconds her best and brainiest friend puzzled. But then Al blinked and snorted in amusement.

"You totally hacked my tablet password."

"I *totally* hacked your password." Clare nodded, grinning. "And spent a few quality minutes speed-reading all the pages you faved about Glastonbury Tor—supposed resting place of King Arthur, possible interdimensional doorway, gateway to the netherworld, and general all-around hippie magnet."

"Cheater."

*"Ingenious* cheater."

"Ingenious ..." Al muttered. "Right. Okay. How'd you guess—"

"You bought yourself that thing as a reward for surviving the Time Monkey Shenanigans." Clare shrugged. "'Monkey' was the second word I tried. Right after 'time.'"

"Ugh. That obvious? I am the worst techno-sidekick ever."

*"Best,"* Clare contradicted her. "I'm the only person in the world who would have figured that out. And anyway, remember how

you boosted Morholt's Bentley with, like, chewing gum and a paper clip?"

"More like with Bluetooth-enabled code decrypters and Milo's cyber connections, but okay." Al grinned. "I'll cop to the amazingness of that feat. Do you remember how pissed he was for what we did to his precious luxury sedan?"

"Oh yeah. I think he vowed catastrophic revenge, didn't he?"

"Pretty much." Al shook her head. "Probably a good thing Stu's stuck somewhere two thousand years in the past. He's gonna have a tough time making our lives miserable from way back then."

"Yeah ... I think you're probably right."

But Clare frowned at the thought and felt a twinge of guilt. She hadn't *meant* to let go of Boudicca's torc during that last, inadvertent time-shimmer—with Morholt hanging on to it for dear greedy life—thereby stranding him with no way to get back to his own time. She felt bad for having let it happen. Then again, it was really Morholt's own fault. He'd been trying to steal the torc. Again. *And* he'd bitten her. That was why she'd let go of the damned thing. Really. She hadn't wanted to leave him stuck in the past—no matter how much of a poseur, super-villain-wannabe, self-serving jerk-ass he was. Still, she couldn't help feeling she could have hung on just a little longer.

"Right then ..." Maggie reappeared suddenly, stepping briskly through the front door of the townhouse and locking it behind her. "That's the last of the gear, is it? Let's get on the road, shall we? All those pot shards aren't just going to lie around waiting for you to find them!"

The girls exchanged a glance.

"Well. I mean, yes," Maggie conceded, "I rather suppose they are. Still."

"It's okay, Mags." Clare grinned and piled into the back of the van, followed closely by Al. "We get it. Tally-ho. Time's a-wastin' and adventure waits for no girl."

2

Allie was awoken by a sudden, bone-shaking jolt.

"Whoops!" Maggie yelped a bit as the van bounced on its suspension. "To the devil with these potholes!"

Startled to full conciousness, Allie sat up and glanced around, bleary-eyed and discombobulated by the bright sunshine that poured in through the windows of the van. She'd been dreaming of darkness. A blood-red moon. And ... fire. And voices. Beside her, Clare was doing exactly the same thing. Well, dreaming, anyway. Allie didn't have the faintest idea what about. She shook off her own unease at the fleeing dream sensations and poked Clare in the arm.

Clare snorted and rolled one eye open.

"You're kinda drooling a little," Allie pointed out. Then she yawned and stretched and said, "Are we there yet?"

"What are you, six?" Clare grinned and ran the edge of her sleeve around the corner of her mouth. "Of course we're not there yet. We've only been on the road for—"

"Here we are!" Maggie announced, pulling off onto a side road. "Um."

"You were saying?" Allie asked Clare.

"I guess I was out longer than I thought."

"Me too, pal," Allie nodded. "Guess time passes briskly in weirdo dreamland."

Clare glanced at her sideways. "You had a weirdo dream?"

The way she said it made Allie glance back. "Yeah. You?"

"Yeah ..."

"What was yours?"

Clare hesitated for a moment and then started to say something, but Maggie was already slowing the van and turning into a parking area bustling with people.

"Well, it's not Bath, exactly," Clare's aunt said, referring to the town with the magnificent Roman ruins not too far to the north of where they were. "But it's a good place to get your feet wet!"

Allie snorted in amusement at the wordplay, but Clare just groaned.

"Tell you later," Clare said, brushing the dream chat aside.

Allie didn't press her on it. She had a feeling she knew the general subject matter of Clare's dreams anyway—fifty percent Milo, fifty percent ancient Britain. And when Clare sighed a little wistfully, Allie figured there must have been at least a little Milo in there somewhere. She knew Clare was trying not to miss him already and she grinned a bit to herself, knowing something—for once—that Clare didn't, and feeling a little smug about it.

AT THE DIG SITE'S DESIGNATED STAGING AREA, their van was approached by a barrel-chested man with—Clare had a hard time not staring—an honest-to-god handlebar moustache. It was iron-grey and bushy and had been waxed into curly points that stuck out an inch on either side. He also wore a pith helmet, a Nehru jacket, jodhpurs, and riding boots, with a bright red scarf tied up high on his neck. The dude looked like a safari guide or a lion-tamer. Or someone's Halloween-party idea of what an archaeologist in the field should look like.

Maggie sighed audibly as the man walked toward them from the field beyond, her hands white-knuckled on the steering wheel for the briefest of moments.

"Wow," Clare said, "that's quite the sartorial statement."

"Be polite now," Maggie muttered out of the side of her mouth. "That's Dr. Nicholas Ashbourne. I've known him since I was a student at Cambridge. And *yes* he dresses like he thinks he's the reincarnation of bloody Howard Carter, but he's also top in his field, and responsible for this entire dig. The Glastonbury Initiative is his brainchild. That means he is, in effect, your boss for the next several weeks."

*Bloody Howard Who now?* Clare was about to ask, but Al had already insta-Wikipediaed. She held out her tablet to Clare, who scanned the article and its accompanying grainy black-and-white photos.

*Ah,* she thought, so *bloody Howard was the guy who discovered King Tut's Tomb. And bloody Nicky Ashbourne thinks he's a bloody fashion plate to be bloody emulated.*

She giggled silently to herself as she mentally employed the Britishisms. Clare got a distinct kick out of the idiosyncrasies of Maggie's Queen's English, especially when her aunt was annoyed—when everything became "bloody this" and "bloody that." Then it suddenly occurred to Clare that perhaps she was fixating a bit unhealthily on the use of the word "bloody." Insofar as she herself had once been the victim of a blood curse, she should probably stop doing that.

*And speaking of curses ...*

"Wait a second," she said warily, handing back the tablet. "Wasn't there a curse or something to do with that whole Tut thing?"

Al shrugged. "It's been largely debunked."

Clare was unconvinced. "'Largely,'" she said dryly.

"What are you worried about?" Al gestured out the window, drawing Clare's attention back to the scenery that rolled away to the horizon in lush emerald waves. "This isn't exactly Egypt."

"Maybe not." Clare shrugged. "And yet I remain wary of tombs. And curses." She grinned sardonically. "Bloody hell, I can't think why ..."

Maggie reached back and patted Clare's knee. "Don't swear, dear. And Alice is right. There are no tombs here. No bodies. Despite its reputation for spookiness—and despite what I've told you about what happened here all those years ago—I don't think you have anything to worry about. In all the years Nicky's grad students have been poking about in the fields around Glastonbury, they've never found so much as a toe bone. It's definitely no tomb. Alas, it's no treasure trove either. This is strictly a training exercise and, for the most part, you girls will be working in what amounts to a midden pit."

"A what now?" Clare asked.

"A refuse dump."

"Gross."

"A very old refuse dump. Nothing fresh, nothing squashy, worry not."

"And we'll be digging what there?"

"Realistically?" Maggie raised an eyebrow. "Mostly pot shards."

"Oh. Yippee." Clare circled one finger in the air. "My very favourite."

"Trust me. You'll be the toast of the dig if you manage to uncover something as grand as a pitted coin."

"I *love* how action-packed you make this sound."

"Don't say I didn't warn you, duck." Maggie grinned a bit evilly. "The pursuit of the past is abundantly tedious in the main, shot through with brief flashes of glorious boredom and steeped in the thrill of repetitive dullness."

Clare grinned back. "You're not talking me out of this."

"Is that what I was doing?" Maggie said mildly.

Clare leaned over the seatback and gave her aunt a peck on the cheek. "Yes. Now stop worrying. I have the gloves."

"And she has me," Al chimed in. "I won't let anything happen to her. Don't worry, Perfesser. I'll keep an eye on Shimmer Girl."

Clare sputtered a bit. "You don't have to!" she protested. "I will *not* touch anything. I'm *not* gonna shimmer. I promise. I—"

At that moment Dr. Ashbourne reached the van and tapped enthusiastically on the driver's side window with one calloused knuckle. Maggie rolled down the glass.

"Nicky!" she greeted Walrus Face with a bright, only slightly brittle smile. "So lovely to see you."

"Ah, Maggie, old chum," Nicky rumbled through his 'stache. He ducked his pith-helmeted head into the darkened confines of the van and peered about, squinting at the girls' faces under the brims of their hats. "Marvellous, marvellous. I see you've brought us a delightful duo of trowel monkeys!"

"Trowel monkeys?" Clare mouthed to Al, whose expression of arid disapproval was so hilarious it almost made Clare laugh in the renowned archaeologist's fuzz-bedecked face.

"I did indeed," Maggie said. "They're all yours. And no need to be gentle with them on my account."

"Marvellous!" Nicky enthused.

The girls would fairly quickly discover that this was Nicholas Ashbourne's favourite saying. He could infuse it with all sorts of different meanings: everything from "Oh, you found a coin! Marvellous!" to "Oh, it's raining. Marvellous ..."

Clare thought briefly about another archaeologist, Dr. Ceciley Jenkins, who at that very moment was lying in a bed in a psych ward back in London (after having wilfully courted possession by the enraged spirit of Boudicca, the Iceni warrior queen), and wondered if being an eccentric—or even an out-and-out loon—was some kind of prerequisite for becoming an archaeologist. Doctors Jenkins and Ashbourne made Maggie look positively sane in comparison, and yet, growing up, Clare had always thought of her aunt as definitely on the nutty side of the party-snacks table. She wondered if she herself would wind up in that same bowl one day.

*I hope I'm a cashew.*

And with that thought, she'd already pretty much proved her own hypothesis. Oh well, nuts or not, it was Bloody Nicky's show now. Maggie was headed back to London later that evening and on the morrow—at a no-doubt obscenely early hour—Clare and Al would be put to work in the trenches. Literally. But for the rest of the day, they had a free pass to play tourist and go exploring.

"First stop ..." Clare said as they left Maggie and Ashbourne chatting awkwardly by the van, "... the Magical Mystery Tor!" And then she broke into a fairly decent rendition of the Beatles tune as, together, she and Al headed off toward the hill.

THE TOR WAS A LONG, wedge-shaped hump of land that rose out of a sea of rolling green fields to loom over the surrounding countryside like some kind of monstrous sentinel. From the top of the hill, the view was spectacular. To the north, on a good day, you could see clear across the Somerset Levels—the rich farmland that had been reclaimed from swamps and wetlands—and on to the Bristol Channel and South Wales. It was amazing, and climbing to the top, Clare could easily imagine what it must have been like back in the days of the Celtic tribes, where it would have been almost entirely surrounded by lakes and marshes except for a few tracts of higher ground.

A series of ridges, like shallow terraces, wound around the sides of the hill in an ascending spiral that led, like a labyrinthine path, to the top where a single stone tower—all that remained of a medieval church called St. Michael's—pointed up into the air like a stone finger. For some reason the Tor reminded Clare of Bartlow Hills, the final resting place of Boudicca and the culminating site of Clare's aforementioned time-travel adventures. Glastonbury had the same kind of feeling, only amplified. Even on that bright, sunny afternoon, it still seemed as if the hill lay like a slumbering dragon, shrouded in mystery, forbidding. Or foreboding.

*Probably both,* Clare thought, a little hazy on the distinction.

As she and Al reached the top of the great hill, Clare had to admit that, even though she was totally winded and sweaty and probably flushed and blotchy from the climb, Glastonbury Tor was a pretty incredible place. And it was made all the more incredible by the sudden, totally unexpected sight of Milo McAllister, who stood at the edge of the summit plateau, a pair of sunglasses pushed up on his forehead, scanning the lay of the land.

Clare immediately forgot all about her sweaty, blotchy exhaustion. Even from a distance, his long, lean build and the way the sunshine lit the dark gold of his hair made him look like some kind of Greek—or was that *Geek*—god, feet apart, one hand shading his brow ...

*What on earth is he doing here?*

"Surprise!" Al said with a chuckle. "Maggie swiped him from the Ordnance Survey to develop a virtual dig-site learning-tool app for the museum in conjunction with our blog. It was Milo's idea, but we thought you'd probably be okay with it."

Clare, hearing herself make a giddy, astonished noise that in no way resembled actual speech, turned to see Al regarding her with a sly grin on her face. Clare turned back to look at Milo, who hadn't seen them yet. And dang, it probably should have been illegal, the way those jeans fit him ...

"Dude." Al elbowed Clare in the side. "You're starting to drool a bit."

"I am not!" She wiped the corner of one sleeve over her mouth just to make sure. "*Gawd.* The way you talk you'd think I had some sort of excess saliva issue."

Al just grinned and said, "I think you left your dribble bib in the van."

Clare rolled her eyes. At least, she tried to. But her gaze just sort of drifted back to Milo. "You knew about this and didn't tell me?"

"Yup. Hence—surprise!"

"Traitor ..."

Al laughed and shook her head, waving Clare away in Milo's direction. "Go on! He's not going to stand there posing winsomely for you all day, y'know."

"I'm a mess. I'm blotchy."

"You look fine. You're pleasantly pink."

"Sweaty."

"Glowing. Now *go*." Al gave her a push. "I'm gonna go check out that tower thingy. You go check out the view of Milo."

"You mean *with* Milo."

"Sure. That too," Al said and turned on her heel.

Clare watched for a moment as her best friend wandered off toward the stone spire that stood at the centre of Glastonbury Tor's summit. She wondered if it was her imagination, or if Al actually looked a little ... lonely. But then Milo called her name and Clare turned to see him waving. There was a big, beautiful smile on his face, and the blazing blueness of his gaze gave the colour of the sky a run for its money. Suddenly, as if released from a spell, Clare was running. And then kissing.

In just that moment, everything was exactly as it should be.

The world revolved around Glastonbury Tor and time stood perfectly still.

3

A llie circumnavigated the old stone tower a total of three times before actually stepping inside one of its four arches. The structure was the signature defining element of the hill's profile. You could see it from miles away—a single stone finger pointing skyward like an accusation. It was, according to everything she'd read, the last remaining ruins of a church dedicated to St. Michael that had stood there until the dissolution of the monasteries in 1539, during the reign of Henry the Eighth.

Once inside, it was a little like standing at the bottom of a well. The top of the tower ruin was open to the sky. Allie glanced up and was startled to see a pair of eyes staring down at her. A raven— the biggest one she'd ever seen—was perched on one of the stone corners. It gazed down at her with its unblinking, obsidian gaze. Allie stared back, the brilliant blue of the sky a stark backdrop that reflected off the bird's oily black feathers almost as if the creature was outlined in an electric-blue glow. It was a cool, if eerie, optical illusion.

Allie stood looking up at the bird for a long time, thinking that *that* was how she had appeared to Clare in the past. Every time she'd shimmered, Clare said it was a raven with Al's voice that had brought her spiralling back home. Of course, there was nothing mystical about the bird on top of the ruined tower. After all, Britain was lousy with ravens. It probably would have been odd *not* to have seen at least one of the things hanging around Glastonbury.

As if sensing her dismissive thoughts, the bird opened its big black beak and cawed at her. The harsh, dissonant sound reverberated off the stone walls, echoing weirdly. Allie put out a hand to steady herself against the tower wall, suddenly dizzy. But the bird just flapped noisily away, and when nothing particularly supernatural happened after a few long moments, Allie breathed a slightly embarrassed sigh of relief.

*You just gave yourself a head rush from staring up for so long, doofus.*

Outside the tower, Clare and Milo must have finally come up for air. Clare was calling her name and, as Allie stepped back into the sunshine, she was reassured to see that there were other tourists—not monks or pilgrims or Druids—wandering around the Tor. In the far distance, there were cars—not horses or chariots—travelling past on the roads below. Allie couldn't help feeling just the tiniest bit ridiculous.

For one thing, *she* wasn't the one the weird stuff happened to.

For another thing, *no* weird stuff was going to happen. Allie's fundamentally analytical mind gave her a bit of a swift kick and urged her to move on.

LATER THAT EVENING, after the girls had settled into the Avalon Mists Bed and Breakfast rooms where they'd been billeted and Milo had checked in at the local inn where the museum had booked him a room, they all met up to have dinner with Maggie before she headed back to the city.

As the waitress wandered back to the kitchen to place their food orders, Maggie sighed deeply and leaned on her hand, staring out the window in the direction of the Tor—even though it was hidden from sight by tall hedgerows and the quaint old buildings of the town.

Clare and Milo and Al exchanged glances.

"Mags," Clare said finally, "what's wrong?"

"Hm?"

"You're fidgeting and sighing and you keep looking out the window. You look as if you're expecting someone to come walking up the road." Clare knew what her aunt must be thinking. "You're *not*, are you?" she asked gently.

"Oh ... no." Maggie laughed wanly and waved a hand through the air. "No. And anyway, I paid my respects today at the Tor and there were no surprises. Still. I suppose this place just ... makes me a bit melancholy."

Back in the eighties, when Maggie had been a student in university, a boy had disappeared from Glastonbury Tor. *Literally.* And Maggie had been there when he had.

"I know he's not really here anymore. Just my memories of him, few as they may be. I hardly even knew the lad. But we *lost* him and I can't help wondering what I could have done differently."

"Maggie ... what ..." Clare hesitated. "What *really* happened back then? That night with Stu and Dr. Jenkins and the others? When the Free Peoples of Prydain—or whatever you guys called yourselves—did that ritual on the Tor?"

Maggie sighed again, took a sip from her half-pint of cider, and told them the story. It was a story about how, as a young graduate student at Cambridge, she'd gone on an ill-advised expedition with her then crush, a self-styled neo-Druid high-priest charlatan named Stuart Morholt. "New Age" was all the rage back in 1986, and there was a handful of them at the university: bored intellectuals who'd decided to band together and form their own, distinctly eighties idea of an Order of Druids. Most of which involved lighting candles, drinking lots of wine late at night out in the quad, and casting quasi-spells designed mainly to increase grades or popularity.

Then someone (Maggie seemed to recall that it was Morholt, although she wasn't entirely certain) had suggested they stop playing around and actually do a road trip to an actual mystical site. Stonehenge had been tossed around as a potential destination, but access to the ancient stone circle had been limited since the year before, when police had clashed with a caravan of hippie types and head-busting mayhem had ensued. Besides, someone pointed out, it was highly unlikely that real Druids had ever had anything to do with Stonehenge. So Glastonbury Tor was decided on.

"The idea—if you can call something so vague, ill thought out, and airy-fairy an idea—had been to cast some kind of mystical New Age spell that would show us all the way to Avalon." Maggie's upper lip twisted in a sneer of disgust. "Maybe commune with some earth spirits or dance in the moonlight with leprechauns or some such ludicrous thing. What a load of bloody rubbish."

Whatever its initial aims, the outcome had been something unexpected. And horrible, in that they'd lost one of their number in the process. A young man named Mark O'Donnell who'd just ... disappeared. Vanished. Never to be seen again.

"I'll never forgive myself. I should have told someone. But quite honestly, I don't know what I would have said." Maggie shook her head, remembering. "I don't know how it happened. I mean, Ceciley took credit for it but I can't say that I believe her. And Stuart is ... well, Stuart. I can't think he'd have had the wherewithal to actually track down a *real* spell. But he must have." Maggie shook her head. "Even to this day, it's all a bit fuzzy in my memory. With Morholt guiding us, we walked the ancient path around and around the hill. I swear he did it wrong—we kept getting turned around, as if it really were a maze—but then somehow we were at the summit of the hill. And then ... and then the world seemed to come apart all around us. It was real magic. *Really* big trouble. Everything felt wrong all of a sudden. They sky looked shattered. And that's all I remember. We all sort of passed out, I think. But when we awoke, one of us ... Mark ... he was gone." Maggie blinked rapidly, her eyes glassy with unshed tears.

"Gone, like ... *shimmer* gone?" Clare asked, suddenly uneasy.

Maggie sniffed and shook her head, reaching out to grip Clare's hand. "Oh, duckling, no. I don't mean to frighten you. I don't know where he went. Or when, or how. But he's not you and it wasn't the same. There were no artifacts, nothing to trigger a shimmering. And *you* always came back. For all I know, it really was Ceciley's spell that spooked him terribly and he *did* just run away—apparently he'd done that kind of thing before—when the rest of us were down for the count."

"What was he like?" Al asked quietly. "The guy who disappeared."

"Oh ... he was very young." Maggie pushed her glasses up on her nose and dabbed at the corner of one eye. "A boy, really. From Edinburgh. I can't think he was more than fourteen or fifteen. He'd gotten into Cambridge on a special linguistics scholarship and had already advanced several grades past his age group." She sighed. "Afterward, back at school, Stuart concocted a story about how the lad had cracked under the pressures of his studies and dropped out. Run away. No one really questioned it all that much, especially once the police confirmed that he'd been a runaway when he was younger. I can't say I blame him. His parents were celebrated academics and, to be honest, I think they'd pushed him hard all his young life and were ashamed at the thought that a son of theirs hadn't been able to handle the workload. The police put out missing persons reports, but after a while, what were they to do? He'd vanished into thin air. His family didn't press the matter. Wrote him off as a black sheep, I suppose. And the rest of us went along with Stuart's story because we were all too frightened and too bloody embarrassed to tell the truth."

"And because Morholt bullied you. I know what that's like coming from him," Clare said, glancing over at Al. "We both do."

"Such a shame. He really was a bright spark ..." Maggie shook her head. "Despite what his parents wound up thinking of him."

Clare smiled and laughed a little. "Jeez, Al," she said, trying to lighten the mood, "he sounds like your perfect male."

"Says the girl who's dating my *cousin*," Al snorted. "Whom we, in secret, have code-named 'Brainzilla.'" She elbowed Milo, who elbowed her playfully back.

"I think I'd prefer 'Brain Kong,'" he mused. "Or 'Creature from the Brain Lagoon.'"

Maggie had gone silent during the brief bout of teen banter, her expression slack with memory, her eyes misted windows looking inward.

"Perfesser?" Al prodded her gently.

"Hm? Oh! Yes. Sorry."

"No, that's okay," Al said. "I was just wondering if that was the end of the story."

"Yeah ... Sorry, Mags," Clare said. "We got a little sidetracky there. You were telling us about this O'Donnell guy."

"Well, as I say," Maggie continued, regaining something of her usual brisk demeanour, "he was young. Soft-spoken. Slight of build, with soft eyes. Soulful, really. And ... he had rather large hair."

Clare and Al exchanged a look. Al said, "What?"

Maggie wafted a hand above her own head. "Sort of poufy."

Clare clamped a hand over her mouth to keep from laughing out loud.

"Now, now. It was the style at the time."

Milo snorted.

"Well," Maggie sighed. "Here. Let me show you."

She hauled up the battered old soft-sided leather satchel that she toted around, full of notebooks and texts and other assorted archaeologist paraphernalia. After searching deep in the bowels of a side pocket, Maggie finally drew forth a scuffed and yellowed Moleskine notebook. She slipped off the elastic band that held the little journal shut and lifted the back cover, taking out an old, bent-cornered photograph. It was a group shot—taken against the backdrop of Glastonbury Tor rising above the trees into a deep blue, twilight sky—and it featured a half-dozen people ranging in age from teens to late twenties.

"Good god, Mags ..." Clare gaped at the picture in disbelief. "You had a spiral perm!"

"And you were hot!" Milo exclaimed, crowding over her shoulder for a look. "I mean—*are* hot."

Maggie's eyebrow crept toward her hairline as she regarded him sideways.

"*Still* hot."

Maggie rolled her eyes and reached across the table to snatch the picture back again, but Clare kept it out of her reach. "Look at the shoulder pads, Al! And is that ... holy crap. It *is!*"

Clare's jaw fell open as she stared at the image of a young Stuart Morholt, who struck a pose in a flowy, open-necked pirate shirt and tight leather pants. His black hair was long and wavy, and his eyes were rimmed with kohl.

"That is some *seriously* egregious guyliner." Clare shook her head in disgust.

Al remained silent, leaning in on Clare's other side. Her gaze was fixed like a laser beam, not on Maggie's questionable sartorial choices or Stuart Morholt's outlandish getup, but on the face of a boy who stood at the end of the line. The boy who'd disappeared. Clare could hardly blame Al for staring—it was a pretty tragic story. She glanced back down at him herself. Mark O'Donnell grinned excitedly at the camera, but his eyes were shadowed by a fringe of—good lord, Maggie hadn't exaggerated, it *was* poufy—mullet-style hair. It kind of reminded Clare of the coif she'd seen Bono sporting in really old U2 music videos. The boy in the picture also wore skinny hip-hugger tartan pants and—

"Is that a *leather* tie?" Al asked, pointing at the narrow strip of neckwear.

"Wait," Milo interjected. "Is *that* Dr. Jenkins?"

"Is she wearing a leopard-print corset?" Clare snorted. "Gawd!"

Clare hadn't managed to muster up much in the way of sympathy for the crazy curator. Not seeing as how Dr. Ceciley Jenkins had tried to kill Clare and her friends and Maggie only a few weeks earlier.

"Jeez, Perfesser!" Al's customary sardonic grin slid back into place and she shook her head. "You guys kinda look like a bunch of avatars from Guitar Hero!"

"I'm not even going to pretend I know what you're talking about." Maggie sniffed and retrieved the photograph, sliding it back into the notebook and returning it to her satchel. Clare thought she might have been beaming just a bit from Milo's "hot" comment. But after a moment she shook her head, the melancholy creeping back into her expression.

"Poor lad ... Morholt treated him like a lackey," she said. "A pet. If he could have had the dear boy carry his books around campus, I think he would have. I wish I could have stopped him. I wish I'd tried. I wish ..." She sighed again and took another sip of her cider. "Ah, well ..."

The crispness returned to her gaze as she glanced around the table at the trio of young people she was about to leave in the place where, all those years ago, she'd lost Mark O'Donnell to the mists of time.

"Now. Enough. I know I don't need to tell you this, but you three *will* be careful while you're here. Do you understand me?" The air almost crackled with the electric force of her stare.

"Maggie?" Clare reached over and laid a hand on her aunt's arm. "Believe me. If there's *anyone* who understands that ... I think it's us. We're probably the only 'trowel monkeys' Dr. Ashbourne has ever had working for him who know just how careful you have to be when you start digging up the past. Trust me. Nothing is going to go wrong. Nothing."

4

The landlady at the Avalon Mists Bed and Breakfast insisted on making the girls a cup of tea before they toddled off to bed. "Dream Tea" she called it: a blend of chamomile and mug-wort infused with valerian root and patchouli and various other hippie-sounding herbs and spices, guaranteed to help facilitate vivid dream experiences, she assured them. So they could better tap into the mystical "Dream Walks" that proximity to Glastonbury Tor bestowed upon the "seekers and the pilgrims." Clare thought it was probably a bunch of New Age hooey—and the tea smelled a bit like cat pee and tasted like watery grass clippings—but she didn't want to offend their purple-haired, crystal-festooned hostess, and so she forced herself to choke back a few tiny sips.

Al, being quicker on the uptake, begged off, claiming herbal allergies.

As it was, Clare went to bed that night dreaming of Milo. *So much for the purported astral potency of Dream Tea,* she thought, smug in her REM sleep state. She dreamt of Milo pretty much nightly these days and didn't exactly require boggy-tasting tisanes to help in that arena.

Clare sighed and settled into her visions of a Thames-side, late-afternoon stroll, hand in hand with the boy genius at her side ... the dream-rich colours of sunshine and blue skies echoing in Milo's blond hair and sparkling gaze ... a gentle breeze wafting the subtle, fresh scent of the soap he used ... Clare losing herself in his eyes as Milo smiled down at her and leaned in for a kiss ...

*Best. Dream. Ever.*

Riiight up until it wasn't.

With her dream-eyes closed for the purposes of dream-kissing, Clare wasn't sure exactly when or how the scene had shifted all around her. But suddenly, jarringly, she realized that the dream-day had turned grimly overcast. She was no longer on a path that ran beside London's famous river, but on a strand of grey beach pounded by the angry waves of a stormy, steel-grey sea. There was a heavy, briny smell in the air—salt and seaweed and wet sand. And Milo, who'd been right there with her, was suddenly nowhere to be found.

*Stupid Dream Tea ...*

With a shock, Clare recognized the pungent dream-odour that assaulted her dream-nostrils. It was the same scent she'd detected in those few moments when she and Stuart Morholt had been locked together in a time-shimmer. In the instant before she'd let go of the Great Snettisham Torc and abandoned Morholt to his fate, trapped back in AD 61.

Right on cue, Stu appeared over the horizon, a whirlwind tangle of arms and legs racing toward the beach and looking pretty much exactly how Clare had left him. In one hand he clutched the Snettisham Torc. In the other, a bulky bag of assorted artifacts also stolen from Boudicca's tomb. And he was being chased by a handful of Celtic warriors astride swift, sturdy ponies. They were gaining on him fast.

Clare curbed her own impulse to run as Morholt and the Celts headed straight for her. She knew that, in the way of dream-logic, she probably couldn't have anyway. The horsemen got within ten yards of where Clare stood before one of them leapt from his mount and tackled Morholt to the ground. The others circled him and then the biggest one dismounted and walked over.

Although the man was cloaked and hooded, Clare couldn't help feeling there was something familiar about him.

He pointed to the torc in Morholt's fist. "That isn't yours."

"Now wait just a second," Morholt protested, shrugging off his tackler and clambering to his feet. "There are certain technicalities to be considered here. I stole this, fair and square. From a museum that—in a manner of speaking—had already stolen it from its *rightful* owner. A charmingly demented lady by the name of Boudicca. Perhaps you've heard of her?"

"Boudicca is dead," the big man said simply. Then he threw back his cowl.

Clare heard her dream-self gasp: it was Llassar, the Druid metalsmith. The one responsible for creating the very same cursed torc that had sent Stuart Morholt back in time and that Stu was now waving around like a Frisbee. Llassar took a step closer to Morholt. "She was my queen and that torc once belonged to her. I know because I made it. But now she is dead."

"Yes, well," Morholt muttered. "She'd been dead for almost two thousand years when I met her. Didn't stop her from trying to kill me."

Llassar's eyes narrowed. "Perhaps I should finish the task."

"Right. Uh, look ... I think perhaps we can come to some sort of mutually beneficial arrangement where not killing me is concerned, don't you? I have power. Wagonloads of it. I could be of great use to you in your ... endeavours."

Clare noticed Morholt's hand creeping toward the hip pocket of his *Mission Impossible*–esque jumpsuit. *Oh, this should be good,* she thought, mentally leaning in to get a closer look at the dream-scene unfolding in front of her. She wondered what Stu was up to and kind of wished she had some dream-popcorn to go along with the drama.

"Behold!" Morholt yelped suddenly, drawing forth a disposable Bic lighter and flicking the little wheel. "I command the power of fire!"

*Seriously?*

Clare felt herself rolling her dream-eyes.

Llassar stepped back a pace—although whether in fear, or awe, or a simple desire not to have his beard ignite was open to interpretation.

"Ha!" Morholt waved the tiny flame in a circle like a warding talisman, keeping the lighter concealed in a tight fist so that it looked as though the fire sprang from the tip of his thumb. "Ha? See that?"

But the others didn't back off in quite the way Morholt had probably anticipated. Rather, they shifted slightly, ranging themselves around Morholt and Llassar as if they were spectators at a competition and wished to get a better view.

Morholt glanced around nervously.

"Ouch, dammit!" he swore, flinching as the lighter grew too hot. The flame went out and Morholt stuck his burned thumb in his mouth, glaring fiercely at his captors. Clearly, the effect was perhaps not as majestic as he'd hoped.

Then Llassar took a single step forward, held out his hand, focused a laser-like gaze on his open palm, muttered a word ... and conjured fire. Out of thin air and *without* having to flick a Bic.

Clare was hardly surprised. She'd seen firsthand what her Druid friends—and Llassar was one—were capable of. Granted, so had Morholt. But apparently he still thought they were a bunch of dimwits he could impress with party tricks.

*That's gonna cost him ...*

Llassar extinguished the flame by closing his hand into a fist. Then he took another step forward, and with the same fist thumped the master thief/self-proclaimed Lord High Druid/academically disgraced archaeologist-turned-crackpot right on the top of his head. Morholt's eyes rolled up and he slumped unconscious to the ground, the torc rolling from his hand. Llassar knelt and picked it up. Clare saw him glare fiercely at the thing and then stuff it into Morholt's bag along with the rest of the booty he'd absconded with.

That surprised Clare. She would have thought he'd treat *that* particular object a little more reverentially. But then she remembered Llassar's resistance when Boudicca had demanded he use Clare's surreptitiously collected blood—along with the Iceni queen's own—to craft a torc cursed with her mad vengeance.

Llassar stood. Turning to his companions, he gestured down the beach to where a handful of ratty fishing vessels—barely more than animal hides stretched over wicker frames—lay upturned on the sand.

"Bring me a fish sack," he said to one of the men. "We'll bag this one and put him in the boat. Mallora will want to see him."

*Mallora? Who the heck is Mallora?*

"Why should the High Druidess have any interest in a common thief?" the other man asked, staring down at Morholt in disdain.

*High Druidess?* Clare thought. *I so don't like the sound of that ...*

"Mallora has foreseen this." Llassar's tone was grim. "And whatever else this one is," he said, glaring down at Morholt, "he's *not* common."

"No," Clare agreed, "but he *is* a dumbass ..."

Suddenly, in that annoying way dreams had of shifting scenes, Clare found herself sitting beside a stream at night, in a place where she'd been before. With a young man she'd known in the past. Connal—handsome, green-eyed, Druid prince Connal—turned to Clare, his eyes reflecting the flames that had suddenly sprung up somewhere behind her.

*"The goddess Andrasta will paint her limbs with woad and wash her hair in blood and hitch twin ponies of smoke and shadow to her war chariot,"* he said, his voice echoing and ethereal. *"The fiery trail from her wheels will scorch the sky and the world will burn."*

And as before, when he'd said the very same thing to her in real life, Clare heard herself reply with the words: "Uh ... that's a euphemism, right?"

But this time Connal didn't laugh. This time he just stared at her until Clare wrenched her own gaze away and willed herself to sink back into the deep, black, dreamless sleep that was her only escape route out of that place. And time.

ALLIE McALLISTER WENT TO SLEEP that night to the sounds of Clare's gentle snoring. In the pale blue glow that filtered in through the curtains of the B&B's tall window, Allie could just make out Clare's face turned toward her and mushed into a feather pillow. She wasn't drooling, but Allie had a sneaking suspicion that she'd fallen asleep thinking about Milo. There was a curve of a smile on her lips.

Allie felt a tiny, stinging twist of envy.

Not that she wasn't happy for Clare. She was. For Milo, too— she adored her cousin and thought the two of them made a delightfully weird pair. It was just that ... she was kind of used to it being just her and Clare. The two of them together, standing united and defiant against a world not prepared to "get" either of them. And, of course, it still was. The two of them.

*The two of us ... plus one.*

It felt uneven somehow.

Also? It somehow felt as if Clare had suddenly acquired some sort of mysterious power that Allie had yet to manifest—or even figure out. Not only had Milo finally made a move, but during Clare's shimmer trips to the past she'd also attracted the undivided attention of a super-hot (according to Clare, at least; Allie had never actually seen him in the flesh) Druid warrior prince. A super-hot Druid warrior prince who'd kissed her under a full moon on the eve of a battle with the Roman army.

Sure, it had been dangerous for Clare in the past. And there'd been bloodshed and death and a bunch of other stuff that Allie's best friend was still, despite her fairly bounce-back demeanour, having a few difficulties dealing with. It wasn't obvious to anyone else, but sometimes Allie would see Clare's gaze turn inward, as if she was replaying the footage of a memory. As much as it had been an adventure and a kick and fun in a kidnapped-threatened-mystical-crazy-let's-not-do-that-ever-again kind of way, Allie knew Clare had seen things that the average contemporary North American seventeen-year-old girl wasn't really supposed to see. And it had stuck with her. Allie supposed death and grief did that kind of thing. Even to a girl like Clare. The last couple of weeks had been better for her, though.

So it wasn't as if Allie begrudged Clare her Milo-time.

Milo helped. The dig would help: if their muscle fatigue from climbing the Tor was any indication, the taxing work of excavation would help keep Clare from dwelling on those events late into the wee hours. It certainly seemed to have done the job tonight.

In theory, it should have worked for Allie too. Her muscles ached from the climb, her head was woolly, and her eyes felt gritty with weariness. And yet there she was. Flat on her back in a cozy little room in the middle of Somerset, England, staring up into the dark while her brain whirred around in her skull trying to make sense of the things she knew had happened to her best friend. And the things that had, to a lesser degree, happened to her best friend's aunt all those years ago.

Maggie's story had really stuck with Allie. She couldn't stop wondering what had happened that night. She wondered how she would have felt if something like that had happened to her instead. Sure—she'd been instrumental in the Shenanigans. She'd been kidnapped along with Clare when Morholt had decided to play hardball to get her to do his dirty work, and she'd shimmered along with Clare into Boudicca's mystically guarded underground tomb. But that was just it. She'd been "along" for the ride.

*Sidekick, accomplice, third wheel ...*

She felt a little weird about that. And she felt weird about feeling weird.

Allie's thoughts looped in and around each other as she finally started to drift off. And then the quiet solitude of the deep, empty night was shattered by an ear-pummelling cacophony.

*What the hell?*

Allie bolted upright, wondering what on earth could be making all that noise—noise that sounded like ... horses. A lot of horses. In fact the thunder of hoofbeats was suddenly so loud that she flinched and dove back under the covers. The drumming of hooves was followed by the noise of a car horn madly beeping and the squeal of tires on asphalt. Allie sat back up in bed. There was a moment of silence ...

And then she heard what sounded like her own voice.

"Help! Clare! *Me!* Somebody ..."

Allie jumped out of bed and flicked on the little bedside lamp.

"Help! *Help!*"

The cries were followed by what sounded like the high-pitched screams of a multitude of furious women. The curtains billowed like sails in the room as Allie threw open the casement and stuck her head out into the cool night air. But there was nothing. A thin ground mist swirled in rolling eddies as if something—or someone—had just run past, but the road was an empty ribbon of gravel. The moon came out from behind a bank of swift-sailing clouds and cast the Avalon Mists's immaculate little yard in a clear, silvery light.

It, too, was empty. Not a potted geranium out of place.

*Dream. It was a dream.*

Allie looked over to where Clare was enthusiastically sawing logs. She considered waking her, but Clare deserved a good night's sleep and pleasant dreams for once. Although her blissful smile, Allie noticed, had bent into something of a smirk.

*I wonder what she's dreaming about now,* she thought.

Whatever it was, it made Clare snort once and mutter "Dumbass ..."

Allie grinned and lay back down on her bed. Her head sank into her feather pillow and she soon drifted back into a deep, and very dreamless, sleep.

5

Three days' worth of digging and the blister on Clare's finger had developed into a mighty, rock-hard layer of scaly reptile hide. The muscles of her forearms had stopped searing and the dull, burning throb in her trowelling shoulder had settled into a soothing, delightful ache. She groaned and dug through her messenger bag for the bottle of ibuprofen that had almost taken over from Al as her bestest friend.

When, on the first day, they reached their assigned area of the dig—the place where they'd spend most of their waking hours for the next three weeks—it was to discover that there was nothing the least bit spooky or even particularly impressive about it. It was mostly just a corner of a farmer's field, surrounded by forest on one side and tall hedgerows on the other. There were no obvious ruins poking majestically out of the ground, no palace walls or broken mosaics depicting naked gods cavorting. No bits of statuary. What there was, however, were several meticulously dug trenches, mostly rectangular, some with varying depths carved like steps within the depressions. In places, stakes were driven into the ground supporting a grid network of hemp strings that sectioned off the areas into checkerboard patterns. It was all very efficient and industrious. And yet, on the whole, the entire operation seemed ... well ... kinda dinky.

But it was theirs. Their own little "Holes Away from Home."

As they surveyed the trenches, Clare and Al had tried their best to mask their disappointment. Milo, on the other hand, was positively giddy from the get-go about *his* new pet project. Every day at around noon he came loping through the field, effusive with geographic praise. Mentally mapping the topography as he went. Or the geography.

*Probably both.*

Clare wasn't particularly certain of the distinction. And she still struggled with the subtleties of strata and striations.

"The stratigraphy of the Tor itself is unique," Milo would say. Or, "The view from the summit of the surrounding terrain is incredible!"

"And if there's anything your cousin loves," Clare said to Al on one such occasion, "it's surrounding terrain."

"Or, really, any kind of terrain," Al had agreed, panting with exertion as she jammed her shovel into a rock-hard patch of soil.

As for the girls, though, so far on the dig they'd discovered ... nothing much. Well, nothing much beyond the fact that digging was hard work. Even if you were only doing it with a weenie baby hand shovel. Clare glanced over at Al, whose blue-pale skin had lost its milky translucent glow and was actually—gasp!—starting to freckle. It messed with her techno-couture, but it was actually kind of cute on her. It made her solemn grey gaze less solemn. Moreover, Al, who'd come with Clare on this dig as a matter of intellectual curiosity—and of riding shotgun on her impulsive BFF—had even admitted at breakfast that she was beginning to enjoy the physical exertion.

Clare had fessed up, in turn, that she was too.

Sure. It hurt. A lot. But the aches and pains and twinges were more than compensated for by the fresh air, sunshine, companionship (including frequent visits—and accompanying blissful shoulder rubs thereof—from Milo), and the fact that they were doing something interesting and different. Something that most of their school friends had never even thought of doing. It would buy them some locker-talk cred when they got back to school at the end of the summer. Even if they still hadn't found anything more interesting than the busted-off handle of a ceramic wine jug.

Also, an unexpected yet strangely gratifying side bonus was that the whole video-blog thing had scared them up a kind of mini cult following, which was in itself kind of cool. Using the camera on Al's tablet and the screen names ClareTheLoon and Al-Mac, the girls had been shooting video entries several times a day and streaming them live to the website they'd set up in conjunction with the museum to record their dig experience. So far, most of the entries had consisted of stuff like "hour three of shovelling ... still nothing ... my calluses are developing calluses ... this is some kind of practical joke, right? ... wait—is that a ... nope ... it's a rock ..." and so on.

Of course, a third of the comments from their followers were pretty obviously posted by twelve-year-old boys and consisted of lewdly misspelled boob jokes. But there were also actively interested hobby historians who'd offered up a decent amount of encouragement to the girls. It was kind of fun.

Clare checked her watch: about a half-hour left before they'd break for lunch. On the ground between the two trenches where she and Al had been assigned to work was a shallow tray that contained a few bits of broken pottery and a random bit of twisted metal that might have once been a horseshoe nail or part of a cloak fastener. Or in all likelihood, just a random bit of twisted metal.

"I'm going to go log our bounteous finds with Command Central, 'kay?" Clare called over to Al.

"Gloves on?"

"Yes, ma'am." Clare rolled her eyes behind her sunglasses.

"Okay then."

"You wanna come with? We can head straight to lunch after."

Clare could see the crown of Al's cowboy hat shake in the negative. "I'll be there in a bit. I finally finished sawing through this nasty old tree root and I feel I should reward myself by digging some more."

"You're in a groove, huh?" Clare laughed, hauling herself out of her own pit and dusting off the knees of her jeans.

"You could say that." Al grinned up at her, tipping back her hat and wiping the sweat from her brow with her sleeve. "Come get me when you're done and we'll head over to the Rifleman."

The Rifleman's Arms was a quaint little English pub they'd found. It had a cute little patio and hearty food. And the owner would serve the girls one little baby half-pint of cider each with their meals, even though technically they weren't of legal drinking age quite yet. The owner said they deserved to be treated like adults because of the job they were doing with such dedication over at the great hill: "Illuminatin' the past and all that. Very important work."

It was nice that the Rifleman's proprietor felt that way, Clare mused as she walked through the long grass, heading for the large canvas tent set up in the far corner of the adjacent field. Especially given the one or two locals who didn't exactly see the excavations in that light. Emphatically so. Even though Glastonbury's bustling little tourist economy traded heavily on the past—and people's fascination with it—some of the town's residents were of the opinion that what's buried should stay buried. And you didn't want to go messing about with the hill, meddling with the natural (some said *un*natural) energies of the place. The girls got opinions from all sides on the matter. Glastonbury itself, and the hill in particular, seemed to inspire strong reactions in people.

Clare got that. What she *wasn't* getting was anything out of the ordinary. No spooky vibes, no shimmer shimmies … and for that she was grateful. She was doing good hard work, she was learning stuff, and she was having fun. She left it at that.


NORMALLY, ALLIE WOULD HAVE JUMPED at the chance to knock off a few minutes early and retreat to the cool comfort of the pub's back patio. But on the third straight day of digging, she was actually finding a kind of rhythm to the work. And after the effort of clearing the roots, she felt as though she just might find something. Something that had lain hidden for a long time there in the shadow of the hill. It felt almost like a premonition. And it was what kept her there digging after Clare had gone to file their log.

The girls had been working side by side since they'd been there, the camaraderie between them an unbreakable bond. They were their usual inseparable duo. And lunches with Milo made for a cheerful, easygoing triumvirate. Even Allie's feelings of third-wheel awkwardness had dissipated. The trio was getting to be known as a familiar sight, with Milo in the middle and the girls on either side. But *something* was making Allie stay in her trench that morning. And in fact it wasn't long before her trowel hit that very something. At first she thought it was a rock. But it was smooth and round in a way that all the other rocks she'd encountered so far were most definitely not.

*Okay. Another pot shard ...*

But a bigger one. Maybe a whole, entire pot!

*Oh, the giddy thrill!* she enthused with silent sarcasm. At least, that's what she was going for. But her inner voice actually *did* sound giddily thrilled.

Allie called out for Clare, but she was nowhere in sight. She thought about waiting until Clare returned, but she was just too excited. Hoisting herself half out of the shallow trench, she reached over and grabbed her tablet before doing any more digging. Almost humming with excitement, Al propped it on its stand, flicked it into video mode, and set it to live-stream to the blog. Then she touched the record button on the screen.

She took off her hat to keep it from casting a dark shadow over her face and waved at the camera eye.

"Hey! Okay, all you dig-diggers out there in Cyberlandia, this is your friendly neighbourhood Al-Mac out here on day three of the Glastonbury Dig, and I'm back atcha with another dispatch from the field. Trench A-3, Sector 6 in the field, to be exact. And you better hang on to your Indy Jones fedoras, kids, because this entry is gonna be one for pot-sterity ..." Allie chuckled to herself.

Clare, if she'd been there, would have thrown something at her head for a pun like that. It was probably a sad commentary on the lack-lustre-y-ness of their discoveries thus far, but Allie was almost quivering with excitement at the thought of maybe, just maybe, unearthing a *whole, entire* pot. Buzzed as she was, though, she still followed procedure. Careful photographing and measuring and recording were her first priority. She blew through that non-sense in about a minute, describing in rapid-fire detail for the blog watchers what she was doing as she went. Then she was ready to take a crack at actually working the artifact free from the sur-rounding soil.

"Okay ... here we go ..."

She gave the thing a gentle tug.

"Here ... we ... gooo ..."

A less gentle tug.

"Go!"

A hearty yank.

The thing didn't budge. Allie wondered if it was being held pris-oner from beneath by another tree root. She felt around blindly with her trowel edge but couldn't tell. Wary about damaging whatever it was, Al laid the little shovel in the dirt beside her util-ity kit. Then she brushed at the layer of compacted soil with her gloved fingertips, but she couldn't get a good feel for the object's edges through the heavy canvas. She muttered a bit under her breath, sat back on her haunches, and wiped the sleeve of her shirt over her brow. It came away pale with sweaty yellow dust. For a moment Allie just glared at the bit of smooth, rounded artifact that seemed cemented into the ground. There was an assortment of tools and various grades of bristle brushes in the kit. There was even a delicately edged chisel.

But for some reason she ignored them all.

It was incredibly unlike her. Out of character. Allie McAllister was nothing if not a by-the-book, methodology-trumps-excitement, procedure-and-nomenclature-and-all-that-boring-stuff rule obeyer. In retrospect, she was never able to adequately explain the impulse that made her strip off the tartan-patterned gloves that Clare's aunt had given her and dig her bare fingertips into the soil on either side of the artifact—potential artifact (probably just a rock, seriously)—and grip its edges.

It was cool.

Not in a "hey, cool" way. But temperature-wise. Cool. Almost ... *cold.*

Allie dug her fingers further into the dirt and felt the powder-fine grit working its way under her black-painted nails. The curve of the buried object extended downward, smooth and slightly irregular. If this was a pot or a bowl or something, it had been made by an amateur. And as the thing curved around its bottom there were even nobby bits that felt out of place—like blobs of clay at the rim. She hooked her fingertips around them and exerted a gentle upward pressure. What she was doing in that moment was strictly against procedure as it had been minutely explained to them at the outset of the dig. And she was capturing it all and sending it streaming out into the world on a live feed. She'd be lucky if they didn't kick her sorry carcass off the dig within the hour.

But she didn't stop.

Allie was caught in the fierce, breathless grip of a mounting impatience. She climbed out of the trench and positioned herself to use her leverage and pull upward to free the whatever-it-was. She reached down. Her fingers burrowed deeper into the sandy soil, curved around the bottom of the object, and one more time, she gave a mighty heave ...

With a sudden sucking pop, she fell backward onto her butt as the thing came free like a stone flung from a catapult. She did a half shoulder roll, holding the precious artifact—if that's what it was—safely over her head and came to a stop a few feet away. Panting from the exertion, Allie lowered the object in front of her face and stared at it.

It stared back.

The empty eye sockets of the skull she held in her hands seemed to grow large enough to swallow her whole. The day turned to darkness, and the world around her faded into ghostly nothing.

"AL?" CLARE CALLED as she and Milo stepped into the sunlit clearing.

The field was empty save for the sound of a single, sweetly singing bird.

"She was here just a few minutes ago ..."

"I thought you said she was going to wait," Milo said, stretching out his shoulder muscles. Clare had found him, as usual, hunched over his souped-up laptop back at Command Central.

She turned to him and shrugged. "I guess she changed her mind. She must have bugged out early and is probably already at the Rifleman. Right?"

Milo checked his watch. "Well, it is after noon—and I am kind of starving. Sure." He swung his arm down and caught Clare's hand in his. "Let's go. With any luck, she's nabbed one of the good outside tables."

"Um. I guess so ..." Clare hesitated. What if Al had gone on ahead because she was tired of waiting, or annoyed, or mad at Clare?

Raging paranoia aside, Clare *was* a little worried about her relationship-y-ness with Milo and how it was affecting her best-friend-y-ness with Al. She didn't *think* Al minded—in fact, Al had already told Clare that she was happy for her and what a doofus Clare was for not having recognized Milo's obvious worth years earlier. Nonetheless, Clare proceeded with caution when it came to balancing the two. Milo was worth dodging flaming arrows for, sure. But her friendship with Al was worth getting *hit* by one. Almost. And—okay—it had been a glancing blow and had barely even scorched the sleeve of the jacket she'd been wearing at the time (which had been Al's anyway), but still.

Al was Clare's anchor. Her bestest best friend. Her blood sister—they'd even done the thing with the pricking of thumbs and elastic bands when they'd been little. And Al McAllister was the only thing that had pulled Clare back from the past again and again when Clare had insisted on shimmering until she managed to put things right.

Clare would never do anything to hurt her and she would mess up big time anyone else who hurt Al, herself and Milo included.

*So there.*

"Hey ..." Milo grabbed her hand and tugged her gently along toward the hedgerow gate. "C'mon, Clare de Lune ..."

He grinned over at her as they walked and Clare melted a little. She still got all fluttery when he called her by that pet name— even though the first time she'd heard it, she thought he was calling her crazy. Not that her behaviour at the time hadn't warranted such an assessment.

The Rifleman's Arms was a brisk five-minute walk from the dig site, up a pleasant laneway called Chilkwell Street. A little on the outskirts of town, situated amongst a few of the less touristy shops, the street was crowded with old, two-storey stone buildings with brightly painted doors. There was a cheese shop, a dressmaker, and an antiques dealer along the way, but Clare had never bothered to stop in at any of them. She was usually too hungry. Also, she wasn't really in the market for a nicely aged Stilton, custom-sewn frock, or granddaddy pocket watch. And yet today she found herself slowing down in front of the antiques-shop window.

Three days of poking in the dirt with a toy-sized shovel hadn't exactly yielded a treasure trove of artifacts and, as much as Clare was enjoying the exercise, she was also kind of pining for the sight of a brooch or a blade or, heck, a slightly tarnished button.

The little bell above the shop's front door tinkled off key as she and Milo stepped inside the dimly lit store. By the light of a laptop's glowing screen they saw the shop clerk, perched on a high stool behind a long counter, half-hidden by an antique cash register that sat crouched like an overfed brass house cat. The clerk was hunched over a piece of antique machinery that looked as though it might be the long-lost cousin of an accordion. At first, Clare couldn't tell whether the clerk was male or a female, given his/her oversized sweatshirt, hood up, and enormous, froggy-looking welder's goggles with dark round lenses. A thin line of acrid smoke that smelled like burning copper rose in a lazy spiral from where he/she was soldering two pieces of metal together.

"Identification, please," the clerk muttered vaguely in their direction, without looking up, as Milo and Clare approached. A girl, by the sound of her voice—which was a rich, deep alto, but still definitely female.

Clare stared in bemusement at the clerk, whose attention seemed wholly split between the object of repair and whatever was on the computer screen in front of her. The ridiculous goggles effectively obscured the upper half of her face and made the rest of her features look tiny and strangely elfin in comparison. And the big, sloppy hoodie made it seem as though she was trying to conceal some kind of hideous physical deformity. Either that or she just found it chilly in the shop. In any case, *not* exactly a fashion plate.

*Glastonbury really is full of an odd assortment of folk,* Clare thought.

"Identification," the clerk said again, tapping the countertop with the glowing red-hot tip of the soldering iron.

"Sorry?" Clare said.

Goggle-enlarged eyes flicked up behind the dark green lenses and then down again. "Store policy. Theft prevention."

"Oh. Uh ... okay."

*Not exactly a trusting soul,* Clare thought, but she and Milo did as they were asked. Milo handed over his driver's licence and Clare dug in her purse for her Canadian passport. The clerk glanced at the ID. Then she glanced at it again. And then, beneath the outlandish headgear, the lower half of her face turned ghostly pale.

*"Gurgle,"* she stammered as she almost fell backward off her stool. Then she lunged forward, slammed the lid of the laptop

shut, yanked the soldering iron plug out of the wall, and disappeared through a beaded curtain into a darkened back room.

"Uhng ... ur ... Bad fish and chips!" she exclaimed over her shoulder. "Store's closed!"

Clare blinked. "Okay. Did that girl actually say 'gurgle'?"

"Some kind of local Somerset dialect, no doubt." Milo shrugged, picked up his licence off the counter and handed Clare back her passport. "Remind me not to order the fish and chips at the Rifleman." His stomach made a rumbling noise despite himself. "Should we go find Allie and food now? Not necessarily in that order? Growing boy, here ..."

He patted the demonically smiling image of the Stay-Puft Marshmallow Man from the movie *Ghostbusters* that adorned his genre T-shirt du jour and Clare grinned at him.

"You know, I'm starting to think the population of this whole island is just one long parade of eccentrics," she said, shaking her head as they left the shop and its intestinally challenged clerk behind.

"You've watched some of the more popular UK sitcoms, right? Even the British wouldn't argue with you on that one."

"Good point. Still. Goggles Baggypants back there actually said 'gurgle'?" Clare snorted.

"She did seem kind of hobbity and strange, didn't she?"

"Oh yeah. I can't wait to tell Al. She already thinks we should be writing a sitcom based on our hostess and the other guests back at the bed and brek."

But it seemed she'd have to wait to share her story whether she wanted to or not. As Clare led the way through the pub's cozy rooms and out to the back patio, one thing became obvious. Allie McAllister wasn't there.

## 6

The brilliant blue of the afternoon sky flashed red and then began to fade to black. Allie had a single, shining-sharp instant to register terror. She knew what was happening—what was *about* to happen—and she dropped the skull like the proverbial hot potato and thrust out her hands to brace herself: the inevitable, mystically induced disorientation was about to overtake her.

*The shimmering.*

The uncanny feeling that all the atoms in your body were flying apart, swirling around and slamming back together again. Her whole being would sparkle like fireflies as she felt herself falling forward into a void filled with nothing but blackness and stars …

… At least that, according to Clare, was what happened.

In reality, all Allie felt as she stood there with her eyes squeezed shut was a sudden drop in air temperature like a shadow falling over her. She gasped, opened her eyes to see the sky rapidly darkening, and felt a brief sense of aggrieved disorientation. Clare had totally misrepresented "shimmering" when she'd described it to Allie all those times …

She stared up into a sky that was an endless deep black except for the place where the moon seemed to punch a hole right through it. Just as in the dream she'd had on the way to Glastonbury, the moon was blood red. But this time her rational mind didn't even bother trying to rationalize it. Besides, it didn't look like any pictures of lunar eclipses Allie had ever seen and she knew it.

She also knew that this time she definitely *wasn't* dreaming.

That's because a glancing blow from the shoulder of a passing horse—galloping by riderless and foaming at the bit—knocked her for a *very* painful loop that spun her around and left her gasping for breath. Where the hell had that horse come from? she almost asked. But when she turned back around, she found she didn't need to. Because several more like it were coming straight at her. Only *these* ones had riders. Roman cavalry soldiers.

*Holy shit.*

The rider closest to her had obviously seen Allie appear out of nowhere. He was staring wide-eyed at her from under the brim of his helmet and hauling on the reins of his mount to avoid running her down. She thought for a second she should be grateful for that, but then he started waving his sword around, pointing it at her and screaming in Latin at his fellows to "Kill the witch!" Or words to that effect.

Suddenly Allie wished she'd never learned Latin.

A couple of the more enthusiastic of the cavalry lads veered sharply in Allie's direction, and she lost her academic, this-can't-possibly-be-happening urge to stand there and see how the whole thing was going to turn out. Instead, she turned and started running for all she was worth. The sound of pounding hooves was so loud Allie thought they must have been almost right on top of her.

Half a foot to her right, a hard-flung spear slammed into the ground. Allie twisted mid-stride to the left, dodging another one, and then zigzagged toward a stretch of forest. There was angry, insistent shouting behind her now but she didn't bother trying to translate.

She was about thirty yards from the trees' safe cover when a crowd of screech-howling figures burst forth from those very same trees.

"*Scathach!*" one of the Romans behind her shouted.

That word Allie *couldn't* translate. But she assumed it meant the horde of blue-painted, red-eyed (*glowing* red-eyed, not just *hay fever* red-eyed), wild-haired women, some running flat out and some riding astride madly careening chariots, all of them brandishing weapons. Or maybe it referred to the raven feather–cloaked figure who strode out of the trees toward Allie, hefted a flaming spear, and launched it in her direction.

*Ha! Gotcha beat, Clare. You only had flaming arrows! I get a whole spear!* Allie thought, shock having utterly disconnected her mind from her emotions. Her next thought, watching the spear coming straight at her, was *I'm gonna die!*

Suddenly she felt a hand reach down and a muscled arm snake around her waist, and with a sharp yank, Allie's feet were no longer touching the ground. Without breaking his horse's stride, one of the cavalry soldiers had thrown her over his mount's withers, driving the breath from Allie's lungs and winding her utterly.

The flaming spear tore into the earth where she'd stood only a micro-second earlier. The rider hauled sharply on the reins, wheeled his mount around, and headed straight back toward the Roman soldiers who'd been howling for her death. And that, shockingly, was the preferable option: from her upside-down over-the-shoulder perspective, hanging over the side of the galloping horse, all Allie could think was that the rapidly approaching warriors looked like a bunch of lunatic groupies at a death-metal thrash-rock concert. She'd never seen such crazy hair and war paint. The weapon-wielding crazy women ran and fought and screamed with such insane levels of abandon that Allie thought they must have been drugged or brainwashed or something before being set loose on the Romans.

And she'd almost run straight into them.

Not that her present situation seemed much better. The motion of the galloping horse was jolting her sharply, her temple was banging into the rider's knee, all the blood was rushing from her head, and she thought she might pass out.

Then she heard her captor shouting: "Gate! Open the gate!"

Horse, rider, and terrified teenage girl from Toronto pounded through the sudden gap in a palisaded wall made of sharpened, lashed-together tree trunks. They were followed by the rest of the cavalry riders—the ones who'd made it through the gauntlet of berserkers. Some of them didn't. Allie saw the scathach—or whatever the hell they were called—actually leaping into the air to take men down, right off the backs of their horses, and then trampling them with their own mounts. The warrior women seemed preternaturally strong and fast. They were like animals—a wolf pack, or hunting cats—savage and brutal.

Safely inside the fortified compound, the soldier who'd grabbed Allie threw himself off his horse and hauled her roughly down behind him. She teetered unsteadily on her feet as he ran back to the gate he'd shouted for them to open so that he could get her safely inside. At least, that's what she'd thought he'd been doing. Maybe he was just taking her prisoner ... she thrust the thought from her mind. There were a half-dozen legionnaires still out there fighting in the field in front of the camp. They fought bravely. Heroically, even. But the howling horde of berserker women cut through them in swaths. It was the most terrifying spectacle Allie had ever witnessed.

And so she was damned glad she was witnessing it from *inside* the Roman encampment—right up until the cavalry soldier who'd called her a witch and howled for her death came careening through the gate that the other soldiers were hurrying to close. He was the last to make it through. And when he fixed his gaze upon Allie, blind red murder was in his eyes.

She stood paralyzed with fear as the soldier, his face a mask of rage, threw one leg over the neck of his horse before the exhausted beast had even slowed to a stop, its withers heaving. The soldier's feet hit the ground almost at a run and he stalked toward Allie, sword raised—

—only to be knocked aside by a powerful shove from the shoulder of the rider who'd captured Allie in the first place.

*What the hell?*

Were they going to argue now over who got to run a sword through her? What on earth was going on? She resisted the urge to cower in a heap on the ground with her hands over her head.

"What in Hades is wrong with you?" The soldier rounded on Allie's captor, looking like he was about to take a swing at him.

But the young man stood his ground. "She's unarmed."

"She's a witch! A stinking Druid sorceress."

"She's a skinny, unarmed girl, Junius. She doesn't look anything like the others. Probably a peasant from a nearby village. Look— just *look* at her." He pointed disdainfully at Allie with his sword. "Killing her would be like stepping on a baby bird fallen from its nest. It's beneath the dignity of Rome."

"The *dignity* of Rome is getting its arse kicked out there, thanks to her kind," Junius snarled back. "Those bitch berserkers are tearing our *dignity* to bloody shreds."

Allie suddenly realized that, with exacting precision, she was understanding an exchange of heated Latin. Which was far beyond what her admittedly excellent scores in high school Latin should ever have allowed her to do. It must have been because of the physical contact (the brutal manhandling!) she'd had with the young legionnaire. Just as it had happened to Clare.

Well, *that* was convenient—although the invisibility thing that Clare'd had going on would have come in handy, too. That particular mystic bonus feature seemed to have gotten lost along the way. Never mind. If her trip was anything like her best friend's had been, then Clare should be showing up in the guise of a bird any moment now to trigger the transition back to her own time.

*Any moment now.*

*Any ...*

Allie glanced around wildly for a raven to appear in the sky and call her name—just the way she had for Clare—and then mystically whisk her away from the cohort of legionnaires. At least, she thought it was a cohort.

*What exactly qualifies as a cohort, anyway?* she wondered. *Maybe this is a maniple, or a century, or ...*

Allie tended to dwell on minutiae in times of stress. It was a kind of default setting designed to keep her from panicking, and it did seem to be helping at that moment. She was too busy mentally cataloguing details to truly give in to the desire to freak right the hell out.

*I'll Google it the second I get back,* she thought. *C'mon, Clare ... Any* day *now ...*

With a painful, irrational stab of longing, Allie suddenly missed her tablet. At the same time, she was glad she hadn't been holding it when she'd shimmered. Shimmering, as they'd learned early on when it first happened to Clare, tended to irreparably fry anything that had an active electrical current running through it. So that at least was a relief. And something Allie could dwell on. Instead of the shouting soldiers in front of her, and the swords they held in their hands.

"It's not your decision to make," her captor was saying. "*I* took her prisoner. And I say we wait for the praefect to decide her fate."

"That's if he ever manages to regain consciousness." Junius shook his head without taking his eyes off Allie. "Not very likely, is it? The Praefect Postumus has been in a death-sleep in the infirmary for five straight days now. In another five he'll most likely be dead for real—just as we'll all be if we stay pinned down to this gods-forsaken hill—killed by those murdering savages. I say *her* life for *his.*"

"Shut your mouth! He'll awaken. He has to," the younger soldier snarled. He looked over at Allie, his gaze travelling the length of her from head to foot. For a long moment his eyes rested on her workboots. Then his glance flicked up over her face and he took a deep breath. "Come on, Junius," he said in a more reasoned tone, lowering his voice. "I know you're angry. And I know you've lost friends out there. I have too. Just ... *think* first before you act in a way you might be made to regret."

Allie fervently hoped he was getting through to the other man, who stood glaring so fiercely at her that she could almost feel the heat of it burn on her skin. She avoided meeting his eyes, glancing instead at the one who was arguing on her behalf.

Suddenly, that heat was replaced with a shocking, icy cold as she looked directly into the other one's eyes for the first time. Now, if there was one thing Allie knew about the Roman army from Clare's experiences, it was this: they were always angry about something. They were ruthless. They'd conquered most of the ancient world by main force, after all. Their soldiers were cold-blooded murder machines. They killed without a second thought. Hobbies included good old-fashioned frontier-style rape-and-pillage potlucks Saturday nights.

*Right, right ... okay. I get it.*

Allie did her best to tune out Clare's voice in her head and concentrated instead on not fainting from fear, caught as she was in the baleful gaze of the legionnaire who'd rescued her. The baleful, angry gaze. She could sense a simmering rage coming off him. But unlike Clare's hypothesis that ire was just the standard Legion grunt's default mode, the anger Allie saw in the young soldier's eyes was more than that.

It felt ... personal.

Allie quickly looked away, but that offered only a less-than-scenic view of another group of soldiers who were—she noticed with a squirming twist of fear—very purposefully making their way toward her. One of them wore the crested helmet of a higher rank. Allie guessed he was a centurion.

Her acrimonious self-appointed captor/guard/possible saviour saw them, too. He turned away from her, sheathing his sword as the other men approached, and Allie got a good look at him for the first time. He was taller than most of the other soldiers and there was something a tiny bit different about the way he carried himself. She couldn't quite put her finger on it. His arms and legs were long and deeply tanned, as was his face, and their planes and contours were all sharply defined under the light of the scary red moon. It was hard to tell what colour his eyes were under the brim of his helmet, but she'd gotten the distinct impression that they were dark. Probably brown or a deep hazel. His posture was upright and the set of his head gave him an air of arrogance. Maybe even callousness.

Before the centurion reached him, he turned and gave her the coldest, hardest stare she'd ever had the displeasure of receiving. And even though he'd ostensibly saved her life—twice—Allie decided that she probably kind of hated him. She mustered just enough spirit, under the circumstances, to glare defiantly back. And was surprised to see him frown a little and blink in what might have been confusion.

But then he turned away from her again and threw a stiff-armed salute to the officer leading the other soldiers toward them—a grizzled, hard-looking man who returned the greeting with casual precision.

"Legionnaire," the centurion growled in heavily accented Latin. "Report."

The young soldier answered back, the words spilling from his lips fluidly and forcefully. He spoke with confidence and passion and—now that these Romans weren't barking at each other—Allie had a chance to really listen to what they were saying. She was surprised to hear just how much actual Latin sounded like modern Italian, all rolled *r*'s and fiery intonation. It was much more dynamic than when Mr. Cavendish, her Latin teacher back in Toronto, spoke it in his nasally, pseudo-English accent. *He'd* sounded as if he were playing a villainous emperor in an old swords-and-sandals movie starring Richard Burton or Charlton Heston. Not these guys. Especially not the young rider with the dark, glittering eyes who'd thrown her over his horse like a sack of grain. Coming from the mouth of *that* guy? Even though she'd already written him off as a pompous macho shithead, she had to admit that the way he spoke was actually kind of ... sexy.

*Sexy dead languages. You really are a high-order geek, McAllister.*

She really was.

*Also? Speaking of "dead"? You* know *you're in mortal peril here, right?*

She really did. She was just trying her best to ignore that fact. Concentrate on the minutiae, avoid the big-picture panic. Right. Or maybe she could listen to what they were actually saying instead of just the sexy way it was being said. *That* might be helpful.

"A Druidess, Centurion." The young legionnaire glanced back over his shoulder in her direction. "At least, Junius here seems to think so."

Junius—a thick-necked bull of a man—stepped forward, glaring sideways at Allie as he passed her. Despite his size and obvious strength, it almost seemed, now that the fever of battle madness was gone from his eyes, as if he was afraid to look at her directly. Junius stopped in front of the centurion and threw a salute forceful enough to make his armour rattle. Then he looked at Allie's rescuer and nodded in agreement.

"She ... appeared in front of me, sir," Junius confirmed, casting glances at Allie. "Just *appeared*. Right out of thin air."

"Right out of thin air, eh?" The centurion walked over and looked down on Allie as if she were something offensive he'd just scraped off the bottom of his sandal. He hawked and spat to one side, plainly unimpressed by the so-called Druidess. "Well, let's see if she can disappear *back* into thin air after we've clapped chains on her and thrown her on a ship bound for the slave markets in Rome along with her fellow barbarians. Take her to the blacksmith and get her fitted. Then put her in with the others." He turned to the young legionnaire. "As for you, attend me. I want a full account of what's going on out there."

The centurion turned on his heel and stalked away. Allie was instantly forgotten in the wake of more important matters. Their curiosity satisfied, the other soldiers dispersed in groups of twos and threes, drifting off down the alleyways between the regimented lines of tents that made up the Roman camp. There were rows and rows of the things, and Allie wondered just how many soldiers there were in the compound. Then she wondered what her odds of escape might be. Probably worse than abysmal.

Junius grabbed Allie ungently by her arm, and she saw the young soldier cast a long look back at her as he followed in the centurion's wake. Then the two men disappeared down a side alley and Junius shoved her forward, prodding her with the butt end of his spear as she stumbled toward a thin line of smoke that rose up between two tents. A blacksmith.

He was going to put her in chains.

Allie felt her heart sink into her stomach.

7

Clare's lunch wasn't sitting very well. And she hadn't even had the fish and chips. Mostly she just had a terrible feeling in the pit of her stomach as she and Milo retraced their route back to the dig site. They'd lingered in the pub for half an hour longer than usual, just waiting to see if Al would show. She didn't. Nor did she call Clare's cell phone to tell her she'd be late. Calls to Al's cell went unanswered. Text messages, the same.

"You know that half the time she's got the thing on silent and stuffed in the bottom of her bag, right?" Milo said, reiterating a version of his standard reassurance. He'd been cycling through several variations with slightly altered wording ever since they'd ordered lunch.

But to Clare's ears, even he wasn't sounding so sure anymore. "So you're saying she probably just stumbled on a really gripping essay on the web about dendrochronology," she said. "Or, I dunno, tree-ring dating—"

"Those are the same thing."

"—what*ever* and is sitting somewhere with her nose happily glued to her shiny new gadget. Oblivious of tummy rumblings or the need to call me and expound on her latest scientific theorizing about ... stuff."

"Clare ... it's Allie. She of the level head," Milo called after her as she quickened her pace and pulled away from him. "Wherever she is, she's fine."

But Clare wasn't so sure and was almost sprinting by the time the fork in the road that led to the dig site came into view. She shoved open the livestock fence that barred the gap in the tall, thick hedgerow leading to the dig field, ran through, and then paused. From the north, she thought she could hear something. A far-off noise that sounded like ...

"Whoa!" she exclaimed, diving for cover in the long grass.

All around her the air shook with the thunder of horses galloping madly past. The ground beneath Clare's feet trembled and her ears rang with piercing neighs and the gruff shouts of many men. A wave of darkness washed over her. Clare smelled smoke and blood and churned mud ... and then, in the sudden silence, it was gone.

"Clare!"

Milo came tearing around the corner of the hedgerow, leaving the gate to swing shut behind him.

"What is it? What's *wrong*?"

Clare glanced wildly around. The day was back to its sunshiney bird-tweety empty-meadow normalcy. And Milo was hauling her up off the ground and gripping her by the arms, staring down worriedly into her eyes.

"You didn't hear that?" Clare pushed past him, looking for the massed cavalry that—she was certain—had just thundered past. "The galloping and the whinnying and the potential trampling?"

He shook his head.

Clare ran back to the gate and hoisted herself up on the rail, looking up and down the road for signs of a nearby rodeo that had just experienced a horsey jail break. Not even a dust cloud to be seen in either direction. Maybe it had been ... thunder? She glanced skyward. Not a cloud.

"Nothing?" she asked.

"I didn't see or hear a thing," Milo said. And then added cautiously, "Are you sure you're okay?"

*Mental breakdown it is, then. Enh. Wouldn't be the first time I've approached that fine line. I still haven't crossed over it. Yet.*

She told herself she was just worried about Al and that it was causing her imagination to run away with her. Milo stood watching her patiently, head tilted, arms crossed over his chest.

"Oh ... quiet, you," she sighed as she stalked past him. "I'm not normal. You know that. Let's go find your wayward cousin. And *not* tell her about my invisible horsey friends. She's already been driving me crazy with the watching-like-a-hawk thing to make sure I don't inadvertently do something enormously stupid like fondle the artifacts without adequate protection. Imagine how she'd react if she thought I was suddenly hallucinating."

"You're not hallucinating. You're just ... you."

Clare didn't know whether that was meant to be reassuring or not.

When they reached the spot where she'd left Al less than two hours earlier, the field was utterly empty. Not even a grumpy grad-student supervisor anywhere to be seen. Clare slowed to a stop on the lip of the trench where she and Al had been working, directly under the shadow of the Tor where the hillside merged into the field below.

"She's here somewhere," Milo said again, sounding even *less* convinced. "And she's fine. Maybe she's found herself a grad student to crush on. Or be crushed on by."

"What?" Clare said absently, turning in a full circle. "You mean all those ruggedly intellectual-looking types always offering to lend Al their vernier calipers?"

Milo, his mouth quirking in a half-smile, seemed reasonably impressed with Clare's correct use of terminology. "That's exactly what I mean. You're not the only geek bait around here, you know," he said wryly. "And I did actually see a couple of the dig guys giving Allie the eye the other day. Is it beyond the realm of possibility to think she might have noticed? And maybe ... reciprocated interest?"

"I guess not ..." Clare muttered, barely restraining herself from turning over rocks in the field to see if Al was hiding under one.

Frankly, she found the idea of Al ditching her and Milo to go make out with a history PhD student—and more to the point, *not* telling Clare about it during their late-night, post-dig gab sessions—even *more* disturbing than a random, unexplained disappearance. Then again, Clare had been preoccupied. Maybe she'd just missed the signals. Did that make her a bad friend? Was Al really off somewhere canoodling with a stubbly, sun-bronzed archaeology nerd?

"Maybe you're right," she sighed. "I just—"

Clare stopped abruptly at the look on Milo's face.

Something had caught his eye and his smile had vanished instantly. Clare followed his gaze but couldn't tell what he was looking at. At first. And then she saw it, too: Al's shiny new tablet lying face down in the dust of the shallow trench where she'd been working. A cold hand of fear closed around Clare's throat. You'd practically have to cut Al's hands off to get her to relinquish her new techno-toy.

*And then beat her senseless with those same severed hands to get her to leave it face down in the dirt!*

For a second Clare feared that was exactly what had happened ... and then realized that it was only Al's *gloves* lying on the ground, not her actual appendages. But that moment of relief was followed by a crushing surge of panic as Milo crouched down and picked up the tablet. He knew just as well as Clare did that his cousin didn't go anywhere without her tech. Not willingly. He pushed the tablet at Clare and ran to the edge of the trees.

"Allie?" he called out, alarm in his voice. "Allie! Where are you?"

Clare looked down at the screen in her hands. It was cool to the touch, so she had no way of knowing how long it had been in sleep mode. She called up the password screen. Hoping desperately that Al hadn't changed it since Clare had figured it out, she entered 6-6-6-5-3-9—numbers corresponding to the letters that made up the word MONKEY. When the tablet glowed to life she checked to see what Al had been doing with it last. It was set to video-camera mode, and Clare called up the last clip Al had shot.

*"Hey! Okay, all you dig-diggers out there in Cyberlandia, this is your friendly neighbourhood Al-Mac out here on day three of the Glastonbury Dig, and I'm back atcha with another dispatch from the field ..."*

Al's familiar voice tumbled cheerfully out of the little speaker. Her grinning face, with its newly acquired adorable smattering of freckles across her nose, filled the screen.

Two minutes and fifty-six seconds later, according to the counter on the video clip, Milo was still hollering for his cousin. Clare didn't bother calling out. She knew what had happened. And she knew—with a certain, sinking horror—that Al was nowhere in the near vicinity.

Or, more accurately, no*when* near.

Moving like a zombie, slow and unthinking and full of dread, Clare traced a path on the trajectory dictated by what she'd seen in the video. And there it was, lying in the grass—the thing she thought she'd seen in the video.

Clare heard Milo come up behind her. "What the *hell*?" he murmured.

Clare nudged the skull with the toe of her sneaker.

In the video, she'd seen Al take off her gloves—*WTH!! Why did you take off your gloves?!*—and work an object free of the ground. She'd seen Al fall out of frame as she tugged the thing free ... and the bright light of day dimming and reddening, washing over the empty scene from the direction where Al had rolled before the tablet tipped over on its face and stopped recording.

Milo walked back to the trench and knelt down beside Al's field kit. Clare nudged the skull again, its rounded bone surface a weathered, bronzey colour. The touch of Clare's shoe sent it rolling toward Milo. He reached out toward it and Clare howled at him: "DO NOT TOUCH! What are you—*crazy*?"

Milo paused, silently raised an eyebrow at her, and held up the long thin dowel of the wooden paintbrush he'd plucked from Al's kit. He very gently prodded the skull until it turned over, exposing the underside where the unfortunate ex-owner's spinal column would have attached.

Clare wondered what had happened to whoever this had been. Who *had* this been?

Then she remembered Connal, the Druid warrior prince she'd encountered during her shimmer trips, saying something about the fierce tribes to the west. She grew instantly frantic: would Al have found herself among a tribe of rather less friendly Britons than Clare had? And by "friendly" she meant a tribe in which one of its members—that very same Druid prince—had held her at sword point more than once. In fact, he'd almost lopped *her* head off before she'd been able to convince him otherwise. She stared at the dirt-encrusted undercarriage of the disembodied skull.

*Holy crap ...*

Al was in a world of trouble. And it was Clare's fault.

Clare *knew* she'd been neglecting her best friend. She knew Al was feeling odd-man-out, and yet she'd still left her alone and gone blithely on her merry, Milo-happy way. Now Al was gone.

"This is all my fault," Clare moaned half to herself.

"Hey ..." Suddenly Milo was there, his arms wrapped around her. "This is not your fault and Allie is *not* your responsibility. If anything, she's mine. Don't worry—I'll be the one her mother kills when she doesn't make it back to Toronto at the end of the summer."

"That's hardly encouraging. And don't *say* that." She smacked him on the chest with the flat of her palm. "She's coming home. Not at the end of summer ... now. Today."

Before Milo could stop her, she knelt down and scooped up the skull bare-handed. The hollow-shadowed, eyeless thing seemed to stare deep into Clare's own head. Her vision seemed to tunnel, fire licking around the periphery, and she went rigid, expecting at any second to shimmer back to wherever Al had gone. Nothing happened. At least, nothing on the order of shimmering.

Only ... ribbons of light and shadow raced over the field, cast by the day's high-altitude, wind-driven clouds. Which wouldn't have been the least bit out of the ordinary ... if there'd actually *been* any high-altitude, wind-driven clouds. There weren't. The sky was a bright, unbroken blue.

"Aw, crap," Milo muttered, looking up into the sky and then down at the ground where the bands of shadows streamed past, confused apprehension on his handsome face. *Some*thing odd was happening, that much was certain. But it *wasn't* something odd that was also bringing Al back.

Awash with sudden despair, Clare handed Milo the skull. She struggled against the urge to give in to the burgeoning panic working its way up from the depths of her stomach and into her throat.

"I have to bring her home, Milo. I have to be Al's anchor." But the realization was inescapable. And the more Clare thought about it, the more she feared the plain truth of the matter. "I just don't know how to make that happen."

8

This couldn't be happening.

*Clare never had anything even remotely this crazy bad happen to her!* Allie thought and was instantly aware that this was in no way accurate. But she was terrified. And panicky hyperbole, she decided, was a valid stress response given her current situation. So she went with it.

*Sure—a Druid had attacked Clare and almost cut her throat,* Allie continued silently in that vein, *but he'd been gorgeous and had made up for it with kissing!*

No hyperbole there. And, really? Clare had never been thrown in irons! She'd only had to help Comorra impersonate a goddess (granted, at considerable risk to her own life and limb), but ultimately that had worked out just fine. Thanks in large part to the fact that Allie had left her well stocked with useful objects like glowsticks and road flares and pocket lighters. What had Clare done for her? Nothing! Allie had been Clare's anchor. Her homing beacon. Her way home when things got too hairy.

"Things are hairy, Clare!" Allie shouted at the night sky as the blacksmith bolted a shackle to her wrist by the light of his glowing forge. "Way too hairy! Now would be a good time for a recall!"

The Legion blacksmith—who, incidentally, rather closely resembled the cave troll that attacks the heroes of the Fellowship in the Mines of Moria back in the first *Lord of the Rings* movie— just rolled one beady eye at her in incomprehension and attached the shackle to her other wrist. Even Clare's *blacksmith* had been cooler than Allie's. He'd been artistic. And a Druid. He had created magic—*real* magic—and objects of beauty and power. Allie wondered if the brute standing in front of her with the hammer even cared about the quality of his work. She doubted it. He'd barely even glanced at her as he'd hammered the irons shut. At least he'd aimed well enough not to accidentally pulverize her hands into salsa, but Allie chalked that up to blind luck.

He grunted to Junius that his task was finished and the soldier prodded Allie with the butt of his spear once more. She spun around and shot out a glare that actually made him back off half a step. But then he set his jaw and, grabbing a handful of her shirt material, half-dragged her away from the smith's forge toward the tent alleys.

The chains felt as heavy as bowling balls tied to Allie's wrists. They pulled her off balance, and she stumbled and fell to her knees. For a moment all she wanted to do was stay there. But Junius picked her up and shoved her forward, down a narrow lane toward a tent guarded by two sentries. The flap doorway was lit by the sullen smoky flares of a pair of torches in a stand. Another shove and she was through the flap. Allie found herself standing in the pitch-dark confines of a prisoners' tent. She could hear the breathing and rustling of others in the near vicinity. The clank and hiss of chains. She didn't know how many others were in there, and she wasn't anxious to find out.

Shuffling her feet, trying not to hyperventilate from fear, Allie backed herself into a corner as far away from her fellow captives as she could get. With her spine up against a corner tent pole, she sank down to the cold ground and pulled her knees in tight to her chest, contemplating how on earth she'd come to this.

She'd *totally* been joking.

The whole "skeletal remains" thing? *Joking!*

What didn't the cosmos understand about that?

Frankly, she hadn't been particularly keen to unearth anything even remotely resembling human remains. Let alone *exactly* resembling. Honestly, Clare's bog bodies—and there'd been thirteen of those dudes—had been more than enough human remains to last Allie a lifetime. And yet? She'd had the audacity to joke about it. Blog Buddies. Skel-e-mail Remains.

*Ha ha, very funny. Stupid irony.*

She should have been at least a *touch* reverential. Especially considering everything she and Clare had experienced since setting foot in Britain, with all of its history and mystery and strange, mystical power. But that was in crystal-clear hindsight, and unless she had some sort of time machine—okay, *less* funny—there wasn't much she could do about it. With the weight of the iron manacles dragging at her wrists *and* her spirit, there wasn't much she could do about anything. Allie rested her head on her forearms and finally allowed silent tears to slide out from under her eyelids as she wept herself into a forlorn, exhausted sleep.


CLARE WISHED SHE WERE HOME. Back in Toronto, even back in London. Anywhere else. She wished Maggie was there. The last time something like this happened, Clare had gambled on her aunt. Not only on Maggie's willingness to believe wild declarations of magic and time travel and nefarious thievery, but on her ability to help sort the whole mess out. Clare could really use Maggie's mad skills in that regard.

But her calls to Maggie's office at the museum, to Maggie's cell phone, and to Maggie's flat all went unanswered. That wasn't particularly unusual—Clare's aunt wasn't one of those tethered-to-technology types, and a phone conversation with her the previous evening—back when things at the dig site were proceeding along quite nicely without any hint of paranormal disruption, thank you very much—had most likely assured Maggie that, well, things at the dig site were proceeding along quite nicely *without any hint of paranormal disruption, thank you very much*. Therefore, she was no doubt going about her business as usual, which for that week, Clare knew, meant an international conference of historians at which Maggie was keynote speaker and distinguished panel-ist. And, as Al or Milo would no doubt say, out of communicator range for the duration.

So Mags was out of the picture, help-wise. That left the only other authority figure in the vicinity: moustachioed, "marvellous," bon-vivant-busybody-in-a-pith-helmet Bloody Nicky Ashbourne. Only ... Clare was understandably reluctant to tell the dig's super-vising honcho that one of his precious trowel monkeys had van-ished, potentially mystically so. So far Bloody Nick had left Milo and the girls pretty much to their own devices. Clare was perfectly well aware that the only reason they were even allowed within a half-mile radius of the excavation was that her aunt had pulled strings and called in favours. Fine. But now she had to put her faith in a man she knew almost nothing about. Still, maybe something like this had happened before. Maybe Nicholas Ashbourne knew something about it. Either way, Clare needed help. She needed to get Al back.

Which was why she now found herself sitting in a torturously uncomfortable folding camp chair outside the Glastonbury exca-vation project's Command Central, waiting for Dr. Ashbourne to finish with a group of grad students so that she could inform him that Al had gone spatio-temporally AWOL and could he please offer some insights as to how to maybe retrieve her from the dis-tant mists of time, thank you. Clare and Milo had been waiting for almost a quarter of an hour.

Milo had spent the last several minutes on the phone. Something to do with ... satellites. Maps.

*Hardly the time,* Clare thought to herself irritably.

But she supposed it was Milo's way of occupying himself while Dr. Ashbourne finished debriefing the PhD candidates who'd unearthed a small hoard of coins. As far as she could tell from the excited chatter drifting through the walls of the tent, the gaggle of grads had found, like, five or six of the things. This was appar-ently a significant find, and the whole camp was abuzz over it. Over pocket change.

*Whoop-dee-doo.*

Not like the grad students had discovered a mystical *torc* or, oh, say, *Boudicca's lost tomb*—like Clare had—or unearthed, oh, say, an enchanted freaking *skull* or anything—like Al had. Clare and Al were way cooler. They'd found magic. Only, the more Clare thought about it, the more it seemed to her that, with what little she could tell from the video blog, there were certain discrepancies between her magic and Al's.

"It's *different* this time ..." she muttered to herself.

Clare watched Milo as he paced back and forth, checking something on his phone's display screen and talking to some computer guru hacker guy named Dan about something technically arcane. Sitting in her camp chair, Clare had a white-knuckled grip on Al's tablet, clutching it to her chest as if it were some sort of enchanted talisman. A looking glass or a magic mirror that she could peer into and see the future. Or the past ...

"Milo?"

She tugged on his sleeve, trying to get his attention as he drifted past her. Whoever he was speaking to couldn't possibly be of any use in finding Al and was thus deeply unimportant in that moment. And Clare desperately needed a sounding board to talk her way through her embryonic observations. Under any other circumstances, that sounding board would have been Al.

"Milo?" she said again. "It's different this time—"

Milo nodded, stuck a finger in his free ear, and kept on pacing, leaving Clare to ponder theories darkly to herself.

"For *one* thing?" she muttered. "It wasn't me. *I'm* supposed to be the one with the whole Druid blood-curse thing happening. Not like I think I'm super-special or anything ... just that it was *my* blood that got all tangled up in Llassar's artifacts in the first place. Al was the one who always brought me back. I don't know how to bring Al back. I'm not good with being the anchor. I'm not ... grounded like she is."

"Clare—" Milo, having finally finished his call, sat down beside her and put his arm around her shoulders.

"—And another thing," Clare continued, "as far as I can figure it, Al didn't touch anything metal. Nothing manmade. No extra-special whammy-imbued time-trip trigger from the ingenious magical forge of Llassar the mystical Druid smith. There is *no artifact*. A skull is not something you can *forge* using someone else's *blood*. I touched the skull and nothing happened. No shimmering. The only thing I'm getting out of all this is a migraine. And I think that's just from stress. Stress is not magical."

"Clare—"

"There is no blood here, Milo!" Clare flailed a bit, growing increasingly agitated.

"I know. But I think—"

"I just don't get it," Clare went on in a low, staccato hiss, glancing warily in the direction of the tent. "There's *nothing* to connect that stupid skull to Al. Nothing!" She waved a hand sharply at Milo's knapsack, as if the skull inside it could hear her and maybe apologize for its presumption. "Unless, of course," she continued with angry sarcasm, "that skull just so happens to belong to *Al*, in which case ..."

She had meant it to be a joke.

"Oh ... god ..."

What if it wasn't? What if the head in the bag really *had* once belonged to Allie McAllister? What if—

"Clare!"

She turned to Milo as if in slow motion. He lunged for her, an expression of alarm on his face, and Clare realized that she'd actually started to fall forward in a semi-faint. The edges of her vision had grown dark with panic at the thought of Headless Allie McAllister.

Milo pried the tablet from her fingers. "Stop."

His voice was like cool water on the flash burn of her freak-out. He brushed back the hair that had escaped her ponytail and tilted her head up. Now she was looking straight into those clear blue eyes that stared back at her, calm and mesmerizing, from behind the angular black frames of his glasses.

"Just stop ... and *listen* to me, Clare." His long fingers cupped the sides of her face. "I've been through this situation before. I've seen it happen from *this* side of things, okay? With you. Every single time with you ... when you shimmered? When you disappeared? I didn't know if I'd ever see you again. And it just about killed me *every* single time, but you have to remember how it all turned out."

She looked up at him, her lip starting to tremble at the remembered anguish in his eyes. She hadn't really ever thought about how it had affected Milo—or Al, or Maggie. Wow, she could be so selfish sometimes ...

"How did it all turn out, Clare?" Milo asked gently.

"Um." She swallowed noisily, willing back the tears that were threatening to spill. "It ... it all turned out okay?"

"Yeah. It did." He smiled down at her and pulled her into another embrace. "It will this time, too. Allie's smart. She's strong. And she's got us on her side. We'll figure out a way to get her back. Together."

ALLIE HAD NO IDEA how long she'd been asleep. She didn't know what time it had been when she'd first arrived outside of the camp, in the middle of that battle. Skirmish. Whatever you called it. Madness. Chaos.

But she'd had a strange dream where she kept hearing a familiar voice. Muttering over and over, like a mantra, the words "I'll kill her ..."

Allie blinked until her eyes adjusted to the dim morning light streaming in through a gap in the canvas at the top of the tent. She was definitely awake now. But if that was the case, why did she keep hearing that same phrase? And whose voice was it anyway?

"I'll kill her ..."

And why was it speaking in English ...?

*Oh god. No.*

Allie watched silently, frozen in horror, from her corner of the tent as Stuart Morholt scribbled away in what looked like a fancy notebook with what looked like a fancy ballpoint pen and continued his chant.

"I'll kill her," he murmured with grim determination. "I'll kill them both. I'll kill Clarinet Reid and her fender-bending minion and her little dog Milo, too. I'll kill Maggie, and I'll kill Ceciley just for the fun of it and I'll—OW!"

That last syllable seemed to be a new addition to the mantra, prompted mostly by the fact that the large bearded man sitting to Morholt's left had turned and casually punched him in the shoulder. Morholt was still wearing his ridiculous multi-pocketed, many-zippered super-spy jumpsuit, but it was coated in several layers of different subsets of filth and hardly recognizable as anything more than a distressed, shapeless collection of rags. His boots were similarly muck-caked and therefore not particularly discernible from the foot coverings worn by the other captives. The other captives who didn't seem to particularly enjoy his company.

*Maybe because he's the most annoying human being on the planet in this or any other era?* Allie thought.

Annoying or not, he was definitely getting the short end of the stick in this situation. His hair was a matted, twig-festooned mess and several weeks' worth of tangled beard crept up his cheeks.

"Shut up," the man said. "Be polite. We seem to have received a new guest in the night." He nodded, not unkindly, at where Allie huddled in the corner of the tent, shocked immobile by any number of things, not least of which was her total comprehension of what the bulky-muscled man had said. Even though he'd clearly spoken in a language she was deeply unfamiliar with. She didn't have time, though, to question that fact. Not in that moment.

Morholt's head snapped up. "What?" he barked. "Who is it? Who's there?"

In the dim light, his ink-black gaze fastened on her face.

Allie held her breath.

Then Morholt threw his arms in the air and shouted, "YES! It worked!"

The handful of other prisoners in the tent gaped at him as he leaped to his feet and did as much of a victory jig as the chains around his ankles would allow. He hobbled toward Allie, a mad grin on his face, and cackled at her when she drew back in revulsion. He *really* needed a bath. Morholt clutched his little book to his chest and did a little spin.

"I win!" he crowed gleefully, giggling like the obvious maniac he'd become. "D'you hear that?" he shouted, pointing at the tent roof as Allie and the others stared at him, agog. "Suck it, cruel Fate!"

## 9

"Seriously. How long does it take to 'ooh' and 'aah' over a couple of stupid coins?" Clare snapped. She was rapidly approaching the point where she'd storm into the tent and lob the skull at Ashbourne in front of his whole posse of grad students.

She'd been sitting there for the better part of an hour, with nothing to do but fret and scroll aimlessly through the web page where Al had live-streamed her explosive find. The comments trail had erupted into fast and furious banter among the regulars as to just what kind of practical jokes @Al-Mac and @ClareTheLoon were trying to pull and whether it was suitable for what was, ostensibly, a serious archaeological dig. That was sprinkled among the regular booby talk. After a while Clare stopped actively reading the comments and just ran her finger up and down the screen, scrolling back and forth through quips and admonishments.

**@GeoffreyMonBouche:** Fake!

**@DirtNap:** The hell??

**@HistoryInTheBuff:** I'm not sure what kind of prank this is, but not convinced it's appropriate for an academic outing. Disappointed.

**@DigFan:** What just happened? Did anyone else see that purple flash at 2:50?

**@BonerWahoo:** BOOBS!!!

"Okaaay ..." Clare sighed. "Flagging this Wahoo guy's comment as inappropriate ... yet again."

The trail of comments continued, gibberish mostly, unabated. Clare scanned away without paying any of it an ounce of attention:

**@SirCharlesQuackalot:** How did u do that?! Was that a skull?

**@ArthurDentsTrowel:** wth? completely agree with history-inthebuff. disappointed. was really looking forward to seeing what you found. dramatics and silly special fx unnecessary. @Al-Mac, please take this seriously. history is not something to be tom-fooleried about with. yes I know that's not a word. also? what are you doing wednesday eve?

**@TardyTardis404:** Must say—interest is piqued. This could be a significant find but would like to know more. What happened after @Al-Mac shimmers off camera? Details please.

"Wait." Clare went cold.

She turned to show Milo, but just then the tent flap at Command Central flew wide and the grad students, beaming smugly at each other, poured out, heading in the direction of the town and—no doubt—the nearest pub to celebrate their find.

"You guys exhumed spare change," Milo muttered, prickly with worry over his cousin's disappearance. "Get over yourselves."

"Hullo! Are you waiting for me?"

Clare and Milo got up and turned to see Dr. Ashbourne, chief archaeologist, beaming genially at them from the door of the tent.

"Marvellous! Marvellous. More eager young people champing at the bit to unearth the past." Despite the cheerful words, there was a world-weariness to Ashbourne's tone. "Come in ..."

Clare froze in place, but Ashbourne huffed impatiently and shooed her in through the flap. Milo followed, and together they stood fidgeting at the large trestle table where the day's precious finds were laid out on a clean white cloth—six small, tarnished metal discs, more or less round, with ragged edges and pitted faces. Clare could barely keep from rolling her eyes at the rinky-dinkedness of it all.

Still, she was surprised when Ashbourne plucked up one of the coins and absently began flipping it in the air, catching it, and flipping it again. His normally goofy-grin expression had crumpled behind his moustache and he looked almost solemn. Lost in thought and weary. But then he seemed to remember that Clare and Milo were standing there, staring at him. He cleared his throat and, with another flick of his thumb, sent the coin spinning through the air at Clare.

She caught it reflexively, and saw Milo's eyes go panic-wide for an instant. But there was nothing. No shimmering ... not even static electricity. Clare stared down at the coin in her palm. It was just a coin, old and crusted with dirt.

"So? Yes? What is it, then?" Ashbourne suddenly barked like a terrier, startling Clare and Milo both. "Have you come to offer up resignations? Are you one of the many who can't take the conditions? Too hot, too cold, too boring out in the field?"

The archaeologist straightened up, threw back his shoulders, and glared back and forth at them. Clare balled up her fists and shoved them in her jacket pockets, taking a step backward away from the table.

"Actually, Dr. Ashbourne," Milo began, "we really—"

"We *really* wanted to congratulate you!" Clare interrupted. "And the money."

"You wanted to congratulate the money?" The archaeologist frowned.

"Well, no. The coins. More like the ... er ... finding thereof." She pasted a big smile on her face and reached forward to give the professor a convivial punch to the shoulder. "Well done! On the money finding. Right, Milo? That's it! That's *all* we wanted."

"Um ..." Milo reined in his confusion admirably. "Right. That's all ..."

"Just, y'know, huzzah!" Clare cheered.

"And … on that note, I should get Clare back to her trench now," Milo said, retreating. "So she can find a coin or two of her own."

Ashbourne shrugged and twisted a moustache end. "Well now, very well. That is the kind of spirited pursuit I like to see in my trowel monkeys. Marvellous. Carry on. Good hunting to you."

"Can hardly wait!" Clare enthused as she let Milo grab her by the elbow and tug her toward the tent flap.

Milo picked up the skull-toting knapsack in his other hand and together they left the mildly bemused archaeologist alone in his tent. Clare led the way through the site excavations, past the few straggling diggers who hadn't yet packed it in to go celebrate the coinage, and back toward her own little secluded hole in the ground the next field over. When they reached the trenches where she and Al had been working, Milo finally pulled Clare to a stop and turned her around.

"Okay," he said. "We're all alone. Now are you going to fill me in on the sudden about-face?"

Clare nodded and wordlessly handed over the tablet, pointing to the comment from @TardyTardis404. "Read that one."

Milo peered at the entry and murmured, *"Shimmers …"* His eyes flicked up and he stared over the top of his glasses at Clare.

"Coincidence?" she asked dryly.

Milo didn't blink. "Yes?"

Clare gave him her best flat glare. Milo continued to gaze at her in the calm, steady, normally Very Sexy (but in that moment Extremely Vexing) way he had.

"Not so long ago," she said evenly, "you said you were starting to think there was no such thing as coincidence."

The staring contest continued until Milo frowned faintly and looked back down at the screen. He read the entry again. His frown deepened. Then he sat down on the edge of Al's trench with his long legs dangling over the side, called up Al's video blog entry, and watched it closely. Three times. Finally he put the tablet down on the grass beside him and pushed his glasses up on his fore-head, hooking a finger across the bridge of his nose. His eyes were still fixed on the screen, which had gone dark, but Clare could see the gears whirring in the mind behind the placid blue stare.

"There's something ... *odd* about this," he said.

*Ah ha! I'm not imagining things,* Clare thought as she sank down beside him. This time it *was* different.

"Allie falls out of frame ..." Milo muttered as he reached over and touched the screen, playing the video through. "And the quality of the light changes. Like suddenly it's a different time of day ..."

Clare leaned over his shoulder, eyes narrowed.

"But there's no shimmer." Milo ran the clip once more. "No coruscation."

"No what?"

"Sparkling. When *you* time-travel," he explained, "you sort of ... light up your surroundings for an instant. Like a birthday cake sparkler. With this," he tapped the screen with his knuckle, "it's sort of the reverse. It looks more like it's the surroundings that change. It's not coming from Allie. At least, it doesn't seem like it ..."

"Right." Clare watched the video looping.

She'd known there was something different. She just hadn't managed to articulate what that something was. But Milo was right. Given her own experiences tearing around in the space–time continuum, Clare had just sort of assumed she knew what was going on with Allie when she disappeared. But now she saw that the ambient light in the video *did* shift dramatically—suddenly becoming tinged with red and purple, as though that part of the video had been shot during twilight against a particularly vibrant sunset ...

But there was no shimmering. None of the telltale fireworks sparkliness that had always seemed to accompany Clare's supernatural jaunts. Light, but no light *show.* Al hadn't shimmered. Not exactly.

*And yet ...* TardyTardis404 seemed to have assumed she had. Just as Clare and Milo did—initially. Which meant that TardyTardis404 knew what "shimmering" *was.*

"Okay," Milo said, coming to the same conclusion. "I'm not saying this comment isn't still a long shot. But maybe it warrants at least a bit of investigating."

"Right." Clare nodded, relieved. "That's what I thought. Listen ... can one of your compu-guru buddies help you track a user address from a comment thread like this?"

"I don't *need* help for that." Milo's mouth bent up at one corner in a devastatingly sexy mastermind kind of smirk. He cracked his knuckles, unslung his computer bag from his shoulder, and flipped open his laptop. "That's kiddie play. Here ... let me see the tablet and give me a few minutes."

Clare handed over the tablet and sat impatiently as Milo tapped away on his laptop, downloading dodgy software and trading chatter on dodgy sites. Seven minutes later he leaned back on one elbow in the grass, and with an only slightly smug grin, turned the screen toward Clare. She watched in fascination as a Google map zoomed in on the GPS coordinates of ... someplace just down the road?

Clare blinked and looked closer. "Can you do a street view?"

Milo tapped at the keyboard and made a surprised noise when the street view popped up, showing the front of a building they both recognized instantly.

"Well, whaddya know," Clare said grimly. "Looks like we get to pay another visit to Goggles McFish'n'Chips and the Old Curiosity Shop."

THE BLINDS WERE ALL DRAWN and the CLOSED sign was hung up. But one stiff push and the door opened wide. Goggles must have forgotten to lock it.

"That was careless," Clare said as they stepped into the dim, dusty confines of the cluttered shop. She glanced around at the shadowy rows of curio cases and shelves jammed with a funhouse assortment of oddities and unidentifiables, from tacky souvenirs to legitimate-seeming antiques and collectibles. Miniature glow-in-

the-dark Stonehenges shared space with fully articulated bat skel-
etons hanging from the ceiling and a suit of armour that looked
as though it might come to life and start wreaking havoc with the
mace in its iron fist.

The place was deserted. And super creepy.

Clare barely noticed. She was on a mission. She had an overwhelming hunch to play out and she wasn't about to let the heebie-
jeebies get in the way. In a half-dozen purposeful strides, she'd
travelled the length of the long, narrow space toward the beaded
curtain covering the door to the back room that Goggles had disappeared through in such a hurry the last time they'd paid the
shop a visit. She was pretty certain now that funky seafood had
had nothing to do with that hasty exit.

She was right.

As Clare was walking in, Goggles was walking out, wearing
entirely different safety eyewear. The girl must have had a cabinet
full of the things. These had magnifying lenses that gave her a
clownishly startled air as—head down, hoodie up—she almost
plowed right into Clare. But she stopped just short and the two
girls faced off like a pair of wary gunslingers in the Old West.

Then Goggles made a break for it.

She got about three feet before Clare had her pinned up against
a shelf, held there by the threat of a rhinestone-handled Charles
and Diana commemorative letter opener she'd snagged off a
nearby table. Behind her magnifying safety glasses, the girl's eyes
were pie-sized and darted back and forth between Clare, Milo, and
the letter opener.

*"You,"* Clare said in her most threatening voice.

All things considered, it wasn't half bad on a one-to-ten menace
scale. She hadn't exactly been taking notes the last time she'd been
threatened with a sharp object (and, really, it had happened more
times in recent weeks than she cared to think about), but she'd
obviously picked up a few "pointers."

*Heh ...*

Out of the corner of her eye, Clare saw Milo do a double take at her. She ignored him to maintain the effect and jabbed the air with the opener.

"You know me, don't you?" Clare said in a low, growly tone.

"I ... um ..."

"*Don't* you?"

"I don't know what you're talking about— OW!"

Another threatening jab, but this time Clare accidentally caught the fleshy bit of the girl's shoulder and freaked herself out enough to almost drop the little blade.

"How?" she asked. "How do you know about me?"

Goggles twisted away from the opener, a mutinous gleam in her magnified brown eyes. Her lips disappeared in a thin line as she rubbed the spot where Clare had poked her.

"Oh, come on!" Clare snorted. "That totally didn't even hurt." Still, she backed off—not much, but enough to give the girl a bit of room. "That wasn't a food poisoning episode this afternoon. You recognized me. How? I've never been here before."

"I swear I don't— GAH! Stop that!"

*Okay. So much for backing off and non-threatening.*

This time Clare didn't pull the letter opener away. Its point made a divot in the material of the girl's sweatshirt.

"You're TardyTardis404." Clare applied a bit more pressure. "And you used the word 'shimmer' in your comment on Al-Mac's video blog. I want to know why you used *that* specific word and I want to know what you know about what happened to Al."

A long pause. "I'll tell you. I'll tell you everything I know."

"I'm listening," Clare said.

"Not now." Goggles's eyes narrowed behind the lenses and she lifted her chin in a defiant gesture. "Come back tomorrow."

"Why?"

"Because I said so. That's why."

"Seriously." Milo shook his head in weary annoyance. "You know you're just quoting *Raiders of the Lost Ark* now, right?"

The girl looked over at Milo, and Clare thought she saw a spark of interest flare in those comically distorted eyes.

"Of course I know," she said with an air of huffy superiority.

Clare was about to lose it, but Goggles seemed to sense she was on the verge of getting stabbed with the letter opener again. For realsies.

"Look. You *really* do have to come back tomorrow," she said.

"And you *really* do have to tell me why," Clare said.

Goggles huffed in frustration. "Because the bank is closed and *that's* where my safe deposit box is. Trust me," she added, her big brown blinky eyes gleaming with a strange, fervent light. "I'll be here tomorrow morning. And I'll have something that you're very much going to want to see. I promise you."

Something in the way the girl said it made Clare think she'd actually keep her word. It seemed that, whatever was going on, it was just as important to Goggles as it was to Clare and Milo. And Al.

And so, while it wasn't much to go on, it seemed clear that Goggles's promise was all they'd get. Clare didn't know what else to do, short of actually stabbing her, and she really wasn't prepared to cross that line. They'd just have to wait until morning. *First* thing in the morning, she made the other girl promise—and took the Chuck and Di letter opener as insurance (there was a tag on the handle that priced the gaudy thing at £150).

As the door to the shop closed behind them, Clare heard Goggles say, "See you tomorrow, Clarinet Reid ..."

Milo just sighed, muttered "Movie geek," and led Clare down the street and back toward the Avalon Mists B&B. All she wanted now was a shower.

Later, she sat down slowly on Al's bed. It took every ounce of strength she had to keep from weeping at the thought that she very well might be spending the night alone in the room, staring over at Al's empty pillow. In all honesty, Clare wondered if she'd ever see her best friend again. And that was messed up.

*Seriously.*

*SERIOUSLY?*

Allie never thought she'd ever see Stuart Morholt again.

The museum thief/kidnapper/all-round overachiever in the ass-hat department had been trapped for good—for*ever*—in the first century. Of course, Allie hadn't counted on travelling back to that very same century herself.

Because, really? What were the odds?

"I beat the odds!" squawked that all-too-familiar voice.

That set Allie's teeth on edge like fingernails down a chalk-board—it was almost enough to stop being terrified.

"I can't believe it worked!" Morholt crowed to the big bearded man, receiving a stony stare in return. "Em ... what I mean is—see *that*, you great lout?" He pointed an outstretched finger at Allie. "What did I tell you? My powers are mighty! For here is the one—or at least the annoying know-it-all Bentley-wrecker *sidekick* of the one—that your high priestess, the Druidess Mallora, has foreseen. I have brought this thing to pass. Me." He waved a hand airily toward the legionnaire standing guard outside the tent flap. "And my magic will save us from the clutches of those wretched imperial drones."

"What *is* that?" Allie asked, incredulous. "Like, a top-ten-rejected *Star Wars* line? Do you even *listen* to yourself?"

When Morholt blinked at her in confusion, Allie realized that the pop-culture reference hadn't been deliberate. He really was *just* that obtuse. In that moment she desperately missed her cousin Milo, who would have totally gotten where she was coming from.

And yet, strangely enough, Allie was almost relieved to find Stuart Morholt there in the prisoners' tent. At the very least, he was something—some*one*—familiar. She wasn't as completely alone as she'd thought. She had company in her misery, no matter how miserable the company might be.

Morholt turned back to the Celtic prisoners, most of whom were either staring at him uncomprehendingly or ignoring him altogether. "She'll get us—and by 'us' I mean 'me'—out of here," he said. "That is, if she knows what's good for her."

Allie just snorted and shook her head. "I can't. I'm stuck here."

"What? *What?*" Morholt's eyes narrowed and he glared at her in disbelief. "What do you mean you're stuck here?"

"See, that's the funny thing." She grinned at him bitterly. "I thought I was speaking English. And even if I wasn't, apparently that's not a requirement." Allie turned her gaze to the bearlike man who'd punched Stuart Morholt in the arm. She wished it had been his head. "I mean, I could understand you perfectly a few seconds ago, and I don't know ... um ... that was Iceni, wasn't it?"

The man's eyebrows raised a little, and Allie could see he'd understood her. Just as she had understood the Roman soldiers—and just as Clare's physical contact with a Druid blacksmith had transferred a comprehension of each other's language between them. Yay magic.

"You're *him*, aren't you?" Allie asked. "Llassar? Boudicca's smith?"

He nodded once. "I am he," he said in Iceni. "And *you* ... I think we have a friend in common."

Allie smiled wanly. She liked Llassar already and could see why Clare had trusted him. "Yeah," she said. "Clare described you pretty well."

Right down to the burn scars on the man's huge knuckles and the singed patches in his hair and beard. And the keenly perceptive gaze—which was now fixed unblinkingly on Allie.

"You and she are bound by blood," Llassar continued. It sounded more like a statement than a question.

"Well ... yeah." Allie shrugged, not bothering to ask how he knew that. He was a Druid mystic after all, a sorceror, and it was a theory she and Clare had come to on their own anyway. "But only, like, a drop."

She stared down at the little black dot in the centre of her thumb pad that she'd acquired when, as kids, she and Clare had pricked their thumbs with a safety pin and tied them together until they turned blue, thereby signifying that they were blood sisters. Inseparable. (Really, really *dumb*, sure, and lucky that neither of them wound up with an infection, but inseparable.) One teeny, tiny drop—Allie supposed that, where magic was concerned, it was more a quality than a quantity kind of thing—but it was why Allie had been Clare's homing beacon, calling to her from her own time and place with the voice of a raven whenever Clare needed to find her way back from the past.

Allie—now stuck in that very same past—could understand Llassar because *Clare* had been able to understand him. At least that part of the equation worked. So why hadn't Clare called her back home? Did she even know Allie was missing? Did she care?

*Oh, stop it. You're being ridiculous. Of course she cares.* Although it *was* possible that Clare hadn't yet noticed. Or figured out that Allie had travelled into the past. Clare had been a mite preoccupied with Milo, after all ...

"Welcome to Ynys Wyddryn, Lady," Llassar rumbled at her. "The Isle of Glass. I apologize for not being able to greet you properly, as a host and a free man, but ..." He held up his manacled wrists and shrugged his bulky shoulders.

"Um. Yeah." Allie frowned down at her own wrists, which were beginning to ache from the tug of heavy iron. "I'm not really sure what I'm doing here. Or how I got here ... but thanks."

"I do not know, either," Llassar said. "But I can tell you that this place—the Tor—is the heart of Prydain."

Allie understood that *Prydain* was his word—the ancient Iceni word—for "Britain."

He lifted his chin and his eyes shone fiercely. "Nowhere is the magic of my people stronger."

"Great," Allie muttered, thinking that if the magic Llassar was so proud of was really all that and a bag of chips, then what was he doing chained, a prisoner in a Roman camp? "I just hope it's strong enough to get me the hell home," she murmured.

"Us! Get *us* the hell home, you rotten little auto wrecker!" Morholt interjected. "I didn't bring you here for a vacation, you know! You owe me."

"*Owe* you?"

"Do you have any idea how much it's going to cost to have my Bentley repaired? A new fender—those things are custom-produced and worth a pretty penny, I can tell you—and a new paint job? You've seen to it my mechanic will retire a rich man!"

*Okay,* Allie thought, *Stu has clearly lost his marbles.* "You've got to be kidding me," she said. "You've been stuck back here for who knows how long and all you've done is obsess about your—admittedly choice—ride?" She *had* thought the Bentley was pretty stylish ...

"I want my car back!" Morholt screeched. "I want my life back! Oh, what I wouldn't give to return to the land of gentlemen's clubs and saunas and proper barbers." His black eyes glinted maniacally. "Well, actually, what I *would* give, Ms. McAllister, is *you.* To whatever misbegotten, bloodthirsty, ancient Celtic deity can transport me out of this wretched era and back into my own. And I'll cheerfully throw Clarinet Reid into the bargain if I can get my hands on her as well. Which, in fact, was rather the plan in the first place. I'm not sure why she countermanded my instructions and sent you in her stead." He sniffed in annoyance.

"What are you talking about, you head case?" Allie's anxiety had pre-empted her normally cucumber-cool demeanour. "Clare didn't send me. *You* didn't give her instructions. You had nothing to do with me being here at all!"

"Didn't I? What about *this* then?" He brandished the little book he'd been writing in as if it were some sort of talisman. "It's finally found its way into Miss Reid's grubby little hands, hasn't it? Mallora foresaw the whole thing, that clever girl. She promised me that it would pass down through generations of our descendants. Hand to hand, mother to daughter to granddaughter, straight down through the ages ... until such time as one of them could ultimately arrange for your ridiculous chum to stumble upon it. And she was right!"

"What is that, a notebook?" Allie squinted at the thing in the dim light, not really having followed Morholt's frothy raving. "Big whoop."

"It's *the* notebook, you little miscreant. The one you and your meddling monkey Bee-Eff-Eff Clare *found*," Morholt scoffed, employing air quotes.

*Wow,* Allie thought. Having his nefarious plots foiled by a couple of teenagers had really turned the guy bitter toward her demographic. Morholt ignored her head-shaking and kissed the book's cover.

"Huzzah for acid-free paper," he chortled. "Oh, it pays to buy quality merchandise—"

"We didn't find that."

He glared narrowly at her. "I don't believe you."

"I don't care what you—Wait." Allie frowned. "What did you mean ... your *descendants*?"

"Yes. Well ..." Morholt stroked his goatee in a way probably meant to convey suaveness, but since the thing had grown ratty with prison neglect he only made it stick out in odd places. He didn't seem to notice. "I *do* have a way with the ladies, you know," he smugged. "Particularly a certain High Druidess—a very power-ful sorceress—who, it just so happens, could not help succumbing to my raging charms. Also, I may have gotten her a little drunk. Or possibly it was the other way around. Really, the whole episode is a little murky—"

"Oh *gawd!*"

"—but suffice to say, there *will* be descendants. Oh yes."

"I'm so gonna barf," Allie groaned, thoroughly squicked out. She involuntarily recalled his image in the photo Maggie carried and shuddered at the thought of the leather pants and pirate shirt ensemble.

"Look. I'm telling you ... I've never seen your stupid journal," she reiterated.

Morholt's eye narrowed further. "But if you didn't get here by way of *this*"—he brandished the book—"then how did you get here?"

"Beats me. All I know is that one minute I'm digging in a field and the next minute I find a skull. Then ... zot." Her hands did a little squiggly dance. "Here I am."

Morholt's lip twitched. "I thought Clare was the, er, zotter."

"Yeah? You and me both."

"Mallora doesn't believe in leaving things to chance," Llassar said suddenly. "This one's—what does he call it? book?—is one path to achieving a goal. But Mallora made sure there was another. There is always a way."

Allie stood up and moved closer to the Druid smith, crouching down in front of him and trying her best to ignore Morholt. "You mean, like a ... a contingency plan?"

Llassar shrugged one muscle-bound shoulder. "I do not know the word," he said in his quiet rumble of a voice. "But I sense that yes, we speak of the same thing. Mallora was intrigued by the things this one told her when we brought him before her in the sanctuary of Mona. What is left of it, that is ... after the Romans burned the oak groves." He tipped his chin in the direction of Morholt, who, no longer the centre of attention, was quietly simmering. "She listened to the stories he told of his time—a time when the Romans had been driven from this land—and it fired her imagination. She devised a ... as you say—a plan. She seeks to bridge the gap between that realm and our own."

Allie remembered Clare saying that Connal, her Druid hottie pal, really had no sense of the passage of great lengths of time. That he couldn't wrap his head around concepts like the distant future. That the Druiddyn lived in the "here and now." Well, it sounded like that was exactly what this Mallora person had in mind. Turning Glastonbury into one big "here and now" no matter where and when you were. It sounded like a terrible idea. But that wasn't all.

"And then," Llassar continued, "she means to send her scathach—her warrior women—out into that realm to claim it in the name of Andrasta, our goddess."

"Oh boy ..." Allie muttered. She knew all about Andrasta. Bloodthirsty, war-hungry, vengeful (probably even more so after what had befallen the Iceni people), and terrifyingly powerful: the Raven Goddess.

"That is why we are in this place. Mallora has seen to it that the Romans are trapped here. They will fight here and die here, at the foot of the Tor, spilling their blood into the soil of Ynys Wyddryn. Once enough of them are dead, the gateway will open, and the worlds will collide. Yours ... and mine."

## 10

Clare had a death grip on a travel mug full of coffee when she and Milo returned to the antique shop just after eight the next morning. She hadn't gotten a whole lot of sleep. Trying to avoid the B&B if Al wasn't going to be there, she'd made Milo go out for dinner with her—which she was too stressed to eat, and then for a long walking tour of every Glastonbury landmark—which she'd been too stressed to pay much attention to, and then finally on a search for a late-night movie theatre—which, of course, didn't exist in the tiny town. It had all exhausted her enough that she was finally able to go back to her room, turn her face to the wall, and catch a few brief winks.

But it had put her in a very touchy mood. And if Goggles didn't have anything to show them that would help bring Al home, Clare was reasonably certain she'd go Defcon One on her baggypants, hyper-bespectacled ass.

The front door was once again open, and they found Goggles squirrelled away in the back room. She was perched on a stool at a workbench wearing yet another set of protective eyewear—clear safety lenses this time, with round, convex magnifying bubbles in the centre for close-up work—and her attention was focused, laserlike, on the object in front of her.

Gone was the oversized sweatshirt. Goggles wore a fitted black tank top instead, negating Clare's earlier suspicion that she'd been hiding some sort of less-than-perfect physique. In fact, Goggles sported a petite but annoyingly sculpted body. She still had on the same baggy cargo pants, but slung low on her hips and with a multitude of belts, they only served to emphasize her lithe figure. She wore stripy fingerless gloves that went up to her elbows and her hair, which was dyed a silvery-white shade of platinum blonde, was pulled up into two winglike ponytails high on either side of her head. What with the eyewear, she looked kind of like an anime character. The kind that nerd boys everywhere developed crushes on. Milo was a nerd boy. Clare felt herself frowning and wondered where the sweatshirt had disappeared to. And why.

*Not the time,* she chastised herself. *More important things to worry about ...*

Goggles held what looked to be a tiny, cordless circular saw, which was whining at the elevated pitch of a kicked hornet's nest and effectively masked their approach. Maybe not *quite* so cool as the image she projected, the girl jumped two feet straight up when Clare tapped her on the shoulder. The mini-saw zanged and whizzed, skittering across the workbench and gouging chunks out of its surface. Piles of junk flew everywhere as Goggles yelped and scrambled after the thing before it could slice through the boxy item she'd been hunched over. She lunged for the saw, Clare grabbed at the box, and Milo went for the electrical outlet, unplugging the cord before the machine took off Clare's fingers at the knuckles.

The silence was deafening.

It stretched out for a long moment.

Then Goggles cleared her throat and pointed tentatively at the box in Clare's hands. "Can I have that back, please?"

Clare glanced down at the little tin box that was sealed with a band of bronze. "No."

"Thank you. I— Wait. What?"

"Not until I get some answers." She hefted the box: it wasn't heavy, but it had the feel of containing something. "You said come back tomorrow. That's now today. You said you'd have something to show us."

"I did. And there's a good chance you're going to think I'm some kind of outrageous fraud the minute I do. But just so we understand each other, I am totally on the level." Goggles crossed her arms over her chest defensively. "And I also locked away all the pointy artifacts, in case you decide otherwise."

Clare had brought the letter opener with her and was about to fish it out from her bag when Milo plugged the little buzz saw back into the outlet. It whizzed maniacally for a moment, then Milo unplugged it again and said dryly, "This isn't pointy, but it'll do the trick. If I were you, I'd do my best to convince us you're not a fraud."

Clare kind of loved it when Milo got all tough-guy like that. But now wasn't the time to indulge her appreciation. "Okay, Goggles," she said. "I'm listening."

"Gogg ...?" The other girl blinked—it was a little like watching one of those YouTube videos of puppies shot up close through a fish-eye lens—and then pulled off her headgear and turned to hang it on a peg. "Goggles. Sure. I get it. How droll."

The girl turned back toward them, and Clare felt her spine stiffen when she saw her unadorned face for the first time. Somehow she'd expected that even without the goggles the girl's amphibian look would remain. Not so much. Probably around nineteen, with dark brown eyes and delicate features currently set in a mule-stubborn expression, Goggles was pretty. Really pretty. Beside Clare, Milo made a small, surprised noise.

*I guess he thought the same thing. And I bet he thinks she's pretty, too—*

*Dude,* Clare admonished her own brain. *Seriously not the time.*

The girl looked back and forth between Clare and Milo and huffed an impatient sigh. Then she turned to face Clare squarely. "My name is Piper Gimble."

"Uh huh." Clare couldn't care less what her name was. And she was unaccountably irritated by the fact that the girl's voice was low and sort of musical, with an accent Clare thought might originate from somewhere around Liverpool. She sounded like a Beatles groupie and it was annoyingly interesting. Clare had always kind of wished she'd had an accent. She wondered if her own voice sounded nasal and flat in Milo's ears in comparison ...

"In one very real sense," Piper was saying, "I suppose I owe my very existence to you, Miss Reid."

"Uh hu— What?" Clare blinked.

Piper rolled her eyes and waved at a couple of stools on the other side of the workbench. "Sit. I'm going to put the kettle on."

"Not thirsty."

"It's not for you," Piper snapped irritably. "It's for me. A cup of tea calms my nerves. Okay, that's a lie ... a shot of brandy in a cup of tea calms my nerves."

Clare could hardly argue with that, even if it would never occur to her to try calming down that way. She looked over at Milo and shrugged. The two of them pulled the pair of stools over and perched upon them while Piper slammed around a tiny kitchenette at the back of the room, concocting her nerve tonic.

"You have to understand something," Piper began as she splashed amber liquid from an antique silver hip flask into a steaming china cup. "These are rather ... extraordinary circumstances for me." She blew on the liquid, took a sip, grimaced at the heat, and then took a slug directly from the flask before putting it away. Colour flushed into her cheeks as Clare and Milo sat waiting, patience thinning perceptibly. "Right. So. I have to commend you, Miss Reid. It must have taken a great deal of effort to piss off someone like Stuart Morholt as badly as you di—"

Clare actually fell off her stool at the mention of the name, but Milo didn't so much fall as *launch* himself off his. And Piper Gimble suddenly found herself backed up against the wall again.

"What the hell do you know about that son of a bitch Morholt?" Milo snarled, one fist cocked at his side.

"Milo!" Clare yelped.

He looked like he was seriously considering punching Piper's ticket, girl or no. In another moment, Clare might just let him. But not before she figured out what on earth this annoying girl was talking about. She stepped up beside Milo and put a hand on his elbow. Lightly.

"Here's something *you* have to understand, *Miss* Gimble. My best friend's continued well-being is at stake here. My best friend *and* Milo's cousin. We're very fond of her and if you're standing in the way of us getting her back, then life is going to become very uncomfortable for you in the next few minutes. Now. What do you know about Morholt? And what does it have to do with Al's disappearance?"

Piper's eyes shifted back and forth, and then she nodded in the direction of the little tin box that Clare still held, forgotten, in her right hand. "Look at it," she said grudgingly. "Look at the lid ..."

Clare frowned, but did as Piper asked. She looked at the box. At the lid. She looked at it for a long time. And then she said, in a quiet voice, "Let her go, Milo."

A prickly sense of foreboding settled over her like an unpleasant acquaintance throwing his arm over your shoulder at a party and settling in for a good, long, excruciating chat. Clare's name— her *actual* name—was scratched on the lid of Piper Gimble's precious little box. In fact, it wasn't just her name, but a set of instructions that included her name. Mostly, it seemed, because they were directed at her:

*This tin is to be kept sealed and held in perpetuity by my direct descendants with my express wishes that it be handed down hereditarily. It is to be opened only by that meddlesome brat* CLARINET REID.

The instructions even included an exact date—that *very day*, in fact—when the box opening was to take place. All of which was disconcerting enough. But then, on the back side of the tin:

*Instructions are to be followed on pain of incurring a* DRUID BLOOD CURSE. *And I can do it, too. Don't think I can't.*

Beneath *that* were initials:

## S. M.

Clare put the box down on the counter as if it contained a nest of vipers. And, really, she wouldn't have been surprised if it had. By the time she'd gotten to the initials, Clare had recognized the handwriting. Stuart Morholt had once left another set of instructions for Milo, warning him not to call the police after Morholt had abducted Clare and Al in an attempt to send Clare on a spatio-temporal treasure hunt for him. Clare would recognize it anywhere— even Morholt's penmanship was snotty and self-important.

She dragged her gaze away from the scratched letters and examined the container itself. The tin was sealed by a thick bronze band that ran all the way around the seam like a collar. It was decorated with a swirling, elegant pattern remarkably similar to a couple of other significant artifacts Clare had come across in her travels. Llassar's distinctive handiwork.

"Hand me the circular saw, please," Piper said quietly. "And the box."

Clare picked up the little motorized blade and handed it over along with the tin, too flummoxed to ask why. And too curious to argue. In a few moments, Piper had carefully sawed through the bronze seal. She removed the band gently and set it down on the worktable.

"So ... what is it?" Clare asked.

"It's an heirloom of sorts, I suppose," Piper said. "A legacy. Passed down through two thousand years' worth of my family's generations."

"Two thou— The thing in the tin is *that* old?"

Piper rolled an eye at her. "The tin itself is that old, Miss Reid."

Sure it was. Except for the fact that it looked more like a mini survival kit that Clare could have bought at a Mountain Equipment Co-op in Toronto, or at any other high-end outdoor lifestyle store—

an emergency camping/road kit that had probably once held candles, matches, and a granola bar.

Inside it now was only a yellowed and slightly brittle heavy-duty waterproof zip-lock baggie. Piper pulled on a pair of blue latex gloves—like the kind coroners in cop shows wore—over her stripy knit fingerless ones and reached into the box, delicately removing the bundled object. She opened the plastic baggie with the care of a surgeon, prying the zipper lock open with needle-nose tweezers. Whatever was inside was wrapped in a strip of what looked like faded black canvas ... with a zipper sort of randomly attached to one end.

Clare stared at it uncomprehendingly, even as something in the back of her mind already recognized the fabric for what it was. A piece of Stuart Morholt's high-tech jumpsuit. The one he'd been wearing at the museum. When Clare had let go of the Snettisham Torc ... stranding Morholt in the far distant past with absolutely no way to get home. She remembered the ridiculous apparel and all the supplies Morholt had packed in its various pockets and pouches—supplies like the mini emergency tin. Clare held her breath as Piper peeled back the jumpsuit fabric to reveal ... a book.

Well. That was a bit of a letdown.

"What is it?" Clare asked, picking it up carefully. It was definitely old, with a slightly musty odour, like a second-hand bookshop find.

"It's a priceless ancient artifact from the first century," Piper said matter-of-factly.

"Oh, it is *not*! It's a notebook from the stationery department at Harrods. Look, you can still just make out the price tag. Try explaining *that* to a museum curator." Clare held it up and pointed to the lower right corner of the back cover. "See? Forty pounds. What the hell kind of joke are you trying to pull? ... Wait." She blinked and peered again at the little tag. "That's, like, *eighty* dollars or something. Who pays that for a notebook?"

"It's a limited-edition Moleskine. They're a venerable company. Archival paper only," Piper pointed out. "Acid-free. Guaranteed to last for hundreds, if not—as is apparently the case here—thousands of years. Under ideal conditions, that is."

Of course. It *was* a priceless—or rather, pric*ey*—artifact from the first century. It had to be. And it had to have belonged to Stuart Morholt. Only an über-status-conscious wanker like Stu would shell out that kind of cash for a freaking notebook. Clare wouldn't have been surprised to learn that Stu was the type to go "glamping," He'd probably used one of those silly super-expensive space-age high-tech gel pens to write in the diary, too. The ones advertised as being able to write upside down and under water and in zero-g. Just in case he ever found himself in the Lost City of Atlantis or abducted by aliens.

"Paper is, in fact, a remarkably durable substance under most conditions that don't include moisture," Piper was saying. "That's why people still find perfectly legible centuries-old newspapers stuffed between the walls of old houses. And then there's the Dead Sea Scrolls, of course. And, as you can see, my, er, ancestor went to rather great lengths to ensure the preservation of this particular artifact."

"Yeah." Clare turned the book over and over in her hands, only half listening. "That. Plus it's probably got a spell cast on it."

Piper actually went a wee bit pale. "Do you really think so?"

"If he thought it would help, Morholt wouldn't hesitate to curse the thing." She waved at the broken bronze seal that Milo had picked up and was examining minutely. "I recognize the designs on the band. It was made by another guy—a metalsmith and a Druid—who could do just that. That is, if Stu could somehow con someone like Llassar into working the magic for him."

"Right," Milo murmured. "And he'd do that because the inane ramblings of Stuart Morholt are considered worthy of posterity and preservation down through the ages."

"Sure," Clare agreed. "By Stuart Morholt."

Milo turned to Piper. "The instructions on the tin expressly say that Clare is the one who's supposed to open this. Clare only." He held up the bronze band. "The seal on this band has been broken. And then re-soldered."

Clare recalled their first encounter with Piper, when she'd sat, hunched over and hoodied, fixing that antique musical instrument—with a soldering iron.

"Of course I opened it," Piper said, huffing defensively. "The minute the thing passed on from my grandmother into my hands. And, yes, I read the diary. And after I was done? I assumed it was a grand, ridiculous hoax. I didn't *really* think you existed."

"Until the day I just happened to walk into your shop."

"Indeed. Just before the very day inscribed on the box. And then you presented me with a passport that had your full name on it." Piper shook her head. "I mean, I'd been keeping an eye on your excavation blog, but you call yourself Clare on the site bio, and there are bound to be more than one or two Clare Reids out there in the world. *Clarinet* Reids on the other hand—as specified on the tin—well, come on now." She snorted. "I mean, I'm descended from a long and well-documented line of complete bloody lunatics, and I don't think anyone in *my* family ever sported a moniker quite that ridiculous."

Milo raised an eyebrow at her.

"What?" Piper protested. "The poor girl's parents named her after the mouthpiece on a musical instrument that sounds like a duck."

"Oh ... shut up," Clare said sourly. *"Piper."*

"Right. Anyway." Piper rolled her eyes. "I suppose I should have known you'd find your way to my shop."

"Only because you made that stupid comment on the blog," Clare said.

"How do you know I didn't do it on purpose?" Piper cocked her head and glared at Clare. "How do you know I haven't lured you into a clever trap?"

"Uh huh. Have you?"

"Er ... no. Not really. Actually, I completely forgot to deadbolt the front door yesterday in all the excitement. Frankly," she said, waving at the diary, "after everything I've read, I'm rather terrified of you." She looked at Milo. "And *you*."

Milo shifted uncomfortably as Clare looked between him and Piper, wondering what on earth *that* crack meant. What exactly did Goggles have to fear from Milo? It occurred to Clare that maybe Piper was actually flirting with Milo in a weird way, and she surprised herself with a sudden urge to tear the girl's pony-tails off. She had to struggle not to let the emotion show on her face. To distract herself, she opened the book and started to read.

The plastic baggie—which Morholt had likely used to keep his strike-anywhere matches from getting damp—had kept the book dry and legible inside the protective tin. Clare had to grudgingly give Morholt credit. Even as the very thought of the guy made her want to punch a wall. Especially once she started reading what he'd written. To wit:

*I, Stuart Morholt, Archdruid extraordinaire, leave this written record as my legacy to you, Miss Reid. A legacy that will allow you to right the dreadful wrong done when you stranded me here in this temporal hellhole. And we both know just how fond you are of doing that sort of thing now don't we, you interfering little twit? So pay attention!*

"Wow," Clare muttered acidly. "Way to butter me up there, Stu. *Gawd* ... What an ass-hat."

Piper had been watching her intently. Now she sat back in her chair and groped blindly for the cup of brandy-spiked tea. "So it's true," she said. "The things he writes. I always thought my old gran had dreamed it up as some kind of elaborate practical joke. She used to own this place and willed it to me when she passed on. She was an absolute nutter. Still ... it's always been in the back of my mind that she might *not* have been having me on, you know?" Piper shook her head and her pale ponytails waggled.

"But then I'd tell myself I was being daft. Only ... I can see now. Watching you read those words. Stuart Morholt is real. And you ... You really are a time traveller."

"Yeah, well. It's kinda less grandly romantic than it sounds," Clare muttered, not really paying one hundred percent attention to what Piper was saying. "How'd you wind up with this again, exactly?"

"I just told you. My gran passed it on to me along with this shop. She was ... oh, how shall I describe the dear old bat?" Piper gazed up at the ceiling. "Ah yes. Barmy. I'm sure it's just the genetics coming out to play every several generations, but she was quite over the rainbow if you know what I mean. Toys in the attic. Gone right round the twist. Kookookajoob—"

"Yeah, okay! I get it."

"No, I don't think you do *get* it, Clare." Piper shook her head in frustration. "What I've been trying to tell you is that I, Piper M. Gimble, am the last in a long line of Stuart Morholt's descendants. *Direct* descendants."

Clare's brain made a noise like a phone that hadn't been hung up properly. If what Piper said was true, that meant Stu had ...

"Yes!" Piper nodded, reading Clare's expression. "That's it exactly. According to his diary, he had a grand old time getting it o— Er, getting romantic, that is—with a Druid high priestess by the name of Mallora. Mostly, as far as I can tell, because she'd foreseen the very moment wherein I was to pass along the notebook to you."

And so it finally sank in. The thought Clare had been actively avoiding.

She and Milo shared a glance.

"Okay." Clare held up a hand. "May I just express—for the record—the unknowably deep depths of my horrification at the very *concept* of Stuart Morholt getting jiggy with a Druid priestess way back in the day, just so he could leave me his diary to read?"

"No need." Milo's expression twisted with distaste. "Right there with you."

"Gech!" Clare shuddered. "Can you imagine? He'd be all like … first-century lounge lizard and stuff."

"Please." Milo squeezed his eyes shut. "Stop."

The two of them cringed in tandem.

"Well, yes," Piper said. "But there's rather more to it than that."

"Is it gonna make me wanna barf?" Clare asked.

"Possibly." Piper tapped the cover of the book. "You see, according to *this* … Stuart Morholt's Druidess lover, Mallora, was an older sister to Boudicca, the Queen of the Iceni. And she was far more powerful to boot."

11

Morholt turned to Allie, slapping the palms of his manacled hands together. "Right!" he said. "Let's get cracking on the time travel then, shall w—"

"Shh!" Allie gave Morholt a fierce look.

There were voices just outside the tent. She recognized one of them immediately—the young one.

"I'm telling you, she's not like the others," he was saying. "If I had to hazard a guess, I'd say Junius is right. I mean, I wouldn't tell *him* that—he'd just want her dead. But I think maybe she *is* a Druidess. And if so, that makes her valuable to us. Or, at the very least, valuable to *them*. We should think twice before simply bundling her off to a slave ship."

"If she's one of those responsible for bringing this red ruin down upon us, then I say I agree with that musclehead Junius."

*That* was the centurion's voice. Allie remembered the flat, jaded tone. It sent ice down her spine.

"Why not kill the bitch? Maybe that'll end it."

"I disagree," the legionnaire said.

Shuffling as close to the entrance of the tent as she could, Allie strained to hear compassion in the younger man's voice, but all she could discern was cold logic. For an instant she'd dared to hope that he'd be, if not exactly a *friend*, at least maybe an ally. But apparently he saw her as only a pawn in a big, deadly game.

"She's a bargaining tool," he continued, confirming as much. "A hostage."

"They're murdering us out here, in case you haven't noticed," the centurion snapped. "We're pinned to this piece of ground. We try to leave, they pick us off one by one. We try to stay, they burn the supply caravans to starve us out. It's not as if they even want us to retreat—they'd be perfectly happy if the whole lot of us stayed here on this gods-forsaken hill to wither and die!"

"I know that," the young soldier answered calmly. "But while we wait for the praefect to regain consciousness, we need to keep her alive."

"So they can keep on murdering us?"

"It's what Commander Postumus would want."

"You presume."

"Aye. But until he awakens to confirm that assumption, I would think it prudent to leave him the option. Don't you?"

There was a long pause. Then the centurion said, "Get her out here."

Allie was already scrambling back from the tent entrance when one of the guards pushed through the flap and glanced around. Then he stepped over the other prisoners and grabbed Allie by the back of her head, dragging her forward.

"What? No!" Stuart Morholt squawked, his eyes going wide in panic above the unkempt goatee. "You can't take her! I need her. Tell me you'll bring her back! You—"

Morholt shuffle-lunged toward them on his manacled feet. When he got too close, the guard simply stuck out his pilum and thrust him back, sending him into a clumsy rolling tumble over the other captives' legs. Then the guard dragged Allie outside.

As Allie blinked in the watery sunshine the centurion leaned over and grabbed her face roughly in one meaty paw, lifting her almost off the ground. But as he held her there, two men hurried past carrying a bloodied soldier on a stretcher between them. The centurion turned, and the rage on his face told Allie that the soldier's wounds had come from fighting the berserker women.

His eyes turned back toward Allie, searching her face. He was so close she could feel his breath, hot on her cheek. She did her best not to actually blubber with fear, even as she felt the hot tears running down her cheeks, collecting in a puddle between the man's finger and thumb as he gripped her jaw.

"Savages," the centurion snarled finally and released his punishing grip.

Allie collapsed onto her knees, chains clanking, a fog of panic dulling her mind. The centurion spat to one side and turned back to the legionnaire. While the two soldiers debated her fate as if she were no more than livestock and they discussing dinner, Allie's gaze roamed over the details of the legionnaire's uniform: the brass fasteners on the plates of his armour, the leather thongs of his sandals, the buckles on the wrist bracers he wore. The thick woollen cloak he'd acquired since she'd last seen him wasn't as nice as the centurion's, but it was brushed and looked cared for, with only a few mud spatters on the hem. The knapsack slung over one shoulder was made of heavy cloth and leather, and looked as though it could have come from the latest Roots Back to School collection. Or maybe Abercrombie and Fitch.

*It's nice. Clare would like that—*

And then she spotted something else.

Something that, she was almost shockingly positive, *had* come from a store in a mall. Sometime in the eighties. A worn, skinny leather tie. Just like the one Mark O'Donnell had been wearing in the photograph taken before he'd disappeared at Glastonbury. She thought of that image—the goofily grinning kid, just a skinny, awkward, pasty-faced, big-haired boy—and, glancing at the hardened expression on the angular, sun-darkened face of the soldier standing in front of her, she could almost picture the two of them meeting unexpectedly on the open moors. Two young men from different eras, unable to communicate ...

*Oh my god,* Allie thought. *This guy must have killed that poor kid!*

It was obvious. The Roman soldier had found Maggie's fellow student lost in time and alone, helpless ... He must have figured Mark was just another outlandishly dressed Celtic local. And he'd killed him and taken his leather tie as some kind of war trophy. Allie looked back up at the legionnaire's face, her chest constricting with anger.

"What a benighted, sorry race these Celts are," the centurion was saying. "Do you know they even kill their own countrymen and collect their heads because they think it gives them power? Mystical power. They're damned headhunters."

Allie thought about the skull she'd found and shivered, wondering.

"We've all fought the scathach, sir." The younger man took a step forward. "And whatever it is they use to fuel their mystical rage ... it seems to work just fine for them. They're winning."

"Perhaps that'll stop if we start collecting some heads of our own. Eh, little witch?" The centurion glared down at Allie. "What do you say? Might be worth a try ..."

"It might," the legionnaire said with a shrug. "Only then the praefect loses a potentially valuable prize. And I don't think he'd approve of the method in which it was lost."

"Quintus Phoenius Postumus"—the centurion turned toward the younger man, his face twisted into a mask of disdain— "'wouldn't approve.' Ha! The coward. Makes me long for a commander like Suetonius Paulinus. *He* had no such qualms about 'methods' when he dealt with that upstart demon-bitch queen in the east." The centurion smiled grimly. "I only wish I'd spent these last few months there with the Twentieth Legion instead of out here in this damp, damned wilderness hunting phantoms."

*Okay*, Allie thought, *at least I know* when *I am. Approximately ...*

It made her feel the tiniest bit better knowing that, at the very least, the vengeful Iceni queen had met her ultimate fate. Boudicca had scared the crap out of Allie. Maybe even more than the Romans did.

"I, for one, am glad I wasn't there," the legionnaire said.

"Squeamish, Legionnaire Donatus?" The centurion's tone dripped sarcasm. "You? Postumus's pampered pet?"

"I can't see how I'm so very pampered. Not when I'm stuck out in this muck hole with the likes of you lot," he answered his commanding officer.

The centurion's flinty gaze narrowed and he drew back his shoulders, chest expanding beneath the creaking harness of his armour. Allie wondered if he was about to strike the young man, who stared back impassively, eventually adding a belated "Sir."

After a long moment, the centurion let his breath out in a gusty, harsh laugh.

If she hadn't been so terrified, Allie might have found herself silently rooting for Legionnaire Donatus. She felt almost as if he was a kindred spirit. As if there was some kind of connection between the two of them—a feeling that intensified for an instant when he turned and she accidentally locked eyes with him. It was like being hit with an electric shock.

"Well then, pet? What 'methods' do you think we should employ?" The officer turned and grinned viciously at Allie.

She felt like her heart would stop. What were they going to do? Torture her? Kill her? Worse?

"I think we should talk to her."

*Talk?* Okay. Allie could handle talk.

Donatus smiled wanly. "As you say, I'm a useful pet, Centurion. Like a well-trained puppy. *And* I can speak her language."

"If that's what you call that appalling barking of theirs," the officer muttered, staring at Allie sideways.

The legionnaire walked toward her where she still knelt on the ground. "I can at least try."

*Damn*, Allie thought. *I don't speak Celt!*

Whatever flavour of Celt she was supposed to be, she didn't speak it. She was doomed. She'd know what he was saying because she understood Latin, but no *way* would she be able to respond in the language he expected her to know—

"Listen to me," he said in a low voice.

*Wait. What?*

He'd said it in perfect, precise, modern English.

Allie *knew* perfect, precise, modern English. She was very good at it. Usually.

"Wha ...?"

Allie had the brief sensation of understanding what the hell was going on, but then her brain recoiled from the thought the second it began to formulate deep in its brainy depth.

*I know what you're thinking,* her brain said. *And you're an idiot. What you're thinking is* not *possible. Clearly. I mean ... look at this guy.*

Allie frowned. Her brain had a distinct point. As her gaze travelled down the young soldier's corded, defined muscles she suddenly felt like one of those *Star Trek* computers Captain Kirk was always talking into self-destructing.

*Illogical ... Illogical ... Does. Not. Compute.*

Legionnaire Donatus and Mark O'Donnell couldn't *possibly* be one and the same person. Allie tried to picture those skinny tartan trousers covering *that* pair of legs.

*Okay, no. Just ... no.*

She felt herself on the verge of blushing as she stared at his muscled calves. Allie wrenched her gaze back up—only to be met by that steely glint in his eyes. How was it that Maggie had described the O'Donnell kid again? Right. "Soft-spoken. Slight of build, with soft eyes ... soulful, really. And he had rather large hair."

*Soulful? Yeah ... again, no.*

How about "arrogant"? Or "pompous"? Allie shook her head. She was catastrophically wrong about this. "Soft-spoken"? Ha! Not this guy. Even compared to the brute manners of the centurion, there was nothing soft about him.

"Well, Marcus Felix Donatus?" the centurion drawled mockingly. "I'm waiting for your useful skills to prove useful ..."

*Marcus ... Mark ...?*

Allie felt her eyes growing impossibly wide. "Holy crap," she whispered. "You're—"

"*Shut* up and listen to me," Marcus snapped.

He crouched down on his haunches and stared into her face, his eyes like two hard, cold stones beneath the bronze brim of his helmet. Maggie had said that Morholt made a pet out of Mark O'Donnell. And the centurion had just baited him with that very same insult. But this boy—this young *man*—was *nobody's* pet. This guy commanded respect.

"The centurion doesn't know that I'm not speaking to you in the language of the ancient Durotriges," he said in a low, whiplash crack of a voice. "But you *aren't* an ancient Durotrigan. Are you?"

Mute, in shock, Allie could only shake her head.

"So we're going to pretend, you and I, that I *am* speaking to you in Durotrigan." His stare burned into her. "And maybe that way I can keep him from getting either suspicious or bored—and killing you—while he waits for his commanding officer to recover enough from his wounds to properly decide what should be done with you. Agreed?"

"How did you—"

"Now is *not* the time," he cut her off abruptly, a stern warning in his gaze. "Just tell me if you agree."

He waited for an answer as she struggled to form a coherent thought.

"Uh. Yeah," she stammered. "I guess. I mean ... Agreed."

He straightened up and turned back to the centurion with a sigh. "Hers is a difficult dialect to make understood," he said, speaking Latin once more as if he'd been born knowing it. He shrugged. "This may take a while, but I think I can talk to her. It will be easier if she's less nervous. I think you should keep her separate from the others. Take her to the praefect's tent. Secure her there, with a guard."

"The praefect's tent!" The centurion regarded Allie with a mix of wariness and distaste. "I think we'd get more answers out of her if we chained her to a stake in the midden pit."

"Except that I don't want to interrogate a prisoner in the midden pit," Legionnaire Marcus Felix Donatus said dryly. "And the more we can manage to put this creature at ease, the better time we'll have of it."

*Creature?* Allie thought. He called her a creature. *Nice.*

The centurion looked as though he was wavering.

"You catch more flies with honey than with vinegar, Centurion."

"Huh," the man grunted. "I like that. Who told you that?"

Marcus shrugged and glanced at Allie. "Just ... an old saying I heard."

"I'll have to remember it."

Allie wondered vaguely if this was when the "old" saying was actually coined. Marcus grabbed her by the shoulder, hauling her to her feet.

"Play along now," he muttered in her ear.

He *did* have a hint of a Scottish accent. She was sure of it.

"Veni!" he barked and gave her a rough shake. "Move!"

Allie winced and cowered away from him, even though his grip on her arm wasn't nearly as punishing as he made it look. *Okay ...* After three years of summer drama camp with Clare? *This* she could pull off. At least until she had a chance to figure out just what on earth was going on.

He dragged her past the lines of neatly laid-out tents toward the centre of the encampment. Behind her curtain of tangled hair, Allie glanced around as she stumbled in his wake. She could see where they'd dug a ditch around the entire circumference of the square-shaped camp and used the dug-up earth to form a defensive embankment inside the ditch. It was topped at intervals by sharpened wooden stakes pointing outward at angles to deter any hostiles from rushing the earthen wall.

These things were meant to be temporary camps, Allie knew from what she'd read about Legion methods and techniques. Except that this one had a slightly more permanent air. She remembered what she'd heard the two soldiers saying about the siege tactics the Celts had been using against them. Rough wooden palisade gates made of lashed, sharpened tree trunks had been put up at the camp's two entrances, and a watch platform seemed to have been hastily erected at the north end of the camp. The south end was protected by the sloping sides of Glastonbury Tor itself.

When they reached the praefect's empty tent, the centurion ordered Allie's manacles to be secured to the central tent pole. He set a sentry guard outside the entrance, then left Marcus alone to deal with his prisoner, citing vastly more gripping things to do than watch the young legionnaire try to wring sense out of a "skinny-arsed barbarian waif."

Allie tried not to collapse in a heap. She needed to focus. To concentrate on the situation at hand, and how the hell she was going to get herself out of it. She needed information. And she needed to know just where (she already knew *when*) Marcus Donatus was coming from.

He stood for a moment after the centurion left, looking down at his hands. They were smeared with dried mud. And blood. So was his uniform, beneath his cloak. It looked as though he hadn't had a chance to clean up after the fight the night before. When he'd saved Allie from a flaming shish-kabob fate.

"Good god, what a mess," he muttered to himself in English.

And he *totally* had a faint Scottish accent. It was ridiculously sexy. Sexier, even, than when he'd been speaking Latin.

*Could we focus on the situation at hand, here, Little Miss Easily Distracted?*

Allie wondered if Clare had experienced something similar when she met Connal, her blue-painted Druid hottie, on her first shimmer trip. She decided to ask the next time she saw her. For the moment, there was a bit more to worry about. Especially since her own hottie didn't seem the least bit inclined to even be polite.

She decided to confirm her theory as to his identity. She was still having difficulties reconciling Mark O'Donnell and Marcus Donatus as far as appearances went. Was *that* what forced marches, fresh air, and legion rations did to teenage boys? Wow. And she thought the high school football team grew up fast.

Allie cleared her throat. "Don't you mean 'By Jupiter, what a mess'?"

Ignoring her, he strode over to a folding stand that held a bronze bowl and pitcher. He poured water into the bowl and began to wash the dirt from his hands.

"I mean ... that *would* be the first-century-Roman thing to say, wouldn't it?" Allie pressed.

He kept washing his hands silently, his shoulders hunched around his ears.

*Okaaay ... let's try a different angle, shall we?*

"Um. So. How long have you been in the army?"

He scrubbed even harder at the dirt.

Allie watched as the skin of his knuckles started to turn red. She tried one more time, only *this* time, she tried it in Latin.

"I *said*," she said loudly, *"Quamdiu militem eras?"*

She was pretty sure her accent sucked big time and her conjugation was a mess, but the attempt had the desired result. And *then* some. Legionnaire Donatus's helmeted head snapped around and his eyes blazed with emotion—anger? fear?—as he glared at her.

"Since they found me," he said in English. "And *don't* do that again."

"What?"

"Speak Latin."

He threw down the cloth he'd been drying his hands with and stalked back toward her, yanking the tent flap closed on his way.

"What if someone overheard that?" he murmured, gesturing in the direction of the guard, whose shadow Allie could see on the tent wall. "If *they* know you speak their language, they won't need me to interpret for them. That centurion could interrogate you himself, and then I wouldn't be around to make him be nice about it. I don't think you want that."

"Oh. Right. No ..." Allie swallowed painfully. He was right. She'd been stupid. Which was really, *really* unlike her. She couldn't afford to be stupid—it could cost her her life. She felt tears of frustration welling behind her eyes.

Marcus stood staring at her. After a moment, he sighed. "Besides which," he said in a slightly less berating tone, "your accent is like a cheese grater to the ears. And your conjugation is a mess."

She glanced up, scowling in indignation, to see him grinning sardonically at her. Allie bit back the sharp retort that was on the tip of her tongue. He *was* trying to help her get the best out of an impossibly bad situation, it seemed. And he did have a vastly superior accent. Maybe she could learn a thing or two from him. Especially if she could manage to ignore how the sound of his voice made the soles of her feet tingle every time he rolled one of his *r*'s.

He shrugged and turned away from her. There was a camp desk in the middle of the sparsely appointed tent and Marcus stared down at one of the parchment maps that lay on its surface. He traced the fingers of one hand over the spidery lines.

"To answer your question," he said in a flat, faraway voice, "I've been with the Second Augusta Legion ever since Quintus Phoenius Postumus, the praefect whose tent pole you're currently shackled to, found me starving to death in the mud below that godforsaken hill out there."

"Oh. Okay. And ... um ... how long ago was that?"

"Four years."

"So you were ... what?" Al prodded gently. "Fifteen? Is that right ... Mark?"

He turned to her, his eyes haunted by the boy he used to be. And it was, Allie thought, the first time he had truly looked at her.

"That's your name, right? Mark O'Donnell? Your *real* name."

He let his breath out in a shaky sigh. "I'm not imagining you ..."

"Uh. No?"

"And I'm *not* mad, then." It was almost a question.

"I don't think so ..."

"Which means you're really from—" He winced suddenly and turned sharply away, his nostrils flaring like those of an animal scenting danger on the wind. He shook his head as if he was having some sort of silent, heated argument with himself. "No," he murmured. "I can't believe that after all this time ... No. If it's true, then why wouldn't someone have come for me before? I don't even know you. Why didn't my— No! I know what this is. It's that damned Druidess. She's sent you to torment me and I'll have none of it!"

He turned on the heel of his sandal and stalked out the door.

It was so sudden, so abrupt, that all Allie could do was watch him go. And once he was gone, she sank to the dirt floor of the tent, hugging the pole that kept her captive. She had never in all her life felt so alone.

"Clare ..." she murmured. "I'm *really* ready to come home now ..."

But the answer to her plea was silence, broken only by the creaking of her sentry's leather armour just outside the Roman praefect's tent.

## 12

Milo's face wore an expression that wavered between disbelief, grudging respect, and outright annoyance. "He planned it. The whole thing."

"Sure." Piper shrugged. "With the mystical help and half the biology of some whacked-out Druid sorceress ancestor-chick of mine who could see the future."

Clare was trying not to think about Boudicca's Druidess sister. That was just too much for her brain at the moment. "You don't understand," she said. "It's *Morholt*. His schemes don't work. Ever. For him to even con*ceive* of a plan—"

"I think it was Mallora who did the actual conceiving," Milo muttered.

"GAH!" Clare covered her ears. "Seriously!"

"Sorry."

"You really find it that unlikely a scenario?" Piper asked.

Clare turned and blinked at her. "I know you've never met the guy, so trust me, the answer to that question is a resounding yes."

She sighed and shook her head, staring at the little book as Milo carefully turned its pages, his eyes scanning what Morholt had written there. "Yup," he said. "A Stuart Morholt plan worked. My worldview is seriously compromised."

"Oh now, mustn't think like that," Piper laughed sarcastically. "I mean, it's only worked up to a point. The book has found its way to you, but it's not as if you've found your way back to Morholt yet, is it? And isn't that his whole point in sending the book forward in time?"

Clare turned to Milo anxiously. "Does he say how? Are there actually instructions on how to go back with*out* a shimmer trigger? Because I don't know how the heck Al managed it ... and without a trigger, I'm not going anywhere. Does Morholt offer any insights?" She waved at the diary in Milo's hands.

"Um ... not exactly," Milo said, shaking his head. "He rambles like a madman. I think being stuck back there in the past really did a number on ol' Stu's brainpan."

"I know, right?" Piper nodded. "Like ... what the hell does the last page mean?"

Milo flipped to the back of the book and frowned.

"See? That." Piper gestured to the page, which seemed to consist of nothing more than a few lines of scribbled numbers. "I could never figure that one out myself. Those numbers range from one to twenty-two. But as far as I can see, there's no pattern. The order and grouping seem totally random."

Clare leaned over Milo's shoulder and scanned the first line. Except that to her eyes there was nothing "random" about them at all. *And* they were written in *her* distinctly crappy penmanship. The message they conveyed leaped out at Clare, plain as day:

19-8 9-8-5 5-18-11-11 10-14-11-8 1-8-4 20-22-9 7-18-22-19 5-15-14-6

But her brain swiftly, automatically, *shockingly* interpreted it:

*do not tell milo you can read this*

Milo, who was looking at the same message, only without the necessary information to understand it. Milo, who Clare trusted with her life. And maybe even her heart.

*Milo ...*

Why the warning, written in a ridiculous grade-school cipher that only Clare would recognize for what it was? The "code"—and it barely even qualified as that—was something Clare and Al had made up in grade four—or maybe it was five—when using secret codes was both fun and a means of avoiding detention when passing notes in class. It consisted of twenty-two numbers, each one corresponding to a letter of the alphabet, starting in reverse. And just to throw anyone off the trail, Clare and Al had omitted assigning numbers to the letters Q, Z, X, and P. They hardly ever used those, and if the notes were ever intercepted, anyone who saw that there were only twenty-two repeating numbers probably wouldn't think to match them alphabetically. And if they tried, the unknown letters the girls had omitted would screw up any attempt at deciphering.

But that had been grade school. The question now was, How on earth had Clare come to write herself a note in Morholt's ancient diary, and why on earth had she found it necessary to write it in code? Whatever it was, it must have been important. But it would take her a bit of time to decipher it all, and meanwhile she couldn't let Milo know she could. She also couldn't risk letting him use his big brain to crack the message. Not until she'd read the whole thing through and figured out why she was warning herself.

"Huh. Random numbers," she said, reaching over to take the book from Milo, casually ignoring his attempts to keep reading, as if she hadn't noticed. "Probably just Morholt playing Sudoku to pass the time. Look—there's even a doodle." She pointed to an elongated squiggly spiral at the bottom of the page, partially obscured by a smudge of brownish dirt, that vaguely resembled the shape of Glastonbury Tor as seen from above. The doodle was in Clare's hand, too.

*What the hell?*

Beside her, Milo was still peering intently at the numbers. Clare could see his brain trying to work out patterns.

"Tell me something ..." She nonchalantly closed the pages and turned toward Piper, holding the notebook up between them. "Why did you open the tin?"

"Because I'm the only one who would." Piper plucked the book delicately from Clare's fingertips and began to rewrap it in its zipper-cloth and baggie. "You really should be wearing gloves, you know ... You want the real reason why this thing has stayed in such marvellous shape? Because for the better part of the last two hundred years it has sat in a dust-free, climate-controlled safe deposit box in a London bank vault. Everyone in my family had heard about it ... and *no* one cared. No one in my family displayed the necessary intellectual curiosity, or the bravery, or even the ... the *mendacity* to open the damned thing. No one except me."

"Not even your whacko granny?" Clare asked.

"She's the one I would have thought most likely to, yeah. She actually believed in things like Druid blood curses." Piper snorted. "She kept newspaper clippings in a scrapbook about the Tutankhamun Curse and the Hope Diamond."

Clare felt a cold shiver run up her spine. The conversation suddenly resembled one she'd once had with Morholt about the very same subject. Okay, so the coconuts didn't fall far from the tree. Even after multiple generations.

"She also kept track of Yeti sightings and collected grainy snaps of the Loch Ness monster," Piper went on, confirming the hypothesis. "Yup. My genetic material was corrupted at the source code. Madman and sorceress. Thanks for making that possible."

"Don't mention it." Clare grinned sourly.

"Right. Nutters, all. But, aside from Gran and me, incurious nutters." Piper finished packing the book away and waved a hand at the curio shop's confines. "See ... me? I actually believe that the past *lives*. It lives in the present and it's our duty to keep it alive for the future. This shop is the very antithesis of a museum. People can walk in here and buy things. Touch things. Take them home and make them a part of their lives. I *had* to know what was in this." She held up the tin. "I needed to solve the mystery."

"What if it had proved to be nothing?"

Piper shrugged. "Then at least I would have known. And I would have sold the thing as a wartime tea tin to some granny to pot a plant in, and made a few quid off it. Also? I'm the last of my line. No siblings, no cousins that I know of. And I'm not precisely the type to settle down and raise a family."

Clare raised an eyebrow. "Sure. You're like, what, nineteen? How do you know? Maybe you just haven't met the right person yet."

Piper's eyes flicked over to where Milo stood silently.

"Maybe," she said. "But maybe not. And I started thinking that, if I didn't open it, chances are no one in my family ever would. And, insofar as you two are here, I know now that I was *meant* to open it."

"What does it say in there about Al?" Clare almost dreaded the answer.

"Well, for starters," Milo said, "she showed up in a Roman encampment that Morholt was being held prisoner in." Clare blinked at him in surprise. Among his other talents, apparently Milo was also a speed reader. "Initially, it seems, Morholt assumed that his demands for *you* to come and rescue him worked. Sort of. I guess he figured you somehow sent Allie in your place."

"Great," Clare said. "But here's the thing—I didn't have anything to do with sending Al back, did I? And now we know that's definitely where she went, I still don't have the foggiest idea how to get her back. Does the book say how we do that? Does it say how *I* can go back without a shimmer trigger? Does it say anything bloody useful at *all*?"

Milo hesitated for a moment. He glanced at Piper.

Clare huffed in frustration as the silence stretched out. "Milo?"

"No. I'm sorry, Clare. It doesn't."

Piper was staring at Milo, the shadow of a frown on her brow. Clare looked back and forth between the two of them. It felt suddenly as if they were keeping something from her.

"What?" she demanded. "Is it Al? Did something horrible happen to her?" Clare felt rising panic again. She'd never gone back for more than an hour or two at a time. Al had been gone since *yesterday*. "Is she in trouble? You have to tell me if—"

"She's fine," Piper said firmly.

Clare turned to her. "What?"

*"Fine,"* she repeated, tapping the tin. "So far. On page thirty-four, *three* days after Morholt first sees her, your friend is still alive and well and—heh—feisty as ever. Apparently she's a bit of a spitfire, that one." Piper laughed a little. "Now, if we extrapolate from how Morholt described *your* travels, the amount of time that passes for Allie *there* is the same amount of time that would have passed for her *here*. The passage of time is a personal chronology—it remains consistent to the individual. You can enter the time stream at any point, but it's like you carry your own stopwatch with you when you do. So. Regardless of how long Morholt's been stuck back there, when he writes about how long *she's* been there, it amounts to the same length of time she would have been here. She hasn't yet been gone three days. Which means she's *still* there, *still* in good health, and will be for at least another twenty-four hours."

"Okay," Milo interjected, "fine. We have a bit of breathing space. And obviously we're still missing a key piece of the puzzle. I guess we're just going to have to wait until it reveals itself to us."

"That's a terrible idea," Clare said, although she could hardly argue with the logic. "I *hate* that idea. Wait? Just ... wait? I hate waiting." She wondered how many times Al had cursed her out loud and in colourful language for not getting her the hell back to the future already. As relieved as she was, Clare still felt terrible. Useless.

"Patience," Piper counselled. "Virtue."

Clare rolled an eye at her. "Patience. Shove it."

"Right." Piper fidgeted for a moment. "You know, maybe this all has something to do with the artifact your pal found. It was a skull, wasn't it?"

Clare nodded, even though she found the idea unlikely. She'd held the gruesome thing in her bare hands and nary a flicker of a shimmer had she felt. Clare's triggers had always been manmade. Not, as it were, made of man. But then again, it *had* been different with Al. The video had clearly shown that. Maybe the bony relic had something to do with Al's temporal displacement after all.

"Could you bring it here?" Piper pressed. "To the shop?"

Clare looked at Milo. The day before they'd decided that wandering around Glastonbury with a human skull in his knapsack was probably a bad idea, so he'd hidden it in his hotel room for the time being. But Piper had spent her life surrounded by antiquities, and she'd read the diary back to front. Maybe there was something she could discover that they hadn't.

Milo must have been thinking the same thing. He shrugged one shoulder and said, "I'm okay with that if you are, Clare—"

Suddenly the clock in the main shop bonged nine, startling the three of them. And only a few seconds later, the front door bell chimed, startling them again.

"Damn," muttered Piper. "I forgot. The teaspoon ladies."

Clare and Milo looked at her.

"They're here every second Wednesday of the month at nine o'clock sharp, all giddy with anticipation, to see if I've got any new spoons in. Be right back ..." She bustled out to the front of the shop.

Clare glanced at her watch and turned to Milo. "If I'm not at the dig site soon, the supervisors are going to start asking questions. They're probably already wondering where the hell Al is."

He nodded. "I'll walk with you. I've got a few things to take care of too, with the virtual-reality dig program."

When Milo reached out to pick up the book tin, Clare thrust out her hand to stop him. As much as she wanted to take it with them, she didn't want Milo examining the line of code any more closely than he already had. She couldn't risk him cracking it.

"Um. Look ..." She struggled to find some kind of valid excuse for leaving the thing behind. "I think maybe we should leave the book here for safekeeping. I don't want to be carting it around in the field. And ... I dunno. It's kind of like a legacy for Goggles. I think we—okay, *me*—got off on the wrong foot with her. Maybe if we show her we trust her with it ... things might go easier."

Clare held her breath as Milo cast a long look at the battered little box.

"I think you're right," he said, smiling as he tucked a stray lock of hair behind her ear. "And I think that's pretty big of you, all things considered."

He bent his head and kissed her lightly on the mouth, and Clare felt herself relax a little and breathe a sigh of relief.

"Anyway," Milo continued, "if Piper's right about Al, and I think she most likely is, then we do have a bit of time. I'll get the skull from my hotel room this afternoon and we can come back and figure out our next move. Okay?"

"Okay ... I just ... Milo, I feel like we're out of our depth here." Clare's anxiety had returned the second Milo stopped kissing her. "Maybe we really *should* tell Dr. Ashbourne about this. Maybe something similar has happened on one of the Tor digs before and—"

"Dr. Nicholas Ashbourne?" Piper asked, ducking back through the beaded curtain to fetch a cardboard box from a shelf labelled SPOONS.

Milo turned to her. "You know him?"

"He was a friend of my old wacky gran's since back before I was born. She used to buy artifacts from him—things the museum wouldn't take. I've bought a few myself from him over the years."

Piper frowned, putting the box down long enough to take Morholt's book tin—she hefted it as if to make sure the book was still inside—and put it away in a cupboard. Piper eyed them skeptically, but when they didn't put up a fight, she gave her head a bit of a shake and returned to the topic.

"Do you trust him?" she asked. "Ashbourne?"

"Of course I do," Clare said. "Why wouldn't I?"

Piper shrugged. "Moustache like that? I never completely trust anyone who finds it necessary to hide half their face from the world."

*This from someone with an obvious affinity for feature-obscuring eyewear?* Clare refrained from pointing out the irony.

"At any rate, be careful." Piper crossed her arms and pegged Clare with a frank, appraising stare. "Surprising as it may be, Miss Reid, you are something extraordinary. You have a rare and precious gift. I believe that rare and precious things should be well taken care of. But there are those who don't necessarily agree with me."

In the main shop, the clamouring for spoons was getting a bit noisy.

"Step out the back way, will you? The spoon ladies tend to clog up the aisles," Piper said. "And be careful. Don't let your*selves* fall into the wrong hands."

"Don't worry about me, Goggles," Clare said as she headed for the back door. "I'm pretty handy with a letter opener, remember?"

But once outside the shop, she frowned. Piper's parting words echoed in her head.

"Wow," she muttered sourly. "Alarmist much?"

As Milo took her hand in his she waited for him to brush off Piper's comment with a bit of his usual disarming wit, but his expression was clouded with worry.

"She's right, Clare."

All of a sudden she was exhausted. She took a step forward and leaned her head on Milo's chest, sinking into his embrace as his arms went around her. Clare didn't give a damn what kind of cryptic warning she'd somehow managed to transmit down through the ages to herself. She wouldn't tell Milo about the code—just yet—but she also wouldn't allow herself to think he'd do something bad or wrong if she did. More than likely she'd been trying to protect him, or Al, from something. That had to be it. Milo was ... Milo. And he loved his cousin dearly. He'd never do anything that would put her in danger—*more* danger.

"I know," she sighed. "I know she's right. But I have *your* hands to fall into and *you* to take care of me. I'll be fine."

"Damn straight. Because I'm not going to let anything—*any-thing*—happen to you." The way he said it made Clare pull away and look up at him again. His handsome face had shifted into a fierce, hard expression.

"Milo? What's wrong?" Clare asked quietly. "I mean, beside the obvious."

Milo glanced back at Piper Gimble's shop.

"Did you get hold of Maggie yet?"

"No." Clare shook her head. "She's in academic-lockdown mode with that conference for the next few days. And every time I pick up the phone, I kind of chicken out anyway. I'm afraid to tell her what's happened."

"Okay. Good."

"What?"

Milo hesitated a moment. "Let's keep her out of the loop on this one for the time being."

"Seriously. What?" Clare pulled him to a stop in the middle of the sidewalk. "Milo! It's *Maggie.*"

"I know." He glanced around as if he expected to catch someone eavesdropping. But of course they were alone on the street in the sleepy little town. "It's not Maggie I don't trust. It's everyone who might know something about this and who has access to Maggie. Look ... that diary? It came from *Stuart Morholt*, shadiest of the shady. He may seem like an incompetent boob most of the time, but he had the wherewithal to make sure that thing found its way down through two thousand years to get to you."

Clare had to agree that, for an incompetent boob, it was an impressive feat.

"And remember, the whole Boudicca museum theft, back when you were shimmering, was an inside job. As far as we know it was only Dr. Jenkins working with Morholt, but that's *only* as far as we know. A bunch of other people were in on the Druid revival thing back in the day. Who knows how many more of those 'Free Peoples of Prydain' freaks are wandering around out there."

Clare thought about that and frowned.

"There were at least three other people just in Maggie's photo alone," Milo went on. "I think we should keep this—all of this— between you and me. And, obviously, our friendly neighbourhood girl-antiquarian in there. Something strange is going on."

"Ya think?"

"I don't just mean Allie's disappearance. That's the *what*. I'm talking about the *why*. We don't have the whole picture. I don't like not having whole pictures." He took Clare's hand again and they started walking back toward the Tor. "I even less like the idea that we're being purposefully kept in the dark."

"Kept in the dark? By who? Why?"

"I don't know."

Clare felt a shiver run down her spine and tried to recall the faces of the other group members in the snapshot.

Milo was adamant. "I'm not running the risk that one of them might be trying to use you—use your gift—and Allie maybe just got in the way somehow."

"And you know you're kind of freaking me out now, right?"

"No ... no, that's not what I'm trying to do. C'mon, Clare de Lune ..." He gathered her into a sudden, fierce embrace. "You don't have to worry about anything. But you do have to be *careful* about everything. Just ... let's take the time to figure this out. To do this right. We need to get Allie back, but in the meantime we need to make sure nothing happens to you. *I* need to make sure. Okay?"

"Okay." Clare nodded.

But in the back of her mind she still wondered what, exactly, she'd been warning herself about ... and why, exactly, she didn't want Milo to read it.

13

When Marcus finally returned, Allie wasn't sure how much time had passed. She'd fallen into a fitful doze, emotionally and physically exhausted. She hadn't even heard him come into the tent. She just opened her eyes and there he was, a cloth-covered wooden tray in his hands. It might have been the smell of fresh-baked bread that had woken her up—the scent of it wafted from the tray as he crouched down, set it in front of her, and then whisked away the cloth. Arranged on the wooden slab was a small, round loaf of bread, a yellow pear, a chunk of what looked like some kind of hard cheese, and a little silver cup half-full of rich red wine. Allie thought she might actually start to drool right then and there. She'd missed lunch at the Rifleman the day before with Clare and Milo ... and she hadn't eaten since.

She looked up at Marcus. "Thank you."

As he slid the tray toward her she reached out with both manacled hands to grab the still-warm bread. The first bite made her think she'd never tasted anything so delicious in her life. Bread in the twenty-first century should be ashamed of itself.

Marcus grinned at her. "There's a saying: 'The Roman Legion travels on its stomach.' We get pretty good grub. Good for morale and keeping up strength. Although, with the way the scathach raids have kept away our supply trains, we'll be dining on peat moss and swamp water soon enough."

"Are you going to get in trouble with that centurion for this?" Allie asked through a mouthful of pear and cheese—which was sharp and tangy and perfectly complemented the fruit.

Marcus shrugged. "Only if he finds out."

Allie figured the best way to avoid that was to leave no evidence behind. She took another bite of pear and wrapped a chunk of cheese in bread and stuffed that in her mouth, too. Marcus watched her for a moment and then stood abruptly. He started pacing, glancing every now and then toward the tent flap where the guard stood. Then he stalked back and lobbed a question at her that was completely, one hundred percent, *straight* out of left field.

"Name the lead singer from Duran Duran."

Allie blinked at him, and swallowed the mouthful of wine she'd just sipped. It was slightly on the vinegary side, but she wasn't about to complain to the maitre d'.

"You're kidding me," she said.

He stooped suddenly and snatched away the platter with the rest of Allie's lunch on it. Her stomach clenched in protest.

"If you come from where I *think* you come from, you'll know the answer," Marcus snapped. "If you don't, you're a creature of that Druidess witch Mallora and a liar and I will let them come in here and cut you to pieces to find out what they need."

His lips were drawn back from his teeth in a kind of snarl and Allie knew he meant what he said. But she also knew she was tired of him trying to intimidate her. The whole split-personality, good cop/bad cop thing was wearying. Okay ... he'd obviously gone through some stuff. But that didn't mean he had to be a total ass-hat. It wasn't *her* fault he'd gotten himself marooned in the past.

"Do you know the answer?" he asked again.

"Of course I do." Allie lifted her chin and looked him square in the eyes. "But only because my lunatic mother has the worst taste in retro bands, like, ever!"

It was Marcus's turn to blink. "Retro ..."

"She listens to all this stupid eighties crap."

"Stupid!" Marcus spluttered.

"Yeah—I mean, you should see pictures of these dudes." Allie rolled her eyes. "They've all got enormo-hair and shoulder pads and wear way too much guyliner and—"

"*Guy* ..." Marcus's hand crept toward his helmeted head. "Enormo-hair?"

"And the bands had ridiculous names. They called themselves stupid things like 'Split Enz' and sang songs with ridiculous titles—"

"'Six Months in a Leaky Boat' is an instant classic!" Marcus almost roared with rage. If he didn't have his hands full of her interrupted repast, he might have actually drawn his sword.

Allie's mouth snapped shut in mid-rant. She blinked at the Roman soldier and realized that he was quite capable of killing her. So she tried to picture him as he'd been in Maggie's snapshot. It worked. Sort of ...

"What?" he asked, suddenly suspicious. "Why are you looking at me like that?"

Allie was trying desperately not to giggle with hysterical nervousness at the mental picture of what his hair used to look like. She wondered what it might look like now, once he took his helmet off. Was it still ... poufy?

*Not cool.*

And not him. No. It couldn't be.

"Could you ... take off your helmet?" Allie drove her fingernails into the palms of her iron-shackled hands to keep from losing it *completely.* "Please?"

"Why?"

"I have issues with authority figures," she snapped sarcastically, trying to regain some of her earlier composure.

He just glared down at her. Allie bit her lip.

*Cut the guy some slack, McAllister. He's obviously just as wigged out about the situation as you are.*

"Please?" she said again, softly.

He hesitated, and Allie knew he was still wondering if she was trying to trick him or make fun of him. After a long moment he put the tray back down in front of her. Then he reached up slowly and unbuckled the chinstrap that held his helmet on. With both hands he lifted the headgear up and off, tucking it under his arm. Then he stood there. Looking—surprisingly—vulnerable. And kind of shy all of a sudden.

His hair, Allie was tremendously relieved to see, was in a short, military kind of cut. No pouffage. No mullet. It made him look like any number of boys she was used to seeing at the University of Toronto library where she sometimes went to do homework assignments and dream of the day when she'd graduate from high school. She wondered, fleetingly, if she'd ever see that library again. She wondered if she'd ever get home.

Mark O'Donnell hadn't.

Legionnaire Donatus seemed to notice that Allie was struggling mightily not to cry. It was the abrupt bleakness of her thoughts that had startled her to tears, but he didn't know that.

"That bad?" he asked, gesturing at his hair.

Allie could only shake her head. In fact it wasn't bad. At *all.*

He sighed gustily and ran a hand over his bristly hair. Then he walked over to the wooden stand in the corner of the tent, hung up his helmet, and then took off the belt that held the sword scabbard around his waist, hanging it on another peg on the stand. Without the weapon, he looked a little less imposing. A little.

He walked back over to where Allie sat tied to the tent post. Her dark hair had fallen across her face and, with her hands manacled, she couldn't do much about it. It stuck to her cheeks—to the tears that had finally spilled over her lashes and run down her face. Marcus, or Mark, or whatever he called himself, frowned faintly and reached out a hand, brushing the strands of hair back out of one eye with his fingertips. His touch was surprisingly gentle.

"What's your name?" he asked.

She looked up at him, blinking. Dazed.

"Your *name*?" he asked again. "You already know mine—both of them—and I'd feel a bit more on even ground if I knew yours." He almost smiled encouragingly at her. Not *quite*, but almost.

"Al. Alice. Um ... Allie."

"Is that the long or the short version?" He brushed the hair out of her other eye.

To which she managed to say, "Meep."

"How about I go with ... Allie."

She just nodded, figuring that was the safest bet. Then she took a deep breath and said, "You're really *him*. You're Mark O'Donnell."

He didn't answer, but she could see the muscles of his throat working as he swallowed convulsively.

"You were a member of the Free Peoples of Prydain—or whatever goofball name it was you guys called yourselves—and you disappeared one night in 1986 from Glastonbury Tor. You *are* Mark O'Donnell," she said again.

"I was," he said. "Once. A long time ago."

"A long time ago that hasn't even happened yet, you mean."

He laughed, a harsh, empty sound, and nodded. "I suppose you're right. But you see, Allie ... That doesn't really matter now. I'm Legionnaire Marcus Felix Donatus, Second Legion Augusta, under the provisional command of Praefect Quintus Phoenius Postumus—assuming he ever wakes up again. That's who I am *now*. For better ... or worse."

Allie's heart sank as she watched his gaze start to turn flinty again. She waited until he locked eyes once more with hers. And then she said, very quietly, "Simon Le Bon. The lead singer for Duran Duran is Simon Le Bon."

Marcus's expression wavered.

"And I heard a rumour," she said, "that they might be going back into the studio soon."

He blinked, and suddenly Allie could see the face of the boy who'd disappeared all those years ago to become the man who stood before her now. "They're thinking of doing a sixth album?" he asked.

Allie smiled as gently as she could. "No. They're thinking of doing a *fifteenth* album." She watched as the blood drained from his face and he went ghost pale. It was, she thought, an appropriate response, given the circumstances—and what she was about to say. "You've been missing for over twenty-five years, Mark. Don't you think it's time we found a way to get you home?"

14

Her mind was *so* not on the work. To the point where, if Clare actually *had* unearthed something in her trench—something really *real*—it probably wouldn't have even registered. Between semi-regular supervisor patrols she would scratch absently at the dirt beneath her knees like a bored hen in a barnyard. And then, whenever the grad students came by, Clare would fake enthusiasm, manufacture cover stories for Al's continuing absence (she'd placed Al's tablet and black cowboy hat on the edge of her trench to make it seem as if she was logging progress or on a bathroom break), and try not to roll her eyes too much behind her sunglasses as ubiquitous coin-discovery chatter drifted down into her trench.

*Whatever ...*

Not like she was jealous of the find or anything. Really. Not like all she'd really wanted on this excursion was to maybe do something cool and worthwhile and *not* time-travelly, even just to prove to herself that she could. *I could find my own stupid crappy pitted coin,* she thought, remembering Maggie mentioning something about being the toast of the project if she could manage even that ...

*Wait.*

Clare sat up and pushed her sunglasses up on her forehead, blinking in the bright sun. She put a hand into the pocket of her jacket. And pulled out a stupid crappy pitted coin. Well. Mission accomplished, then.

*Oops ...*

It was the coin that Professor Ashbourne had tossed at her when she and Milo went to see him in his tent. Back in the early days of the Shenanigans, Clare had almost convinced herself she was a klepto. It was Al who'd convinced her she wasn't. Now, it seemed, there was no convincing to be done either way and Al wasn't around for an I-told-you-so in any case. She'd nicked the artifact from Ashbourne's tent without even realizing it.

And frankly, she was rather hard-pressed to give a damn.

Bloody Nicky—the guy who was supposed to be all reverential about the past—hadn't seemed to really give one either. Clare wondered if he'd even noticed that one of his precious finds was missing. She somehow doubted it. The archaeologist had seemed awfully distracted when she and Milo talked to him ...

Her other jacket pocket began to buzz. Clare pulled out her phone and read the text message Milo had sent.

> Hey, Clare de Lune ... Meet me at Goggles's place as soon as you can after you're done. Don't worry about dinner, I'll stop at the Rifleman and get takeaway. Have something to show you both.

She almost had to tie herself to a tree root to keep from leaping out of her gopher hole and running to the rendezvous. But if she went MIA again before the end of her shift, she'd either raise suspicions or someone just might rat her out to Ashbourne, who might even relay to Maggie that Clare was a slacker. She didn't want that for two reasons. One, she wasn't. If it hadn't been for the Al crisis, Clare would still be happily, achingly, enthusiastically digging away. And two, she needed the time and space to figure out how to get Al back. So she just had to bide her work time and stay in her dig space. Until 4:45 at least, when the supervisors had knocked off and were already half-pints into the evening.

When, finally, quittin' time rolled around, Clare headed in the direction of Gimble's Antiquarian Shop on Chilkwell Street at a dead run. She was out of breath and gasping when she rounded the corner and saw Milo entering the shop just ahead of her. Clare bolted through the door right behind him, almost taking Milo—and Piper Gimble, who'd met Milo at the door—down in a tangled heap.

Piper directed them toward the back room. "I just have a few lookie-loos to shoo on their way," she murmured, gesturing at a middle-aged couple who were peering into one of the cabinets.

"Good. The sooner the better." Milo pointed to the front door. "And then *lock* it this time."

Piper hesitated, then flipped the OPEN sign to CLOSED.

Clare tugged at Milo's sleeve as he stalked between the rows of curio shelves, the brown paper takeaway bag he carried wafting mouth-watering smells in his wake. She suddenly couldn't remember the last full meal she'd eaten. Oh … yes, she could. It was the dinner she'd been unable to choke down after the lunch of the day before that hadn't sat well. No wonder she was damn-near-starving hungry, even with Al still MIA.

"Hey," she said a bit breathlessly.

Milo half-turned and flashed her a warm smile. "Hey, Clare de Lune."

Clare breathed a silent sigh of relief. She'd been wondering if Milo had begun to think a relationship with her was getting to be all just a bit too much. Especially since it had cost him his cousin.

*Temporarily.*

Before Piper managed to ditch the browsing couple, Clare and Milo had laid out a bit of an impromptu picnic. Milo wouldn't tell her what he'd discovered before Piper joined them, but the tang of malt vinegar from the steaming-hot, crispy-battered fish and chips mollified her curiosity for the moment. As she wolfed it down Milo grinned at her.

"That's my girl," he said. "I know *I* always function better on a belly full of food."

Clare grinned back and snarfed a plastic forkful of coleslaw. She had no idea where he packed it all away—he was built like a long-distance runner, all long legs and not an ounce of fat. Still, Clare wasn't about to quibble. Not when he brought her food and called her "his girl." She even forgot to be stressed. Then Piper Gimble, yet another pair of goggles perched on top of her head (vaguely steampunk this time, with ruby-coloured lenses; Clare was beginning to suspect they were strictly for show), rattled her way through the beaded curtain, platinum ponytails flouncing, and it was back to business.

Once Clare had cleared away the cardboard takeaway containers, Milo reached into his knapsack and pulled out his laptop, positioning it on the counter between the three of them and flipping it open. Clare tried her best to ignore the skull-shaped bulge still left in the bag.

"I've been in communication with a ... *friend* of mine over the last couple of days," Milo began.

"A friend?" Clare asked, curious about the way he'd emphasized the word.

"Well, he's more of a ... a contact, really."

*Why does that sound as if Milo's been doing something most people wouldn't do?* Something ... illegal. Or at the very least, suspect. She was staring at him, she knew.

"Just someone I know through work," he went on, shrugging off Clare's frown. "I mean, I've never actually met the guy face to face. But he's a tech genius who works at a multinational geotech survey company. He's seriously hooked in and I asked him to look into something for me. So he did. With some pretty spectacular results."

Milo's fingers danced fluidly over the keyboard as he called up a log-in screen for some kind of official-looking website. His expression set and serious, he plucked his cell phone out of its holder on his belt and punched a number on the screen. It didn't take many rings before someone picked up. Milo murmured something into the handset that was too low for Clare to make out.

She heard the faint chatter of a terse response.

"Thanks, Dan," Milo said. "I owe you one."

The screen had begun to fill, seemingly of its own accord, with overlapping pop-up windows: satellite images, in dizzying variety, of Glastonbury and the surrounding area.

And they didn't look as though they were meant for the average digital customer. Clare saw "classified" tags at the bottom of some of the windows before Milo repositioned them on the screen.

"Most of this stuff comes from oil and prospecting companies that use geomagnetic surveys for help in locating underground resources," Milo murmured as he began to scroll around the various windows, cycling through the data to find what he was looking for.

"*Most* of it?" Clare asked, one eyebrow creeping up her forehead.

Milo seemed to be avoiding eye contact. "Yeah ... some of it comes from military satellites. Dan's got access to the raw data—I mean, he can't patch me in directly to a live feed or anything, but he's posted these latest passes from a geosynchronous bird plus a couple of orbital ones to a secure server site and given me temporary passcode access."

"You're totally not supposed to have that, are you?"

"No." Milo's mouth disappeared into a fine line. "But I needed to see something, and Dan has ... flexible scruples. That's not the point now."

Clare wisely shut up. She knew Milo was worried sick about Al, even though he tried his best to hide it—just to keep *her* from worrying. If he thought the data was worth the risk, the least she could do was pay attention and try to follow the techno jargon.

Piper was close enough to the screen she almost left a nose print on it.

Clare shouldered her out of the way.

"Okay ... here's what I think is happening." Milo's finger hovered in a circle over one of the rainbow-hued images. "This is what the electromagnetic fields surrounding Glastonbury looked like last week. Before we got here."

"What am I looking for?" Clare asked, leaning in. "I don't see anything strange. I mean, other than all the strange stuff. The colours are pretty ..."

"No. You're right," Piper said. "There isn't anything strange. The colour gradients are fairly uniform across the spectrum."

Clare suddenly felt like an idiot for calling them "pretty." *Stupid showoff Piper.*

"There are no large-scale distortions to speak of," Piper continued. "Is that what you're getting at?"

"Right." Milo nodded. "I mean ... this wide inner ring of orange-red indicates some substantial electromagnetic energy readings emanating from the hill, but for this region, it's nothing too off the charts. It falls within the range of normal. Barely, but still normal."

"Okay ..." Clare frowned.

"I mean, as near as I can figure out," he explained, seeing the confusion on her face, "the whole area surrounding the Tor is ... 'in flux' is the only way I can describe it. But it's usual *for the area.* I remember a couple of months ago—when you were still in Toronto, Clare—I was doing some topography mapping of this area and I got kinda fascinated with the quality of its emanations: background radiation levels and that sort of thing. And sure, it's weird. But last week's weird was the same kind of weird as last month's. And the month before that."

Clare worked that through. "So ... uniform weirdness."

"Exactly. Now ..." Milo continued cycling through the graphics Dan had sent him until he got to the one he was looking for. "Here's a shot of the area—taken by the same satellite as the one I just showed you—but *this* one was taken yesterday. At 11:45 A.M. local time."

"That's right around the time I left Al to go log those pot shards," Clare noted. "Just before lunch."

"Just about the time we figure Allie went AWOL. See anything different?"

Clare and Piper both moved in for a closer look. The image was basically the same—rainbow rings flowing out in wobbly circles from the summit of the hill—except that, in one corner of the screen, the coloured rings suddenly buckled inward. And the colour gradient shaded sharply from red to purple to indigo ...

And then, like a pinprick of darkness at the very heart of the anomaly, to black.

"What ...?" Clare squinted at the dot.

"I think that's Allie," Milo said quietly. "At least, I think that's where she went."

Clare's mouth went dry.

"If that was yesterday ..." Piper said, "what does it look like *now*?"

Milo glanced up at her over the rim of his glasses, his mouth set in a grim line. Then he clicked on another image window, enlarging it so that it filled the entire screen.

Clare gasped.

Piper sat back and said, "Whoa."

Instead of uniform rings of colour spreading out from the Tor, streaks of darkness—angry, squiggly threads—snaked through the image like the telltale signs of blood poisoning from a wound gone bad. And what had been a dark pinpoint in the previous shot was now a small, smudgy blur.

"What the *hell* ...?" Clare whispered.

"It begins," Piper said quietly.

Clare's gaze snapped up from the screen. The other girl's expression was calm, serene. Almost cold. But her eyes glittered darkly, like chips of black ice. Suddenly there was no doubt—not a shred of uncertainty—in Clare's mind that Piper Gimble truly was a direct descendant of Stuart Morholt. And that the yarn she'd spun about her ancestress being Boudicca's Druidess sister was just as true.

And if this Mallora chick had been anything at all like her sibling, then …

"How do we stop it?" Clare asked.

"You don't," said Nicholas Ashbourne, walking through the beaded curtain from the shop. "Not yet." The archaeologist nodded at Piper, who shifted uncomfortably on her stool. "Thanks for the tip, my dear."

Clare turned and stared daggers at the other girl. "Don't trust *any*one, huh, Goggles? You bi—"

"Tut, tut, Miss Reid." Bloody Nicky stepped further into the room. "Miss Gimble was only following my instructions for the betterment of all. Never mind that now. We have work to do. And I'd like to start off by having you return something that belongs to me."

He gestured to Milo's knapsack on the workbench. "My skull."

As Bloody Nicky reached for the bag, Milo stood up abruptly and slapped his hand down on the hard round contour shaped by the lump of bone inside. Clare could see that Milo had just about had enough game playing. She heard the knuckles of his other hand crack as he clenched it into a fist.

"All right," Milo said, daring the archaeologist with his glare to take the knapsack from under his hand. "I think you'd better tell us what's going on here, Dr. Ashbourne. What do you mean we don't stop *that*?" He nodded his head sharply at the computer screen with its disturbing, distorted rainbow.

"Just what I said. You don't. You can't." Under one corner of the crumb catcher that festooned his upper lip, Ashbourne's mouth quirked upward in a cold, unpleasant smile. He looked back and forth between her and Milo. "Because it hasn't started yet."

Clare stared at the screen. Ashbourne was clearly off his rocker: the phenomenon was in full swing.

"What I mean is that it hasn't started yet *then*." His eyes gleamed with a fevered light. "But you can make that happen, young man. You *will*. Two thousand years ago. And then *I* will take it from there, twenty-five years ago. And *that's* how we're going to get

Miss McAllister back *and* save the lives of a lot of good men. It's the only way. By using your ... unique abilities to activate the mystical Glastonbury portal. With my help."

"I don't think I want your help," Milo snapped. "I think I want your answers. *Without* all this cryptic bullcrap. What good men? What 'unique' abilities? You seem to know a thing or two about what's going on here, Professor. Well, what *I* know is *this:* my cousin disappeared in that electromagnetic shitstorm of a spatio-temporal funhouse you call the Glastonbury portal. I don't know how it occurred. I don't care. But I want her back. *Now.* And I'm not partial about who I have to hurt to make that happen."

Milo was *dead* sexy when he was all pissed off like that, Clare thought. She felt her heart flutter at the sight of his clenched jaw and the muscles standing out along the forearm above his knotted fist. But ogling opportunities aside, the whole situation was about to become something of an alpha-male debacle.

"Okaaay ..." She took two steps out from behind the workbench, positioning herself between archaeologist and topographist. "I'm going to take over from Milo in the threatening department now."

"Oh, goody." Piper rolled her eyes. "Shall I find you another letter opener?"

"Shut it, Goggles." Clare kept her eyes on the archaeologist. "Let me give you *my* unique perspective on events, Professor Ashbourne. My best friend is lost, some*when*, out there. And as Milo said, you don't seem particularly surprised. You also said you can help us get her back. That's great, and I'm willing to hear what you have to say."

Ashbourne nodded graciously.

"But I swear—I *swear* to you—if something bad happens to Al? I will *not* be a happy little trowel monkey. I happen to be on speaking terms with a vengeful war goddess and I'm not above calling in a favour or two." Okay, so that last bit was strictly for dramatic effect. Still. Whatever game Bloody Nicky and Goggles thought they were playing, Clare wasn't about to go meekly along without getting a few things straight first. Not when Al's well-being was at stake. No freaking way.

"I've met those who are on more than just speaking terms with your goddess, Miss Reid," Nicholas Ashbourne said. "Up close and personal."

He stepped forward to tug the knapsack out from under Milo's hand. Reaching in, he pulled out the skull and held the grisly artifact up in front of his face. Now it looked as if they were staring at each other. Clare's stomach heaved a bit.

"This was an auspicious find," Ashbourne remarked. "Well, not terribly auspicious for *him*, poor chap ..."

"How d'you know it was a he?" Clare asked.

"Hm?" Bloody Nicky seemed awfully distracted all of a sudden. Just as he'd been in the tent, with the coins. He took a moment to process the question. "Oh ... oh, I know. Definitely male. Early forties. In rugged good health right up until the moment of his death. A fine specimen, really. Don't you just wonder what it was that made someone want to go and chop the dear fellow's head clean off?"

Piper winced. Clare and Milo blinked at each other.

Clare turned back to the archaeologist. "How ...?"

"Here. You see?" he said, pointing. "At the base of the skull near this opening, where the spinal column would have joined up with the medulla oblongata—the brain stem—you can see a very distinct mark below the occipital bun, which is that slight bony protrusion there. That mark, the scar on the bone, indicates a blow made by a blade. Clean, sharp. Excellent aim. Someone who'd been well trained in the art of war did the deed. Took this fellow's head off in one fell swoop."

"How do you know the blow came before and not after?" Milo asked. "I mean, the Celts thought the head was the seat of the soul, didn't they? Couldn't this have been a case of head hunting? Trophy gathering after a battle?"

Clare blinked over at Milo through the wooziness that was beginning to make her feel dizzy. She supposed it was only natural that he'd done some in-depth reading on Celtic beliefs and practices. After all, as relatively normal as he seemed, Milo had spent several hours possessed by the disembodied soul of Connal the Druid back when they'd faced off against Boudicca. The experience had probably piqued his intellectual curiosity.

But Bloody Nicky dismissed Milo's suggestion with a wave of his hand. "No. This was the killing blow."

"So ... you're saying this was a sacrifice?" Clare asked. "Like a ritual?"

"More of an execution, really," Ashbourne said with a trace of bitterness in his voice. "But I dare say it wound up serving the same purpose, ultimately."

The archaeologist stared into the empty, shadowed eye sockets as if they stared right back at him. A good minute ticked by. Piper fidgeted, and then stood abruptly and went to fetch the silver hip flask she used to spike her tea. She set it down forcefully in front of Ashbourne, who blinked, grunted a word of thanks, and took a long swallow of the brandy.

"Wait ..." Clare frowned. An uncomfortably morbid thought was assembling itself deep in her brain. "You said that thing belonged to you. Then how did it wind up out in that field? Did you lose it?"

"I did indeed," the professor mused. "Almost two thousand years ago, when I ordered one of my own men to decapitate me on top of Glastonbury Tor."

Clare glanced back and forth between the skull ... and Ashbourne's head. When he said he'd come to reclaim his skull, he meant he'd come to reclaim *his skull*. Suddenly, quite clearly, Clare could picture a handlebar moustache on the bone relic. The anonymous old skull wasn't anonymous anymore.

In that instant, the fish and chips Milo had so thoughtfully provided rolled over violently in Clare's stomach and she bolted for the shop's back entrance, took a hard left in the alleyway, and threw up in the bushes.

15

Marcus stared at Allie, and she could see the implications of what she'd just said sinking in. He turned and sat down heavily on a folding stool. "A ... quarter of a century?" he asked.

She nodded. "Give or take."

"My friends. My ... family ..." His mouth twisted in a bitter grimace and he shook his head slowly. "They must think I'm dead. Disappeared. Some of *them* are probably dead ..."

"I'm really sorry." Allie didn't know what else to say.

"And you ..." His gaze, full of dawning realization and dull hurt, drifted back to her face. "Who *are* you? And after all this time, why have you come only now to find me?"

"If you want the honest truth, I *didn't* come here for you. I didn't actually mean to come here at all." She shrugged apologetically and the manacles around her wrists clanked. "It was an accident. I hadn't meant to find you. But ... now that I have ... maybe together we can find a way to go back."

"Back? Back to what?" he scoffed. "To a world I never really fit into in the first place and probably wouldn't even recognize—let alone find a place for myself in—now? I'd be a walking anachronism. Obsolete. At least here, I belong. I *have* a place here. For as long as I'm likely to stay alive, that is. Which—with the way things have been going lately—should be another few weeks at least ..."

Allie felt her lower lip start to tremble again and, as hard as she tried, she couldn't seem to keep the tears from welling in her eyes. Suddenly it hit her: she really *hadn't* wanted this. And all that time she'd spent thinking she might be a tiny bit jealous of Clare and her adventures in the past ...

How stupid was *that*?

The past was cold. It was uncomfortable. It was very possibly lethal. And all Allie wanted in that moment was to be home. Seeing how Marcus had reacted made her want it more than anything. She wanted to get the hell back to her own time and she didn't care how she had to do it. She didn't care if it meant leaving Mark O'Donnell behind.

*I don't know him. I don't* owe *him anything.*

He seemed perfectly, grimly happy to stay right where and when he was. If there was some way she could convince him to come along if—no, *when*—she made her return, then fine. Otherwise, Legionnaire Donatus was on his own. Of course, she wasn't at all sure how it would come to pass. Especially since Marcus Donatus didn't even seem particularly inclined to unchain her from the tent pole. Allie would have to play to his sympathetic side. Win him over. She decided to gamble on a tactic she thought might work.

"You know ... you *wouldn't* be totally alone if you went back," she said. "I mean ... Maggie's there. And she will totally lose her mind when she finds out you're still alive—"

His head snapped back as if she'd just slapped him.

*"Maggie ..."* he said, his mouth moving around the word as if he found it almost impossible to say. "Do you mean ... Magda? Magda Wallace?"

"Yes!" Allie nodded excitedly. "She's ... well, she's been really upset about it. For years. She ... um ..."

Allie stammered to a halt as she watched Mark/Marcus's expression turn hard and cold. And angry. Then she remembered that Maggie and Stuart Morholt had been some kind of an item back in the day. It was entirely possible that Mark held her partly responsible for what had happened to him—

"That bitch."

*Okaaay ... maybe not possible. Maybe definite.*

"Um," Allie said again and swallowed nervously.

As he glared at her, she found herself asking—out loud—just what the hell had happened to him to change him so much. To make him so cold. When he turned away from her she knew she'd pushed him one step too far. The question was barely out of Allie's mouth before he was across the tent's dirt floor and almost nose to nose with her. His teeth were bared again in that frightening grimace and the breath heaved in his lungs.

"What happened to me?" he snarled between clenched teeth. "What *happened* to me? Look around you. This war happened to me. In *this* time, in *this* place. Those ... *things*—demons—out there happened to me. I was fifteen years old. A child. I was ripped from my world, thrown into this one, and I almost died. I found myself in a place of savagery and sorcery and I. Almost. *Died*." He spat the words. "And Magda Wallace stood by and let it happen and did nothing."

"I'm sorry ..."

"No more sorry than I am," he said in a voice rough with emotion. "If she's the kind of company you keep in your own time, then I don't know that I want anything to do with you in mine." He spun around and headed toward the tent flap.

"Wait!" Allie couldn't handle being left alone again, regardless of how terrible the present company was. "Maggie's sorry, too. I *know* she's sorry."

Marcus uttered a short, brutal laugh. "I'm sure she is. Did Stuart make her run all his errands for him after I disappeared? It must have been a great hardship."

"That's not fair. I mean, yeah, Morholt's like a complete tool, but it was Dr. Jenkins that set the whole thing up."

"Doctor ...?"

"Mags was just kind of along for the ride." Allie kept talking, kept trying to explain. "And Stu is *way* too much of a doofus to actually make anything happen. Really. I mean, the guy's a lame ass. And Maggie was devastated when you disappeared. She's come back to Glastonbury every year. Just to mark the occasion. Even after all this time. She hasn't forgotten you and—"

Marcus silenced her with a smouldering glare. She was about to tell him he was more than welcome to take it out on Morholt— who was in the tent just down the way—but then she wondered if he even knew that. It didn't seem as if he did. Allie's brain whirled furiously, stacking up the pros and cons of telling Marcus that his hated former classman, the one he obviously blamed for his temporal misfortunes (no doubt rightfully so), was sitting in a filthy huddle not fifty yards away.

But then a commotion erupted outside the tent. Allie could hear soldiers running and yelling and the centurion's voice, braying like a mule, above it all.

Suddenly the tent flap flew wide and the centurion's helmeted head appeared in the opening. "He's back," he said to Marcus. "Postumus is awake! The wily old bastard is alive and well and back on his feet again."

The relief on Marcus's face was palpable. And as the tension seemed to flow like water from him, Allie realized that it wasn't just her presence in the camp that had set the young soldier's nerves jangling. It was everything else that was happening, too. She could hardly blame him for being on hair-trigger response. The fact that he'd been only fifteen when he was thrust back in time—and an awkward, sheltered bookworm, by all accounts— was part of it too, but as he stood there beside the centurion, all leather and armour and hardened muscle, she could barely imagine him as that boy.

Marcus grinned widely at the other man. "An hour ago you were calling him a coward."

The centurion grinned back. "An hour ago I thought he was as good as dead!"

Marcus crossed to the wooden stand and reached for his helmet and sword belt. "Where is he?"

"Headed straight for the mess tent. It's nothing short of amazing—he's full of fire. Wants to address the troops, assure the men, all that. And the cooks are setting a welcome table for him. You coming?"

Marcus glanced back at Allie. "Go on. I'll follow you shortly. I want to get cleaned up before I face the praefect again."

"Well. Don't dawdle. You'll miss all the best inspirational speeches." Junius rolled his eyes and ducked back out of the tent.

Marcus stalked back over to Allie and gazed at her intently, a wealth of unspoken emotions swimming behind his eyes. His gaze fixed upon the manacles circling her slender wrists. Allie had to bite her tongue from mentioning that she was only two years older than the "boy" he'd been when he'd gotten stuck back in this awful place ...

*Girls mature faster than boys,* she thought sourly. *Just don't tell him that ...*

When he finally spoke again, the sharpness was gone from his tone.

"Listen to me," he said. "The praefect will want to question you at some point."

"You mean interrogate me."

Marcus hesitated. "Just ... remember what I told you. He'll need me to interpret for you, and I'll try to help you as much as I can. But for heaven's sake, don't let on that you can understand him. Or that you can speak his language. All right? It's the only way I'll be able to keep you safe."

Allie nodded and kept her expression as neutral as possible. *Like you actually care about my safety ...*

"I'll return soon."

*Good for you,* she thought. *I won't be here when you get back.*

The impromptu camp assembly was just the opportunity Allie had been waiting for. It had always kind of galled her that, despite a deeply female need to accessorize her techno-ninja style with black and silver bangles, her wrists were just way too skinny to accommodate that need. Clare could wear bracelets. She could stack them to her elbows. But everything just kind of slid off Allie's hands. And yet that had proved quite useful growing up: every time her brothers would gang up on Allie and tie her to the apple tree in the backyard during one of their stupid games of cowboys and Indians, she'd let them lash her with their hemp rope, wait five minutes after they'd gone in search of more captives, and then wriggle her skinny little hands free and scamper away to Clare's house three blocks over. It never mattered how tight the McAllister boys tied the knots; she'd always pull a daring escape, and her brothers could never figure out how she did it.

And now, tied to a tent pole in the middle of a Roman army camp somewhere in the wilds of first-century Somerset, an overwhelming sense of déjà vu washed over her as she squished and squeezed the bones of her hands together, contorting in ways that would make Houdini proud.

Once free, she glanced around the dim confines of the tent, taking thorough, analytical stock of her situation.

There was only one entrance—the flap-covered doorway guarded by some poor schmuck sentry who'd have to hear about the praefect's remarkable recovery secondhand. Allie could see his shadow as he paced back and forth, but he had yet to poke his head in to check on her. The other three sides of the square, spartan enclosure consisted of blank canvas walls stretched and pegged tight to the ground. Allie tried to remember what she'd learned about the configuration of a Roman marching camp from all she'd been reading. The thing about the Legions was that they were all about conformity. Everything they did, they did with as little deviation from established procedures as possible. They were a machine. Ruthlessly efficient. It was one of the reasons they'd been so successful in their military campaigns. They didn't waste time screwing around trying new things like different camp layouts.

Allie knew with certainty that this, the commanding officer's tent, was usually situated somewhere close to the centre of the camp. She was pretty sure that the forward half of the camp quartered the elite soldiers—the best fighters—and that the rearward half quartered the auxiliaries, along with the supply tents and the cavalry if there was any. At least some horses were attached to the Second Augusta—there had been during the battle—so there'd have to be some kind of stabling or picket lines for them. Allie figured the tent opening faced forward, toward the enemy. So she turned now and tiptoed to the back wall.

The thing about the terrain around Glastonbury was that, because the Somerset Levels had yet to be drained and converted into arable farmland, most of it was in a state of perpetual marshiness. The ground on which the camp stood was spongy. Spongy enough to let a slender, seventeen-year-old girl—wriggling like an eel and with a reasonably modest set of boobs mashed flat—squeeze herself under the edge of the heavy canvas and out into the narrow alleyway. She could smell meat cooking from somewhere north of her, wafted on a hint of a breeze. Okay, so ... the mess tent was off to her left. She turned to her right.

Allie knew that the camp would have two main "avenues" leading north-south and east-west, cutting the enclosed area into quarters. She'd have to avoid those. She edged her way to the corner of the tent. The coast was clear down a side alley between two rows of tents that looked as though they might be used for either storage or the infirmary—they didn't have the same sort of inhabited air she'd seen when Marcus had led her to the praefect's tent. She heard the soft whickering of a horse off in that direction. So she'd go south: it was her best bet to make it undetected to the bank-and-ditch enclosure that surrounded the camp. Thank goodness for the kind of mind-numbing fear that drove her forward without hesitation—and that silenced the voice asking her what the hell she was going to do once she managed to get outside the walls. She had, frankly, no idea. But it couldn't be any worse than being a prisoner. And if the Romans had captured Llassar the smith, it wasn't entirely inconceivable that—scathach notwithstanding (Allie didn't want to ponder what might happen if she ran into any of *them*)—other Clare-friendly Celts were roaming the moors nearby. And if Al could maybe get to them ... or something ...

*Whatever. It doesn't matter. Anything has got to be better than chains.*

Allie ran from tent to tent. When she was close enough to see the defensive fortifications, she found a spot to hide in the shadows beneath a provisions wagon. She willed herself to be patient as a pair of soldiers passed by on patrol. Then she willed herself to be even more patient until they'd passed her for the second time, heading the other way. They were discussing the evening's feast with anticipation. Apparently, with provisions growing thin thanks to the scathach siege, the cooks had been forced to ration things like seasoning and the better cuts of meat. From what Allie gathered, last night's stew tasted as if it had been made from cavalry mounts fallen in battle (she thought she might barf on hearing that and really hoped they were joking). Finally the sentries moved on, muttering to each other about "just what in Hades the Second Augusta was doing in this gods-forsaken marsh-ridden demon-plagued land anyway, by Mars and Mithras ..."

Allie held her breath until she could no longer hear them, and counted to ten just to make sure. Then she wriggled out from under the cart, leaped to her feet, and made a run for it. Scrambling up the earthen bank that surrounded the camp was easier said than done. At least the sharpened stakes were on the other side, pointing out—the Romans hadn't expected having to keep anyone *in* the camp—and so she didn't have to worry about being impaled. But the dirt was only loosely packed, and it was hard to find hand- and footholds. Still, desperation gave Allie the determination she needed, and she reached the top of the bank, tumbled over it, and rolled all the way down the other side into the surrounding ditch, just as she heard the sentries returning.

Her mouth and nose were filled with grit, her eyes stung, and her hair was a matted mess. Her clothes were a mass of grass stains, dirt, and ripped bits. It was not, sartorially speaking, her finest hour. Still, she was elated. Almost as elated as when she'd made another escape—in Stuart Morholt's limited-edition Bentley, which she'd driven into a utility pole just to let him know that kidnapping two teenage girls wasn't the best idea he'd ever had and he should think twice before doing it again. Ha.

Okay, maybe Marcus hadn't exactly kidnapped her. Maybe he'd saved her life. Maybe he'd continued to do so in weird, off-putting ways. Still. He'd left her tied to a tent pole. That—in the language of his eighties upbringing—was bogus. And Allie wasn't about to hang around waiting for that Junius guy to decide that maybe she wasn't so scary with her hands shackled and maybe his superiors wouldn't mind so much if he did just run a sword through her guts. She was *so* getting out of there.

Once outside the camp walls, Allie ran for all she was worth. She headed west, not because she knew where she was going or what she'd do when she got there, but because that was, in some other world, where home was. Even if it was an ocean and a couple of thousand years away.

It was probably, in retrospect, the exact wrong direction in which to head. As Allie soon discovered, and in such a way as to make her think some higher power with a really twisted sense of humour had broken out a big ol' bucket of popcorn and was sitting on a couch somewhere just waiting and watching to see how she'd deal with this one.

She had to stop running because there was a river in front of her.

And there was someone in the river.

And damn it all, that someone was Marcus.

Maybe Clare *shouldn't* have had the fish and chips. But in retrospect it wouldn't have made much difference, since it was Nicholas Ashbourne gazing into the eye sockets of his own damned cranium that had flipped Clare's stomach to the point of no return. Back inside the shop, she took a long swallow of water from the bottle Milo handed her and tried not to heave again.

But ... the thing was *staring* at her.

She imagined a faintly amused expression on its grim, bony visage.

"For crying out loud," Clare muttered peevishly. She picked up a dust rag lying on the counter and tossed it over the skull.

Nicholas Ashbourne emitted a small, mirthless laugh. Then he took another slug of brandy, sighed, and removed his ridiculous pith helmet for the first time since Clare had met him. She noticed that the professor's demeanour had subtly changed. His posture seemed more relaxed. His gestures were less flamboyant. Even the goofball moustache seemed almost ... dignified. *Almost.*

Ashbourne ran a hand down his face, smoothing the bristles as if he were distantly longing for a straight razor.

"I'm not exactly sure where to begin," he said in a voice that was lower, more solemn. And apparently less inclined to add the word 'marvellous' to every utterance, although he did seem to have stocked up on a few other adjectives. "It's a complicated story. Fantastical. Unbelievable ..."

Clare refrained from rolling her eyes, but only because she was becoming well and truly freaked out. Still, she could give Bloody Nicky a run for his money when it came to those three things.

"Go on," she said. "I'm pretty open-minded when it comes to complicated, fantastical, and unbelievable. I promise I won't laugh or anything."

Milo grinned wanly. "She won't. Trust me. Neither will I."

Ashbourne and Piper exchanged a glance and the archaeologist shrugged.

"All right then," he said. "I am not Nicholas Ashbourne. Well ... that's not strictly true, I suppose. I suppose I am he as much as I am anyone. But it is certainly not who I started out as. A long time ago, a young man by the name of Quintus Phoenius Postumus was born in the year AD 20 by our present calendar standards and grew up to become an officer in the Roman army, serving at the siege of the Druid stronghold of Mona under the command of one Gaius Suetonius—"

*"Paulinus?"* Clare interrupted, agog with astonishment and disgust. "Not *that* guy again! I'm seriously *so* sick of hearing about that bloody Roman wanker."

Milo turned and raised a grimly amused eyebrow at her. It seemed that, in the few weeks she'd been across the pond, Clare had acclimated nicely. Peppering her speech with bon mots like "bloody" and "wanker" just like a native; Maggie would be proud. Ashbourne, for his part, did a double take.

"Spoken like someone with firsthand knowledge of the man," he murmured.

"I am," she snorted. "Oh, the good old days."

"Clare ... is special," Milo explained. "In a lot of ways, but temporally speaking, *really* special."

"Oh yes. I know all about that."

"You do?"

"About the fact that Miss Reid carries a Druid blood curse in her veins?" He chuckled at Clare's reaction. "Come now, Miss Reid, surely you don't think you're the only one who's fallen prey to a centuries-spanning Druid blood curse?"

"Um. No?" Clare blinked. "Well ... yes. I actually kind of did."

She was startled to the core. But then her gaze locked with Ashbourne's and it dawned on Clare that he knew about her ... *condition* because it was something they shared.

"You," she said quietly. "You were this Postumus guy ..."

He nodded.

"... and the Druiddyn blood cursed you."

Ashbourne's mouth half-bent in a mirthless smile and he nodded faintly. "I suspect, though, that mine was rather more malicious than yours."

"Yeah, well. I was a girl in a sundress who time-travelled by accident." Clare couldn't help the abruptly snarky tone; her mind had just flashed on the mental picture of him in full Roman armour, standing against a backdrop of fire and smoke. "You, on the other hand, were a commander in the army that was kind of busy trying to wipe out a large percentage of the native Briton population. I imagine that didn't exactly stir up the warm fuzzies among the Druiddyn, y'know?"

Ashbourne sighed. "I'm sorry you think of me that way."

"I'm sorry you *make* me think of you that way."

Milo put a hand on her shoulder. "Clare ... this isn't getting us any closer to finding Allie. Dr. Ashbourne, please. Go on."

"Sure. Right. Go on." Clare bit her lip and struggled to keep a lid on her temper. She couldn't help seeing Bloody Nicky Ashbourne not for who he was now but for what he'd been. Comorra had died—before Clare had altered the course of history just a teeny bit—because of the actions of men like him. A lot of the Iceni had died. Boudicca, her daughter Tasca, her husband ... and those were just a few of the faces Clare could put to the dead. There'd been so many more. All because a bunch of stupid men from a stupid country thousands of miles away decided they wanted a little more space to spread out.

She simmered silently while Ashbourne told them about the siege of the Druid Isle of Mona, where the Roman governor, the brutal Suetonius Paulinus, had ordered the sacred oak groves burned before he had to hurry east to take care of Boudicca's rebellious uprising.

"He commanded me to follow him once we were done with the job on Mona ..."

"Job?" Clare muttered. "Is *that* what they called a massacre back in the day?"

Ashbourne's shoulders stiffened, and a slight flush—whether of anger or shame, Clare couldn't tell—suffused his face. But otherwise he ignored the dig.

"I declined to follow that order," he continued.

Clare swallowed another knee-jerk snark.

"Declined?" Milo said. "You mean you disobeyed a direct order from your commander?"

"I did. But only because I had other orders—imperatives, really—from higher up the ladder. Paulinus was a ... driven man, shall we say. He was single-minded in his quest to beat the Britons into submission—especially when it came to Boudicca and her rebels. And the Druiddyn. What happened on Mona was ... not honourable. And I knew it would be even worse with the Iceni: Boudicca and her people would fight to the bitterest end, and Paulinus and his men would be merciless. The Fourteenth—the Legio Gemina—had a reputation as the most brutally efficient of all the Legions, and it was not an unearned one. Under the command of Paulinus, the Fourteenth was a well-oiled killing machine. My own men—the Second Augusta—had cultivated a different reputation. One of honour. We were in Britain as keepers of peace. Arbiters of civilization and progress."

"Even if the Celts didn't want you there?"

Ashbourne sighed. "Perhaps so. Yes. At the time I didn't see it that way. None of us did." He ran a hand over his face again, his expression betraying a bone-deep weariness, and Clare felt her righteous indignation faltering somewhat. "At any rate," he continued, "I had no wish to put my own men in the middle of such a ruinous clash. And so I manufactured a viable excuse for avoiding the conflict. A *golden* excuse, one might say."

"What was that?" Milo asked.

"Emperor Nero was a man thirsty for the riches of his provinces. And Britain was nothing if not rich. In gold. Druid gold. After Paulinus left to go fight Boudicca, my men and I discovered masses of the stuff, hidden in caves on Mona. Magnificent workmanship, torcs and brooches and bracelets ... all manner of jewellery fit for kings and queens ..."

Clare thought back to the treasure hoard buried along with the body of the queen in Boudicca's grave barrow, and she knew that Ashbourne wasn't exaggerating.

"I sent a missive to Paulinus describing the treasure caches and telling him that, as per the emperor's mandate, my men and I would escort the captured booty to ships sailing for Rome. I thought I was being clever. But in trying to save my men from unnecessary slaughter and destruction, I succeeded only in damning them more thoroughly than I ever could have imagined."

"What happened?" Clare leaned forward, fascinated in spite of herself.

"After we left Mona, we travelled south with a caravan of wagons to deliver the gold to one of the supply ships that anchored at a place called Parwydydd, on the south shore of the River Severn where it empties into the Bristol Channel. But the gold weighed us down. Slowed our progress. And, I suppose, fuelled an even greater anger in the Britons—who attacked us for having stolen their Druids' sacred treasure. Eventually they laid a trap for us. We were ambushed in the Mendip Hills, not very far north of here. A lot of my men were killed in what became a long-running battle ..."

His eyes went glassy with the memory and Clare felt a chill crawling across her scalp. She'd been caught in the middle of a Celt versus Roman battle once. She still had nightmares about it.

"Eventually we had to abandon all but one of the wagons, giving up the gold to be recaptured. Then, under cover of darkness one night, I sent my best men out with the remaining booty in sacks upon their backs. They were to hide the gold somewhere in the Mendips while the rest of us provided a distraction and then meet us again at the foot of Ynys Wyddryn—what you now know as Glastonbury Tor—and that's what we did. Unfortunately, we never made it back to retrieve the gold and we never made it any further. Instead, we set up camp in order to regroup. But when I tried to lead a patrol out, I was captured. Briefly." Ashbourne's expression darkened as he spoke. "I don't remember much of what happened ... only jumbled images of a shadowy place and a woman in a cloak of raven feathers standing over me, her eyes red and terrible ..." He shook his head. "And then, the next morning, some of my men found me just outside the camp gate, unconscious. With a heavy gold torc wrapped around my neck that I could not remove no matter how hard I tried."

Clare shuddered, remembering the dream she'd had—the one with Morholt and the scary chick in the feathered cloak. Obviously, it *hadn't* been only a dream. Clare was still mystically tied to the torc, just as, it was now apparent, Ashbourne was tied to it. And she was tied to Al. And Al had found Ashbourne's skull ... She remembered watching as the woman took the Snettisham Great Torc from Morholt ... and now she knew what had happened to it.

"The Great Torc," Milo said, grasping the significance only a moment after Clare had. "Somehow it wound up on Mona instead of buried in a hole in the ground in Norfolk."

"That's correct," Ashbourne said. "And Mallora—Boudicca's Druidess sister—took what power the torc already had and ... amplified it. Augmented it with her own magics and the magics of this place." He waved a hand in the vague direction of the Tor. "From that moment on, we were doomed. Regular Celtic warriors we could fight our way through—with casualties, certainly, but our superior numbers and techniques would eventually win the day.

But after they found me outside the gate, we were besieged—not by Celtic warriors, but by demons. The scathach. They appeared out of nowhere—literally *no*where, right out of thin air—and they kept us pinned down in that place.

"You see, Glastonbury itself is a mystical doorway that can be opened—or closed—with a key made of blood. After my capture, I had unwittingly become that key. And Mallora called forth those monsters with it. They were like ... primeval berserkers. Wild-eyed and tattooed, they seemed almost from an earlier time. Perhaps they were—Celtic lore and legends are stuffed with accounts of mystically empowered women warriors from a shadowy time when the magic of the island was rife. Perhaps Mallora used me to bring them forward into her world. Used them to exact her revenge for the Roman predations upon her people. Revenge for our theft of their treasure ... At any rate, I found myself the instrument through which the curse worked its will."

"Welcome to the club," Clare murmured.

"Yes." Ashbourne leaned back in his chair and regarded Clare as if she were some kind of scientific curiosity. And then, even more annoyingly, he started *talking* about her that way. "Now, insofar as I understand Miss Reid's abilities," he said with a meaningful look at Piper, "she is temporally linked to certain objects that have been forged using minute amounts of her blood. Although I will admit that I am somewhat foggy on which came first: the time *travel* or the time-travel *curse* ..."

"Don't ask." Milo put up a weary hand. "Because, frankly? I have a bank of microprocessors sitting in my apartment back in London that have been trying to sort out that conundrum for the last few weeks, and I think one of them is about to start singing 'Daisy, Daisy, give me your answer do' any day now."

"You do?" Clare blinked, not entirely certain he was joking.

"Heh," Piper snickered. "*2001*. Gotta love a movie with a homicidal computer—"

Clare glared her into silence.

"The upshot of the whole thing," Milo went on, "is that—chicken/egg conundrum notwithstanding—Clare wound up flipping back and forth between the present and the Boudiccan rebellion for a few days. And Boudicca's spirit wound up following her back to modern-day London, briefly, where she proceeded to possess a museum curator, raise a bunch of bog-zombie warriors from the dead, and wreak a little havoc. Until Clare forcibly evicted her and everything went back to normal. Relatively."

"Don't forget, *you* got to share your brain with a Druid warrior prince who showed us a magical pathway between dimensions," Clare chimed in. "Don't forget that."

"I'm unlikely to," Milo said.

He shot Clare a look so intense it startled her. She wasn't quite sure how to interpret it. But just then Ashbourne snapped his fingers.

"And *that*, my dear fellow," he said, "is the very crux of the whole matter."

Milo and Clare turned to him.

"You see, *you*, Mr. McAllister, are also a kind of key," the archaeologist said. "The key to bringing your cousin home."

Clare didn't know quite what to think of that. In some ways, she'd wholly expected Dr. Ashbourne to throw the "Here is what you must do to save the day" curveball into the conversation. But she'd also assumed he would throw it at *her*. And she was feeling vaguely guilty for thinking she was kind of ... irrelevant, all of a sudden.

"You mean ... I'm the key. *Me*. Girl Time traveller over here."

"No, Clare." Milo shook his head. "Not this time."

He'd said it quietly. And yet the *way* he'd said it was enough to make Clare spin around and stare at him, her mouth drifting open in astonishment at something she'd just figured out. Something that should have been apparent to her for weeks. Ever since the Shenanigans. Something she'd been actively ignoring, hoping it wasn't true.

"What did I *do* to you?" she whispered.

It was just loud enough for Milo to hear and he half-turned, gazing at her over the rim of his glasses, a strange, haunted look in his eyes.

"God ..." Clare put a hand over her mouth to keep from crying out. "What have I done? He's still in your head, isn't he? Connal?"

"No!" Milo protested. "No ... It's nothing. Just ... he left behind some of his knowledge."

"Knowledge? You mean magic?"

"I mean knowledge, Clare. Information. I *like* that stuff, remember?"

Milo stared down at the cup made by his laced fingers as if he held secrets there that only he could see. Maybe he did. The tiny gold hoop in Milo's ear reflected off the work light on Piper's table and winked at her. She still couldn't remember if he'd always worn it. But she knew that Connal had worn one just like it. Two thousand years ago.

Clare had no idea what to say to Milo. It was she who had pleaded with him to host the disembodied spirit of Connal the Druid, and so it was her fault that Connal had left Milo changed. Altered in ways she couldn't even begin to imagine.

Milo had done it for *her.*

And now?

She turned to Ashbourne, almost grabbing him by the front of his jacket. "What does Morholt say? About Milo. What did he write?"

"Miss Gimble," Dr. Ashbourne said, "would you be so kind as to fetch the book? I'd like to show Miss Reid and Mr. McAllister what we're talking about."

Clare turned to see the other girl's expression of concern for Milo. She almost lost it. If *anyone* was going to feel bad for Milo it was going to be her. Clare turned her Piper-glare up to withering.

"Oh yes," she said. "*Do* indulge us, Miss Gimble. Fulfill your meddlesome evil-henchgirl stereotypical duties and fetch."

Piper blinked in surprise and then frosted up a glare of her own. "Oh, please. Talk about meddlesome. I wouldn't even exist if it wasn't for you. And as for stereotypes? You're a *time* traveller. If that isn't a hackneyed B-movie stock-character role, I don't know what is—"

"Ladies ..." Milo sighed wearily, finally looking up. "Not helping."

Piper's mouth snapped shut. Then she tossed her pale ponytails and huffed over to the cabinet where she'd put the tin box earlier in the day. A moment passed while she opened the cabinet doors and rummaged around a bit. Another moment passed, and the rummaging increased in intensity. And then random articles began flying out of the cabinet as Piper started chucking stuff over her shoulders in a seeming panic. Now she was making high-pitched chirping noises like some kind of baby animal in distress. Clare glanced over at Ashbourne, whose brow creased in a worried frown. He started to rise up off his stool just as Piper's head poked around the cabinet door. She was deathly pale and her eyes were almost as big as when Clare had first seen them peering out of her magni-goggles.

"It's gone!" she blurted.

Ashbourne finished his rise off his stool so fast the thing toppled over behind him with a loud crash.

"What in the name of all the gods do you mean *'It's gone'*?" The ferocity of his snarl brought a sudden flush to Piper's ashen complexion. Clare was starting to see the man behind the moustache very clearly now. The whole "marvellous," genial, slightly bumbling, overdressed professor of archaeology act was just that. An act. Nicholas Ashbourne was an elaborately constructed persona. The reality behind that facade—the real man behind the facial-hair curtain—was a commander of men. A soldier. And capable of ruthlessness and cold calculation. Clare suddenly felt a bit—a *tiny* bit—sorry for Piper, who swallowed nervously and pointed to the cabinet.

"Gone," she said again in a dry whisper. "I put it in there. Right there! For safekeeping. I hid it behind Nigel."

"Nigel?" Clare asked.

"The badger!"

Piper threw the cabinet door wide and Clare realized she was talking about a moth-eaten stuffed badger mounted on a drift-wood stand. Just another oddity in Piper's emporium, the thing grinned hideously at her from an otherwise mostly empty cabinet. Clare stared at the other girl, speechless. When she glanced back at Milo, his expression was unreadable. She wanted to say something to him. Comfort him and utter all sorts of reassurances that Al would be fine. That they'd find his cousin and bring her home. But the hollow pit opening in the bottom of Clare's stomach seemed to have swallowed up all her words. They'd been counting on the diary to give them some kind of answer. Clues as to how to get Al back. But now that possibility was slipping further and further from Clare's grasp. Just as Milo seemed to be drifting beyond her reach.

*This can't be happening. How on earth has everything gotten so screwed up?*

Piper suddenly hauled off and violently kicked the cabinet.

"I'm doomed!" she exclaimed, a sheen of tears unexpectedly glimmering on the lashes of her dark brown eyes.

"*You're* doomed?" Clare was aghast. "What about Al?"

"What about her?" Piper rounded on Clare fiercely. "At least she bloody still exists! Without the diary, we have no way of sending you back. And if you don't go back who knows if I'll even ever be born? This is my *fate* we're talking about here! I expect I'll start disappearing soon, like the people in Marty McFly's family snapshot in *Back to the Future*!"

Okay. Maybe she had a valid point. Still, there had to be a way forward. A way out of this mess.

"But ... you guys have read it, right?" Clare glanced back and forth between Piper and Ashbourne. "The diary? You know what it says. You can just tell us and we can take it from there. Right?"

"Not ... well, not exactly." Ashbourne shrugged helplessly.

Clare felt her fists clenching in frustration.

"There are ... things. Symbols and such." The archaeologist struggled to explain. He looked at Milo. "Things Morholt wrote that only a Druid would understand."

"A Druid? Milo? *You* read it. Right?" Clare said. "And ... and you know Druish. We just established that. You have knowledge. What things did Morholt write?"

"I only had the chance to skim the thing, Clare." Milo shook his head, glaring flatly at Ashbourne. "I must have missed that part."

"Who on earth would take such a thing?" Piper moaned.

"Maybe one of your stupid spoon ladies was back here rummaging and got sticky fingers," Clare said accusingly.

Before she and Piper could get into another scrap, Milo suddenly stood up. "Stop. Look ... it doesn't matter who took it or why. All that matters is it's gone and that means we're out of luck on this road. Without the diary, we'll just have to do a U-turn and find another way."

"But—"

"You said we still had some time," he snapped, cutting Piper's protestations short. "You said that according to what Morholt had already written in his diary—as of right now—Allie is still safe. And frankly—as of *right* now—I need to get some air and clear my head ..."

He turned away from them abruptly and, in three long strides, was out the back door of Piper's shop. Without asking Clare to go with him. Without even a backward glance. Clare watched him go, too stunned to even think about trying to call him back. She just sat there, confused, and feeling a little like she'd been thrown overboard off a ship in the middle of the ocean.

The whole stupid situation had Clare treading water as fast as she could, but she knew perfectly well that, unless help arrived— and arrived soon—she was going to drown. And now Milo, her life preserver, had just floated away. She turned back to Piper and Ashbourne, both of whom were—for a merciful moment—rendered speechless by the suddenness of Milo's exit.

He hadn't even taken his laptop with him. Clare gazed dumbly at the thing where it sat on the worktable, screen glowing gently. As she watched, another screen cap from Dan popped up on top of the others. Clare's breath caught in her throat. The dark, branching veins of time-travel distortion appeared to be growing, spreading out.

"You said this whole place is a portal. Is that what you meant?" She pointed to the screen.

Ashbourne blanched when he turned to look at it. "Yes. That's exactly what I meant. Your ... *shimmering*, as you call it, is restricted to your immediate person. Or, you and anyone you happen to be in contact with. Like the unfortunate Mr. Morholt. Correct?"

Clare nodded.

"This"—Ashbourne pointed to the screen—"seems to be a location-based version of the same kind of magic. Or rather, an *in*version. Instead of an individual stepping backward in time, time—these ribbons of temporal distortion that you see here— seems to overtake individuals. But the effect isn't as strong as it was with you. Nor as tangible. I've heard stories of the locals wandering through fields and suddenly finding themselves knee-deep in a bog that was drained generations ago. Or having night turn into day. One chap claims to have spotted an Iron Age fortress off in the distance. Or hearing a passing Celtic war band. Some claim to have seen the Church of St. Michael sitting atop the Tor—the whole church, not just the tower—and *that* hasn't existed since the mid–fifteen hundreds."

"Oh."

"Most of those ... encounters have, of course, been written off as the delusions of hippies in various states of psychotropic alteration. Because the time distortions are weak. They sweep on and the poor bloke experiencing the phenomenon is left with no proof of it ever happening beyond a pair of muddied shoes."

"Has anyone ever vanished *into* one of the portals?" Clare was wondering whether Ashbourne knew about Maggie's classmate's disappearance. She didn't want to mention it in connection with her aunt, though.

But it seemed Bloody Nicky was in the dark about that. He just frowned and shrugged and turned his attention back to the screen.

"Perhaps there will be now," he said. "Those distortions look to be getting stronger ..."

Most of them, so far, snaked across open fields and forested areas and down the steep, terraced sides of the Tor itself. Places where people were less likely to wander. Which was a good thing. Clare wondered how long it would be before a mailman taking a shortcut or grad students cutting through a pasture on their way to the pub got sucked into the vortex.

"Do you think this has something to do with Al unearthing your skull? With the whole 'the head is the seat of the soul' thing Milo was talking about? Do you think it triggered an increase in these ... temporal incursions?" As proud as she was for working her way through as much of the puzzle as she had, Clare silently wished Milo was still there. She could really use his brain power. And a hug.

Ashbourne nodded his still-attached head (a facet of the whole puzzle that was still deeply confusing to Clare but, y'know, one thing at a time) and said, "Yes. I do. Miss McAllister is connected to you through blood. You are connected to the torc. The torc was the engine of my curse, and the skull is my skull. It then follows. Mallora's designs were for this very thing to happen. Morholt has said she was a visionary. And she wanted to bridge the gap between her world and ours—to bring her scathach to this place and time. To take it for her own."

Clare turned back to the screen, envisioning the moment when Bloody Nicky's unpronounceable, death-dealing warrior women would come pouring through a rip in the space–time continuum to wreak havoc amongst the day-tripping busloads of New Age enthusiasts and granny cavalcades out for a spot of touristing. Hell, if they were lucky, maybe Mallora would bring along a bunch of bog zombies like her little sis Boudicca had. Because *that* had been fun ...

The spiralling areas of darkness on the screen mesmerized Clare and reminded her of the darkly beautiful designs on Llassar's creations. She thought about the deadly, cursed torc he'd made for his queen. About how it had transported Clare through time ...

"Professor Ashbourne." Clare frowned, thinking hard. Something was niggling away at the back of her brain. "When, according to historians, was the Snettisham Torc finally buried? Y'know ... *at* Snettisham?"

She could almost see him fight the urge to reach up toward his neck. And she wasn't surprised that he knew the answer off the top of his head.

*Er. So to speak.*

"Experts think it was sometime around AD 74 or 75. That's thirteen or fourteen years after the death of Boudicca," Ashbourne said. "And ... well, of yours truly."

"Why did they settle on that particular date?"

"It was found buried with a number of other artifacts, including a Celtic coin caught in the torc's coils that, judging from the designs on it, indicated that time period."

Ashbourne reached up to a shelf crammed with reference texts and pulled down some sort of archaeological catalogue that had the size and heft of a phone book. He thumbed through it, muttering. Eventually he found the entry he wanted, complete with black-and-white photos, and pointed. "See, here's a picture of the torc, catalogued shortly after it was discovered, along with the other pieces found in that hoard. Including the coin that—"

"Aw, hell ..." Clare interrupted. Muttering darkly, she reached into the pocket of her jacket. "You mean this coin right here?" She slid the tarnished little metal disc across the workbench to Ashbourne.

He blinked at it in disbelief. And then at her.

Clare waved a hand in weary dismissal. "*Yes*, that's a coin from the grad weenies' triumphal find. *No*, I'm not a klepto. Much.

That's the one you flipped at me yesterday and I accidentally put it in my pocket. I was going to return it but then, y'know, I got a little distracted here ..."

"Extraordinary," Ashbourne said, openmouthed. "This is not a similar coin. This is the *same* coin. Look, you can see that the irregularities in its edges—here and here—match the image precisely."

Piper crowded in to see. "So it doesn't mean the torc was buried that many years later, it just means the damn thing is still in play—in Morholt's timeline—right *now*."

"Right," Clare said. "Or, y'know, *then*. With Morholt. And more importantly, Al. And, I guess, you." She looked at the archaeologist and shook her head in a kind of overwhelming frustration. A feeling of defeat, almost galactic in proportion, descended like a heavy fog. "Damn it. When we beat Boudicca we didn't end *any*thing about that stupid curse! We didn't *finish* it."

"It would appear not," Ashbourne agreed, still looking a bit gobsmacked.

"It's like the torc is some kind of temporal monkey wrench," Clare continued. "When I stranded Morholt back there with the thing I thought it was near Snettisham—I travelled part of the way back with him and I could smell the sea—and I figured he probably just buried the thing right away. I thought *that* was how it got there in the first place."

But it wasn't, obviously. Clare had made a terrible mistake. The smell of the sea hadn't been the Norfolk coast, it had been the strait separating the Welsh coast from Mona. The Druid Isle. She thought back to her vision/dream/thingy and pieced it together anew: when Clare had unwittingly left Morholt and his dangerous booty stranded in the past, she'd left him near Mona in easy reach of the Druiddyn, who then took the cursed gold and gave it to the sorceress Mallora, who cursed it even more.

And then wrapped it around Quintus Phoenius Postumus's neck.

"It was your friend Allie, Miss Reid," the ex–Roman commander explained, "who told me what must be done in order to finally break the torc's curse." He shrugged. "At least, she will. Of course, *you'll* have to tell her first. After *I* tell *you* what *she* told me, that is."

"Okay—BOOM!" Clare exclaimed, flinging her hands out from either side of her head like her brains had just kablooeyed out her ears. Which, to be fair, they might have a little bit. "You know?" She smiled acidly at Goggles and Bloody Nicky. "I thought I was getting pretty good at doing the whole follow-the-bouncing-ball thing where time travel is concerned, but ... what the *hell*? How am I supposed to tell Al anything? And how is she ... and then you ... aargh! I don't ... I can't even ..."

Ashbourne waited patiently for Clare to cycle through her mini-meltdown.

Finally she dropped her head in her hands, infinitely weary. "Okay. Fine. Hit me. What did Al tell you to tell me to tell her so she can tell you what to do because you told me to tell her so?"

Ashbourne told her.

And Clare thought she might just have to go barf in the back alley again.

*Right. The beheading thing ...* She swallowed against the sick feeling clawing up her throat. "There's really no other way?"

"I don't see how. For every one of my men who dies at the foot of Ynys Wyddryn, that's one step closer to the doorway opening. And one more brave legionnaire dead," Ashbourne added grimly. "The only way to break the curse that torments my men—and powers the widening portal—is to shut off the life force feeding the torc's magic. Mine. You, Clare, conveyed that information to Miss McAllister, and she in turn convinced me to order one of my men to cut my head off on top of Glastonbury Tor. At least, that's what happened before. With the diary gone and no way for you to get to her, I don't know what will happen now."

Clare stared at him, horrified by the idea that he would have to make—had already *made*—that sacrifice. She'd always thought the Romans were selfish. But what he proposed was an act of extreme selflessness. And unfathomable courage. She shook her head. "One thing I don't get. This Mallora chick. If she was Boudicca's older sister, how come no one's ever heard of her?"

Ashbourne laughed mirthlessly. "The Roman historians would not dare to even commit her name to record. But I can confirm that she held the highest of high offices amongst the Druiddyn during the time when the Romans were sacking Mona and decimating the Iceni. She was a priestess unparalleled. A seeress and a sorceress. And not one to be trifled with. Unless, apparently, you were Piper's ancestor. This Stuart Morholt of yours had rather a grand old time trifling with—"

"Gah! Stop." Clare put her hands over her ears. "I know. I heard. I'm scarred for life."

Ashbourne was still toying with the tarnished coin in his hand, and Clare found her attention returning to it. There was a question that neither Piper nor Nicky had managed to ask yet. Clare couldn't blame them. It took some getting used to, thinking in terms of temporal loops, but she'd obviously had some experience. And so, plucking the coin from Ashbourne's fingers, she asked the question for them.

"So, if this coin is the one they found with the torc, and I'm sitting with it right here and now, then that means only one thing." She felt herself smiling, even though she had no rational solutions to their current problems: namely, how to go back in time, find Al, save Al, have Al give Quintus Postumus instructions on how to break the curse (Clare widely circumnavigated the decapitative practicalities of that), and make sure the torc got buried good and proper this time. In Snettisham, where it was supposed to be.

"What one thing can that mean?" Piper prompted when she got tired of waiting for Clare to finish.

*Gawd,* Clare thought. *I miss Al so much.* Goggles was a disappointing step down in sidekickery. She rolled her eyes at the other girl.

"It means," she said, as if explaining to a six-year-old, "that we're still in the game. We may have lost the diary but *somehow* the coin goes back. Which means that whoever has the coin in their possession goes back. I have the coin. And that someone is going to be me."

She pocketed the coin and closed Milo's laptop, tucking it under her arm.

"I just haven't quite figured out how ... yet."

## 17

Whate the hell was Marcus doing in the river? He was supposed to be yukking it up in the mess hall with his returned-
from-the-dead praefect. If he'd wanted to tidy up first, there were
dozens of places along the riverbank he could have chosen. Places
that weren't directly in the path of Allie's escape route.

*Seriously. This guy is easily the most infuriating human being I
have ever met.*

Also, very possibly the most ... stunningly handsome and ...
sculpted ...

Allie clapped a hand over her eyes as Marcus, with his back to
her, suddenly stood in the shallow water and waded ashore just
downstream of where she crouched, hidden from view, in a stand
of long grass. But she wasn't quite fast enough, and the image of
his naked, muscled torso and legs, not to mention his ridiculously
chiselled backside, was already burned into her brain. She thought
of the one and only time she'd seen male buttocks that hadn't
belonged to a toddler—when her brothers had thrown her into the
guys' locker room at school after football practice for a joke—but,
really? No comparison. None.

Somehow her fingers slipped and she accidentally snuck
another peek.

*Now* that *is what I call a tight end*, she thought.

And then felt herself blushing furiously at the pun. This was
why Clare was dead set against puns. They were inappropriate.

The whole situation was inappropriate. Allie groaned inwardly and wrapped her arms around her head. This was not happening. NOT.

For one thing, she was not suddenly having *those* kinds of thoughts about Marcus Donatus. Or whatever he wanted to call himself. She was getting out of there and she was leaving him. Behind. And *not* thinking up cheesy puns about it, present circumstances notwithstanding. So ... what then? One accidental glimpse of Legionnaire Gluteus Maximus in the altogether and ... what? She wanted to date him suddenly? No. No, no. He was arrogant. And annoying. And bossy. He wore armour and he spoke Latin ten times better than she did. With a really stupid, stupidly sexy accent.

*Those last two things are not contraindicative of relationship potential, McAllister,* she chided herself. *Try harder.*

Okay. He was a soldier in the Roman army in AD 61. And it looked like that's how he was going to stay. So, by that logic, he'd already been dead for almost two thousand years by the time she was born. Talk about dating older men.

*No,* don't *talk about it! We're* not *talking about i—*

"Allie? What in hell are you doing out here?"

Allie cringed and opened her eyes.

"Are you trying to *escape*?"

Marcus's bare feet were planted on the ground in front of her. Her gaze travelled up his lean legs to the short length of linen he'd wrapped around his waist like a bath towel and held bunched in one fist. Just below the hollowed curve of his hip bone ...

*This was a guy who once wore a skinny leather tie,* she thought. *How?*

"Are you okay?" he asked, frowning.

Allie's mouth worked soundlessly. She kept trying to say things to make him go away but nothing was coming out. He held out his free hand to help her stand.

"Oh, for the love of— Get up. If anyone finds you out here you'll be in a lot of trouble. And so will I."

Allie hesitated.

"Come *on.*"

Allie reached up reluctantly and took his offered hand. Marcus lifted her effortlessly, one-armed, with enough muscle behind the assist to propel her a few inches airborne. And then to land really—*way too*—close to him. Eye level with his collarbones, which glistened with water droplets in the sun. It was like he sparkled or something, and who knew that could actually be sexy on a guy? But it was. Without all that armour encasing him—without much of *anything* encasing him—he seemed less of a pompous jerk. Without the harsh lines of his helmet framing his face, his cheekbones and jaw seemed less severe. His straight dark brows less frowning. And after his bath in the river, his short black hair was as tousled as it was likely to get and Allie kind of wanted to run her fingers through it, shaking off the water that beaded on it like rain.

But she just stood there looking up at him as he stared back down at her with his clear hazel eyes. To cover her tongue-tiedness, Allie tried to shrug casually and utter a disarming laugh. But instead what she did was jerk her hand out of his grasp and snort in disdain.

Marcus shook his head. The frown returned to his face with some gusto. The spark in his eyes turned flinty and his lip curled up in a shadow of a sneer. "Where in hell did you think you'd go once you left the camp?"

"I—"

"The countryside is lousy with hostiles where it isn't treacherous swampland."

"I—"

"Seriously. What's *wrong* with you?"

That was it. She cracked.

"What's wrong with *me*?" she half-shouted, gaping at him in astonishment. To think for a moment that she'd almost ... that she'd thought he was ... She smacked him on his broad, damp chest with the flat of her palm. "What's wrong with *me*?"

Marcus was so astonished that he actually took a half step back.

"What the hell is wrong with *you*?" Tears pricked at the corners of her eyes. "You know, I'm starting to think that maybe Clare's right about you guys. All of you. You've been here for so many years, living this way for so long, that it's who you are now. A soldier. A killer. A conqueror."

"And you expected—what?" he snapped back at her. "That some kind of sensitive nerd-o linguist was still trapped inside my hardened exterior?"

*It certainly is a hardened exterior— Oh, will you stop?!*

"You thought I'd just go all melty and forgo my obligations to the Legion at the prospect of a glorious return to the twentieth century and stuffy academia?"

"It's the twenty-*first* century now."

"Right. Where I'm a castoff. And I'm supposed to thank you for showing up to rescue me from a life of noble service to a greater cause?"

Allie snorted. "And don't forget all that fresh air and exercise you get invading the locals and grinding them under your hobnailed sandal! How exactly is that *noble*?"

That stopped him cold. For a moment. His anger seemed to dissipate a little and he sighed. "Allie ... these men ..." He waved a hand in the vague direction of the camp. "They're good men. Most of them. They're soldiers, yeah, but they're not slavering kill machines and psycho berserkers."

"Tell that to Boudicca's tribe."

"Boudicca?" He barked a harsh laugh. "Are you kidding me? The most enthusiastic killing machine around? She butchered her own people, Allie. Just for wanting to live peaceably with the Romans. And yeah, I know." He put up a hand to keep her from interrupting. "Maybe they shouldn't be here. In Britain. The whole conquering thing ... I know. I struggle with that one, too. But they do a lot of good. Roads, water, technological advancements. Things that, more often than not, have meant more prosperity to the lands they occupy. Better crops. Better water supplies. Trade. Longer, fuller lives for the common people."

"God. You sound like a recruiting brochure."

He made an exasperated sound. "I have to get back to camp. And you're coming with me. But first I have to get dressed. You can either stand there and get an eyeful or turn around and wait."

Trying desperately to cover her disappointment and look non-chalant and uncaring, Allie rolled her eyes and did a one-eighty. She thought she might have heard Marcus chuckling behind her and was glad he couldn't see her face, which she could feel had turned a vibrant shade of pink.

"What if I don't want to go with you?" she asked, listening to the sounds of him shrugging into his linen tunic and strapping on his various and sundry bits of leather and armour.

"Suit yourself," he grunted. "It's marshland on all sides of this forsaken hill as far as the eye can see. And what the eye *can't* see, hiding in that marshland, will most likely make a quick and brutal end of you inside twenty-four hours. Have fun."

*All right, fine,* said the rebellious voice in her head. *I will ...*

And so, as Marcus was busy getting dressed, she made a break for it.

In a flat-out sprint, she got maybe fifty yards away from him when the air suddenly shivered like a heat wave and Allie experienced a sensation akin to her launch into the past: a moment of strange disorientation followed by an abrupt shift from bright sunny day to deepest night. With a full moon hanging overhead.

"What the—"

Ululating cries sounded from somewhere close behind, and glancing back, Allie saw red eyes coming at her in the darkness. Then a small voice in the back of her head said ... *Run!*

She poured on a burst of speed as Marcus suddenly appeared at her side, half-dressed in his Legion gear and running just as hard.

"What the hell are those things?" she cried out.

"Scathach!" he said, arms and legs pumping.

*There's that word again ...*

"Crazed Druidess warriors!" he elaborated, ducking to one side as a trio of short, black-feathered arrows peppered the ground between them. "They're fuelled by blood magic and they live only for the destruction of their enemies—if they catch us they'll tear us limb from limb. Run! Do *not* stop—no matter what happens!"

*No matter what happens,* Allie thought wildly. *Easier said than done!*

The rapid, muted slap of Mark's legionnaire sandals on the soft earth of the goat track suddenly became snare-drum thwacks of leather on a hard surface. Allie stumbled and almost fell when the ground beneath them transformed into a ribbon of fresh-paved asphalt, coal black in the wan blue light of a crescent moon.

"The hell?!" she exclaimed. The ancient Britons hadn't exactly been known for having paved roads.

Then the ribbon of road was gone again and soft, marshy ground sucked at Allie's feet. She stumbled and would have landed on her face if it hadn't been for Marcus's strong hands gripping her by the shoulders and hauling her forward, her feet windmilling through the air before the soles of her boots found purchase again. The sky above was bright blue and dotted with fluffy white clouds.

"This way!" Marcus said, dragging her through a gap in a stand of trees—which turned into a gap in a farm-field hedgerow when they were out the other side.

Something that looked an awful lot like a utility pole appeared directly in front of Allie. She dodged to one side, narrowly avoiding an astonished-looking black-woolled sheep that—she could have *sworn*—hadn't been there a second ago. A thatch-roofed hut appeared in the distance and, off to the left, a group of horsemen on massive chargers went thundering by swinging longswords, brocade cloaks flying behind them.

Dark night descended once more with dizzying swiftness and Allie screamed again as they dove through another hedge gap and into the path of a pair of blazing white lights barrelling down on them—the eyes of a monster. Or maybe a blue Honda minivan, beeping its horn and swerving crazily to avoid running them down.

It vanished before her eyes and another stand of trees sprang up in its place. Allie could hear the howling of the warrior women. Closer this time. She poured on another burst of panic-speed and made for a street edged with a row of shops that suddenly glimmered into view. She recognized the cheese shop and the antiques store they always passed on the way to the Rifleman. A little further down the way ...

"Hey! That's my bed and breakfast!"

Allie glanced up at the darkened corner window on the third floor as she ran past. But with the scathach probably still hot on their heels they dared not stop.

"Help! Clare! *Me!* Somebody ..." she shouted at the top of her lungs. "Help! *Help!*"

"Don't stop!"

Marcus almost pulled her arm out of its socket as the scenery shifted again and a hard-flung flaming spear flew through the space between them—just above their joined hands.

Allie whimpered as she kept on running. She thought she might have seen a light flicker to life in the bedroom window. Not that it mattered—another glance over her shoulder as she ran showed her that the B&B was gone. She would have wept if she hadn't been so busy dodging impossible things.

Post office! *Duck* ...

Sudden, massive oak tree! *Dodge* ...

Dead Roman soldier! *Hurdle* ...

Thirty yards ahead a soaring cathedral shimmered into view right out of thin air. Allie could see rainbow light shining from the prisms of the tall stained-glass panels—scenes of angels and demons—and then, in the blink of an eye ... only a crumbled shell. A few ragged stone curtain-walls reached toward the sky, roofless and cradling empty air, overgrown grass growing where once there was polished flagstone.

"Allie! Look out!"

"Ow—!" Al's shoulder had slammed into a metal mailbox on the side of the road—neither having existed a moment earlier—and she spun sharply sideways, her hand ripped out of Marcus's grip. He hurtled past her, carried by his own momentum, and—right in front of her eyes—he vanished. Allie tripped over her own feet, tumbled for another several yards, and fell senseless to the ground. She lay there, pain blooming out from her shoulder in waves of fiery agony.

The sound of Marcus's voice still echoed in the misty night.

It drifted away and silence descended on Allie McAllister like a blanket of new-fallen snow. She couldn't even hear the sound of her own heart and she couldn't make herself stop holding her breath. And then, just at the edge of her awareness, she heard something. For a long moment, she couldn't think what it was. Then it dawned on her ... the distant drone, carried on the still air, was the sound of an airplane engine, coming from high overhead. She was home. Or was she? She almost didn't dare hope.

For a brief, shining instant, she thought she heard Clare calling her name.

But then, as she lay there, the dark/dusk/dawn sky seemed to fade back to a solid, normal, afternoon blue. The very same sky that had domed the world in the moments before everything had gone haywire. Back on the riverbank with Marcus. The howls of the scathach faded too, quickly replaced with another, single voice. Marcus's voice again, ragged with the harshness of his breathing, as he fell to his knees beside her and gathered her in his arms.

"Allie ... Allie!" he called. "Oh, *shit* ... Say something. Please be okay! Allie ..."

So close. She'd been so close to going home. The bitter taste of that nearness made her throat ache and she felt a single tear slide out from under her closed eyelid.

"Oh, thank god ..." she heard Marcus sigh in relief. "You're alive."

"What makes you think that?" she murmured through the pain.

"Corpses don't cry."

Carefully, he took his arm from around her torso as Allie struggled to sit up under her own power. It felt almost as though she'd dislocated her shoulder, but she could still move it, so she knew she'd be fine. At least they seemed to have outrun the scathach.

"Weren't you *listening* when I said you'd never survive out here?" Marcus asked, exasperation soaking his every word. "I told you there were things that would try to kill you."

"What happened?" She glanced around. "That was crazy. It was like multiple shimmer doors opening one right after the other ..."

"They're like ... waves," Marcus said, sitting back on his heels. "Bands of temporal distortion. I've experienced them before. Most of the soldiers in the Second Augusta have. It's one of the reasons they all think this place is haunted. The anomalies appear without warning, but usually they're barely even tangible. Not like these. And certainly not like the one that sent me—and, I'm guessing, you—here."

"Um, yeah ..." Allie kept glancing around, but the distortions had vanished like heat waves after the sun goes down. "That was close, but not, obviously, the same. Because I'm still here. With you."

"Try not to sound so excited," he said dryly.

Allie just wiped the dampness of the tear from her cheek and rolled an eye at him.

"Right. Anyway. You walk through one, or one washes over you, and you come out the other side," Marcus continued. "Back where—*when*—you started. It's just that there are pockets of weak temporal displacement. I think they emanate from the Tor itself. They're a nuisance, but usually if you just stay in one place, they're harmless. Unless, of course, you happen to step into the path of an oncoming war band or a beer delivery truck. Like you just did. Uh—repeatedly." He shook his head. "You either have the best or the worst luck I've ever seen."

"Thanks." Allie shifted and groaned in pain.

"Can you stand?"

"Do you care?"

His expression was unreadable.

Allie pushed herself up onto her hands and knees. "How come you never tried to use one of those things to get back home?"

"You think I didn't? Every time we came up this way on patrols over the last four years I've tried to find one. But I never could. They're unpredictable. And like I said ... it used to be you just walked through and came out the other side. But what just happened: that was weird. I've never seen that many at once. And the sensations have never been so corporeal." He shook his head. "Something's changed ... and I don't think it's for the better."

"It could be my friends," Allie said, a glimmer of hope stirring. Maybe they're trying to get me back home."

"Yeah?" Marcus's lip quirked up in an irritating half-sneer. "That's great. Mine never did."

Allie looked down. He was definitely bitter.

But then, maybe realizing how upset she really was, Mark gave her a sad smile. "Here's hoping they don't get us both killed in the process, yeah?"

"Maybe ... maybe if you could keep pace with one of the distortions for long enough—"

"Forget it, Allie. It's too dangerous."

"Right. The scathach." She glanced around nervously.

"No," Marcus said. "I mean in general. The scathach attack the camp itself only after the sun goes down."

"Only?"

"So far. Thankfully. But when we actually send out a patrol they appear out of nowhere and wreak bloody havoc, day *or* night. We can be out on a wide-open moor and then ... wham. Surrounded in the blink of an eye. It's like evil magic. We can't leave. If we stay hunkered down inside the walls, at least the men have the daylight hours to recuperate and regroup after the attacks. But it also means very little sleep, and the stress is starting to wear the men down." He stood and held out a hand to her. "Can you stand?"

She could. And she did. Wordlessly and without any help. And she absolutely would *not* let him see how much it hurt.

He huffed a sigh at her stubbornness. "Great. Can you walk?"

"Of course I can walk."

"Then follow me. And I mean it this time. Because if you don't, I won't run after you again. Next time you bolt, you're on your own." Marcus stalked past, heading back in the direction of the encampment. Ten feet in front of Allie he stopped and looked at her over his shoulder. "So what'll it be? Should I say goodbye and good luck now? Or are you going to be a good girl and let me save your life? Again."

She gritted her teeth, biting back the retort she knew would just get her abandoned. Marcus was pretty obviously at the end of his tether where she was concerned. Moment of tender panic when he thought she might be dead—what the hell was *that* about, anyway?—notwithstanding. In all honesty, Allie was hard-pressed to find the fault in him for that. Running away had been a pretty bone-headed thing to do. Temporal whammy waves or no. Her chances of survival out in the Somerset marshes would have been slim to none under *normal* circumstances.

"Fine," Allie muttered. "Whatever. 'Lead on, Macduff.'"

He grinned (a bit evilly), and set off at a brisk pace.

Trailing behind as Marcus stalked sure-footed over the uneven ground, Allie got a good look at the lean, defined muscles of his legs—at the way the straps of his armoured leather kilt slapped against his thighs and how the laces of his sandals tightened against his sinewy calves with every stride. Marcus Donatus had muscles on his muscles.

*Thews,* Allie thought. *This is what all those romance novelists mean when they talk about the hero's "thews." Muscles.*

There was simply no denying the fact that, irritating personality or no, the guy was positively ripped. Not in a bulgy, pumping-iron kind of way. More like in the not-an-ounce-of-fat, nicely defined, ridiculously manly kind of way. One thing was certain:

EVERY NEVER AFTER  181

Marcus Donatus *wasn't* Maggie's Mark O'Donnell. And if he ever had been? He sure as heck wasn't anymore.

*This* Marcus was Allie's very own—

*Okay, wait. Stop* right *there.*

Allie shook her head sharply to dispel any such random, unfortunately worded thoughts. Whoever this guy was, he was not "hers." He had nothing to do with her. Other than the fact that he'd taken her captive. He'd made her a prisoner of the Roman Legion, for crying out loud! Unacceptable. It didn't matter how sexy his accent—either of his accents—was. Were. Or how tanned and chiselled his features. Again: he was a ruthless Roman killing machine.

And she couldn't even imagine how that had come about in the first place.

"Hey," she said, lengthening her stride a bit to catch up. "How did all this happen to you? I mean—the army thing. Not the time-travelling thing. I've already got a handle on that part."

He walked in silence for another minute or so and Allie thought he might not even deign to answer. But then he said, "When they found me I'd been here, hiding in the forest beneath the Tor, for about three weeks. Lost. Alone. I managed to convince them that I'd served with the Twentieth—the Valeria Victrix, one of the Legions stationed in the north. And that I'd been captured by the enemy, had managed to escape, and had been running ever since. I'm pretty sure Postumus didn't entirely believe it. But he did take pity on me."

"That was, uh, good of him," Allie said, panting a bit to keep up. "I guess."

Marcus shrugged a shoulder. "Over time, I proved myself useful. I could communicate with the locals, and so he used me as a kind of emissary in dealing with the friendlier tribes south of here, closer to our permanent camp."

"Right!" Allie said. "That happened to my friend Clare. Once she came into physical contact with Comorra, she found that she could understand the Iceni language—and they could understand her. It's part of the functioning of the magic. I guess that's what happened to you, right?"

Marcus barely glanced at Allie and didn't slow his pace. "No. In fact, I didn't discover that until I'd been here for some time. The Legions aren't known as being a particularly touchy-feely bunch and I certainly wasn't going around pawing at the locals just so I could communicate with them."

So the way the magic worked *had* been different for him, too, Allie realized.

"Oh. Right," she said. "I mean ... everyone could see you right off the bat, I'm guessing ... like you could all see me. Maybe it's only Clare who's invisible when she shimmers. Because it's her going back into the past, and not the past swallowing her whole. Like it did us."

For her and Mark, it was just ZOT! and they were there. Fully corporeal in that world and time. It must have been specific to Glastonbury. But it didn't explain how Marcus could understand the Celts—or be understood by them. Allie frowned, puzzled.

"But then how—"

"Linguistics prodigy," he said. "Seven years of intensive study before I ... found myself here. When I was eight my parents realized that I was watching foreign-language programs on the telly and understanding them. I can pick up the basics of almost any language usually within a few hours of listening to someone speak it. Brilliant for winning scholarships, not so great for developing anything even remotely resembling a social life. Still ... I suppose it's what's kept me alive here. That, and the praefect."

"Right. Because he thought you were a Roman." Allie snorted. "I'm guessing it would have turned out a little differently if he'd thought you were just some random Celt. Like your Legion buddies seem to think *I* am."

"Some of the men have cause to be wary—even hostile—toward the tribes, you know. They've lost friends to the scathach. Then again ... some of them are just maladjusted jerks," he conceded with a tilt of his head. "Postumus isn't one of those. He saved my life. He's a good man. A decent one—even though it's cost him."

"Cost him how?" Allie asked, curious.

"He was left in charge of the Second Augusta when our legate was killed during the raids on Mona. When Suetonius Paulinus was setting out to exterminate Boudicca, he ordered Postumus to send the Second to help him rout the Iceni. Postumus basically told him to go to hell. He thought it was the wrong way to deal with the uprising. Said it would end badly ... and it did."

"Boy, did it ever." Allie thought about the hundreds of thousands of lives lost.

Marcus nodded. "Mostly for the Iceni, but still. It'll prove to be career suicide for Postumus, though, once Governor Paulinus gets around to dealing with him."

"Suicide ..." Allie murmured, frowning at a niggling memory. "Wait. The name Postumus ..." It was familiar. "Oh! I *remember* that guy. I read about him. And it wasn't just career suicide— he actually killed himself!" She blurted out the words before she could stop herself.

"What?" Marcus rounded on her. "No ... it *can't* be. You're wrong!"

"Um ..." Allie felt immediately terrible for having said so. She had the distinct feeling that, whoever this Postumus guy was, he'd been more than a commander to the young, lost linguist trapped in the past and utterly alone. He'd been a mentor. A father figure. A friend. "Um. M-maybe. I mean ... That's just what I read, at least."

Marcus had turned positively ashen. "Read where?"

At the gutted expression on his face, sympathy twinged in Allie's chest. But then she *also* remembered that they were talking about a commander in the Roman army here. The same Roman army that had been cheerfully responsible for the death of Queen Boudicca. And her husband and her offspring and *most* of her people. And they'd almost (accidentally, but still) killed her best friend.

*So this Quintus Postumus guy decided not to join in the fun. So what? Big deal,* Allie thought.

It didn't mean he was any better than a guy like Suetonius Paulinus. In fact, from what she'd read, it just made him a coward. Why should she feel sorry for him? Or for Marcus Donatus, who so far hadn't directed very much sympathy her way?

"Where did you read such a thing?" he demanded again.

"Um. Tacitus the historian. Actually, Tacitus via Wikipedia, but since you won't have the faintest idea what that is, let's just leave it at Tacitus." She frowned again. "Wait. You're a Latin super-geek and you don't know your Tacitus? I thought you'd have read his stuff for fun."

"Actually I read Pliny the Elder for fun," he murmured. "I read Tacitus when I was nine and he bored me. I don't remember him mentioning the praefect. I ... I can't believe Postumus would have done such a thing. *Why?*"

"Tacitus said it was because, once he saw what a success the Boudicca smackdown was for the Legions, Postumus couldn't live with the shame of having denied his troops all that glory. So he offed himself. Real noble."

"It's not true!" Marcus exclaimed. "He doesn't think that way. He thinks the whole mess was a tragedy. A bloody, unnecessary slaughter. Postumus thinks Suetonius Paulinus is a monster. And I agree with him. We all do!"

"Junius doesn't."

"*Most* of us agree with him." Marcus squeezed his eyes shut. "Men like Junius ... they think with their swords. Like I said: maladjusted jerks. They're little better than mercenaries. Governor Paulinus lauds them but Postumus has weeded most of that brand of soldier from the Secunda. He believes in the Legions as a force of peace and progress. That's why I just don't believe what you're telling me."

"All I know is that's what I've read." Allie crossed her arms over her chest.

"Do you believe everything you read?"

"Ye— Um. No. Of course not."

"The man you're talking about is not the man I know." Marcus shook his head. "He saved my life ... and then he taught me how to survive on my own. I used to conjugate verbs for fun." He laughed a little. Ruefully. "Look at me now."

She was. Looking at him. She did that a lot, it seemed.

He turned to her and the habitual hardness of his expression softened. "Allie ... I know what you think of this situation. I know what you've read. But look around you."

That meant looking away from Marcus. As infuriating as he was, as conflicted as her feelings about him were, she wasn't sure she wanted to do that. Or, really, that she was entirely capable. But okay ...

"Go on," he urged.

She dragged her gaze away from his face and looked out over the rolling landscape. In the distance, sunlight reflected off the multitude of lakes that dotted the marshy moors, lying still and serene like pools of spilled ink. To the north were the rolling purple contours of the Mendip Hills. The view was breathtaking on all sides. And this was the first she'd stopped to notice it—at Marcus's insistence.

"What am I supposed to be looking at?" Allie asked quietly.

"The future," Marcus said. "Right now this land is a wilderness. Beautiful, yes, but treacherous. Untamed. One day there'll be vineyards here. Villas. Peacocks. Peace ..."

"Sure. But at what cost?"

Marcus sighed gustily. "You just don't get it, do you?"

She was trying to. She really was ... "No. I guess I don't."

He mustered up his stern face again. It was remarkably effective in shutting down conversation. Without another word, he turned and started walking.

Soon they were approaching the main gates of the camp, Marcus's stoic demeanour firmly in place for all his stoic Roman soldier buddies to see. So stoic was he, in fact, so purposeful and unhesitating as he marched her through the gates back toward the centre of the camp, that not one of the other soldiers questioned what Legionnaire Donatus had been doing taking his captive little Druidess out onto the moors.

When Junius found them, he told Marcus that Postumus was waiting for him—not in his own tent where Allie had been chained to the post, but in the camp legate's quarters. Those were, after all, his now. What with the legate being dead and all, and Praefect Quintus Phoenius Postumus, Interim Commander of the Legio Secunda Augusta, freshly revived from his long deathlike sleep. Marcus seemed pleased. Junius, on the other hand, seemed to think the praefect was taking on airs with the accommodations upgrade. But then Junius, apparently, had very little respect for authority. Particularly Postumus's authority.

Marcus and Allie ducked their heads and entered the spacious but dimly lit confines of the tent. The praefect was slumped wearily at his desk, dressed in a voluminous toga, a fold of which he'd draped over his head and around his neck and shoulders like a hooded cloak. A single oil lamp burned on the desk, casting deep shadows.

He glanced up as Marcus saluted sharply enough to make his gear rattle.

"So this is Junius's little Druidess," Postumus said in a gruff voice.

Allie did her best to play dumb and pretend she didn't understand a thing he said. She couldn't make out the man's features under his hood and in the gloom, but as his gaze took in her bedraggled appearance she saw his eyes glitter in the lamp flame. Then he turned to Marcus, who—Allie was surprised to see—had taken up an almost protective stance beside and just slightly in front of her.

A hint of a smile might have tugged at one corner of the praefect's mouth. "Or ... is she yours?"

"We're not exactly sure what she is, sir," Marcus said.

The older man nodded contemplatively. "Junius tells me she appeared out of nowhere in the middle of a fight with the scathach."

"That's what he says, sir. I didn't see that." Marcus's voice was neutral, stripped of emotion. A simple reporting of the facts. "All I saw was the girl running from the berserkers—who I suspect would have killed her if they could have. They didn't seem to think she was one of them. To that end, I deemed it prudent to remove her from harm's way."

"A Druid trick?"

"Your guess is as good as mine, sir. Better, no doubt."

The praefect turned to Allie, the glittering gaze narrowing as he contemplated her. "She doesn't look like much of a threat. And not much of a power, either. But she might be the only hope we have," he muttered darkly. "The only hope *I* have ..."

Allie saw Marcus frown in confusion as his commanding officer glanced at the open tent flap. The praefect got up and released the tieback, letting the flap fall closed and shutting out the bustle of the camp outside. Then he stood before Allie and threw back the fold of the toga, exposing his face. The blood froze in Allie's veins as she looked up into the eyes of Professor Nicholas Ashbourne.

*What. The. Hell ...*

Astonished, she stared at a much younger, non-moustachioed version of the slightly pompous archaeologist. In her mind's eye, she tried to overlay a pith helmet and a grey walrus moustache and goofy grin, but it was almost impossible to reconcile that genial professor with this stern, world-weary commander of men. She blinked and lowered her gaze, hoping that her confusion registered on her face as fear. Around the praefect's neck was a bright crimson scarf—the only splash of colour in the tent—and she watched as he raised a hand and untied its knot.

Then he pulled the scarf away. "Tell me," he said. "What is this?"

Allie heard herself gasp and she took an involuntary step back.

Gleaming in the lamplight, the Great Snettisham Torc sat circling the praefect's neck. The golden symbol of Celtic tribal rule rested there as if he were the king of the Iceni. Just as it had once sat around Boudicca's neck.

*Right before she'd cursed it with her own blood. And Clare's ...*

"She recognizes this," Postumus said to Marcus. "It means something to her, I can tell."

"Sir ..." Marcus was staring at the torc. Clearly it wasn't one of his praefect's usual accessories. "What *is* that?"

"The physician tells me that it was around my neck when the men found me after my capture. He discovered it when he attended me here in the camp and removed my cloak and kerchief." Postumus's eye never left Allie's face as he spoke. "For my part, I do not know how it got there. All I remember from my time in captivity is a woman, fierce and angry, cloaked in feathers, chanting in front of a fire. Telling me—and her Celt accent was so thick I could barely understand her Latin—telling me that my men would die here on this hill. That our blood would soak the soil and change the world. And that it would be my fault."

"Sir—"

"Ask *her*," he snapped, cutting Marcus short. "Ask her why it is around my neck! Tell me *this*, little Druidess—is this thing the engine of the curse that plagues my men? Is that why I can't take it off? Is that why we cannot leave this place?"

Marcus turned to Allie and repeated the question in English, keeping up the pretense that he was translating into her Celtic tongue.

It was just as well he did. Allie was almost too dazed to follow what the praefect had said. Dazed and terrified. She'd seen what wearing that particular torc had done to Dr. Jenkins. But nothing in the tent was on fire yet and the praefect didn't seem demonically possessed—at least, not in the way Dr. Jenkins had been. Maybe there was still time. So to speak.

"You should really tell him to take that off," Allie said in a panic-shaky voice to Marcus.

"He just told you he can't."

"Tell him to try again. *Now!*"

Marcus relayed the sentiment to Postumus, who said simply, "I cannot."

To illustrate the point, he tugged on the ends of the torc. Allie saw that he wasn't kidding. Postumus strained against the metal, his muscles bulging, the tendons in his neck standing out like taut ropes. The thing might as well have been made of adamantium— the super-strong metal that made up the Wolverine's claws in the *X-Men* comic books—for all it budged. What should have been soft, malleable gold didn't give so much as an inch.

"As you see ..."

The torc dropped back down onto his collarbone and he let go of the ends. The two men stared at her expectantly, waiting for some kind of answer she didn't have. She had to stall. She had to figure out how in the world the Snettisham Torc had found its nefarious way out of Stuart Morholt's grubby paws and onto the neck of Quintus Phoenius Postumus ... and how and why Postumus and Nicholas Ashbourne were the same person. She was pretty damn sure that—yeah—he was cursed somehow. But she didn't know *how*, exactly, and anything she said then would probably just dig her a deeper hole than the one she was already in. There was something going on here that she didn't quite understand. Not yet. But she had an idea of how she'd find out. Unfortunately, that meant ... horror of horrors ... she'd have to talk to Stuart Morholt again.

"I don't have any answers for you," she said to the praefect, listening while Marcus translated. He spoke haltingly, as if he didn't believe her. She couldn't help that. "I'd like to go back with the other prisoners now," she added, and watched as the praefect contemplated her response.

"No," he said eventually. "If that is what she wants, then we will keep her apart from them for the time being. You may be right, Marcus. She may have no connection with the others whatsoever. She is ... different. But until we know who—and what—she is, I do not want her conspiring. Keep her where she was. In my old quarters. See that she is taken care of. And bring her to me again if she decides she has anything useful to tell us."

"Aye, sir," Marcus said and led Allie from the tent.

She could feel his cold disapproval coming in waves as he walked her back. "I don't know what you wanted me to say," she muttered as she walked. "I'm not a Druid. I don't know how to remove the torc."

"Perhaps. But you know more about all this than you're saying."

Allie stubbornly kept her mouth shut. Knowledge was power, and anything she knew might become the only bargaining chip she had. But she didn't trust Marcus enough to tell him that.

He glanced at her and shook his head. "He was kind to you. He could have had you whipped."

"Oh, well. How disappointing. No whipping!" She glared at him mutinously, not wanting to believe he'd let such a thing happen. "Because, you know, I'm all about the whipping. Yup, Allie McAllister, masochist at large. Must be why I get such a grand old kick out of hanging around you!"

Marcus blinked at her.

"What? What d'you expect from me?" she shouted. "You might be having the time of your life here, but *I* have a life *there*. Then. And all I want is to get back to it. I understand if you don't get that. From the sound of things, maybe there's a reason no one ever tried to bring you home!"

He drew back slowly, not quite able to hide the raw hurt that flashed in his eyes, and Allie felt suddenly, scorchingly, like the biggest bitch in the world. She remembered the boy's look of eager glee in Maggie's old photograph. The awkward fashion sense, the blatant attempt to fit in. To be a part of the cool crowd. She knew what that felt like. Before Clare, Allie had had no one. How dare she throw the same thing in someone else's face? Mark O'Donnell had found a place where he *did* fit in. So it happened to be as a soldier in an invading army at the beginning end of British history.

What right did she have to tell him that that made him an undesirable? Especially when the experience seemed to have made him anything but. She wanted to say she was sorry. But he'd already turned away. And she just couldn't find the words that would take back what she'd said.

She might as well try to turn back time.

Or, rather, try to turn it forward again.

## 18

So. Milo had gone AWOL. And despite her spectacularly unfounded optimism that the coin meant she'd be time-travelling again, Clare was starting to get slightly frantic. Back at the B&B, she began to think that maybe Milo had been sucked into the past just like his cousin. Swallowed up by one of the temporal tendrils that, according to the screen-cap updates that kept popping up on his computer, continued to wind like a nest of serpents all around the Tor.

And then he texted her. She calmed down—a little—but the message was cryptic and un-Milo-like:

Sorry I took off. Need to take care of something. Back soon.

And that was it. No calling her "Clare de Lune." No pop-culture quip. No Dr. Who–ism. Not even a *Star Wars* quote. So Clare used one of her own.

"I've got a bad feeling about this," she muttered to herself.

She glanced over at Milo's laptop on the nightstand between her bed and Al's. The screen caps were coming every fifteen minutes now—Dan must have set the feed on automatic. The dark swirls and blotches seemed to be forming into a pattern that started at the bottom of the Tor, at its most southerly point, and ascended in semi-regular switchbacks up the terraced sides of the hill ...

Suddenly Clare recognized the slowly coalescing, swirling pattern.

It was no longer a random series of squiggles, whiplashing out from the Tor. It was a spiral. A spiral *path,* to be precise. And just like that, Clare knew *exactly* where Milo was.

"Aw, damn!" she exclaimed. "No, no, *no*, Milo! No!" She started frantically searching for her shoes. "You need to 'take care' of something? *This* is what you meant? Argh! Stupid, overprotective man!"

The image on the screen looked just like the unseen, labyrinthine track that Milo had walked on Bartlow High Hill weeks earlier, when he led Clare and Al and Maggie on a journey through a mystical gateway and into the heart of Boudicca's tomb.

*He's trying to do it again,* Clare thought. *Without me!*

Only *this* time, in *this* place, the path would tunnel not into a tomb, but right through the walls of the space–time continuum itself. Milo must have thought he'd open up a doorway himself, walk in, get Al, and walk back out again. And for all Clare knew, he could probably do it, too. If he still had a nogginful of Druid brain, he could. And if the latest screenshot was any indication, he was already halfway there. She'd have to hurry. With one foot in a found shoe—the wrong foot, sadly—Clare glanced back at the screen and stalled for an instant, her thoughts frozen in apprehension.

Then something solid hit the window beside her head. She jumped, tripped over the corner of her bed—almost doing a header through the casement—and looked down into the little garden courtyard. Her heart leapt: a figure with dark hair was standing below. But when she saw the gleam of light reflected in twin circles—the lenses of a pair of ruby goggles—she huffed an impatient sigh.

Clare ran, mono-shod, downstairs and then hauled Piper Gimble back up to her room. When she showed her the screen-cap progression, the other girl frowned worriedly and then pulled her phone out of one of the many pockets of her cargo pants. Even *that,* Clare thought fleetingly, kind of reminded her of Morholt, with his ridiculously multi-pocketed jumpsuit. But she decided to hold that observation in reserve, depending on how much the other girl annoyed her.

"Look," Piper said, handing over the phone. "I remembered that I'd taken a picture of the last page of Morholt's diary not long after I'd first read it all the way through. The page with the numbers on it. I did it ages ago and forgot it was there. I once thought of scanning the whole diary just in case, but the binding is too fragile to stand it. Still, I was intrigued by the last page and used to try to figure it out every now and then. Never did. If it *is* a code, it's a pretty sophisticated one."

Clare snorted. "Yeah. *Or* ... a painfully stupid one. Same diff in this case, I guess."

"So I was right!" Piper narrowed her eyes at Clare. "You *do* know something about this. I thought so from the way you acted in the shop. You're terrible at nonchalance, you know."

Clare sighed, gazed heavenward, and wished the Chuck and Di letter opener wasn't buried in the bottom of her shoulder bag. Shaking off the urge, she turned the phone to horizontal view and zoomed in.

"Piper. Get me a pencil and a piece of paper."

At the top of the page, the words were still in Morholt's ostentatious handwriting:

*My master plan now—obviously—set in motion, I will commit this diary to safekeeping in the hands of Llassar, the Druid smi~~*

The writing scrawled off the page. Clare could almost hear herself saying "Gimme that!" as she snatched the thing out of Morholt's hands to write herself her coded note. Then she zoomed in on the dirt-smudged spiral doodle at the bottom of the page. But even close up it was still just a squiggle. No hidden meaning there, at least none she could decipher. Probably she'd just been trying to occupy herself to keep from punching Stu in the face. She turned her attention once more to the lines of numbers.

Beneath Morholt's truncated sentence, Clare already knew the first line: her self-instruction not to tell Milo she could read the code. Okay. So. She hadn't. Wondering briefly if that had been a mistake, she started to work through the rest of the numbers. It took her almost no time at all, considering she hadn't given a thought to the damn silly grade-school encryption in probably over a decade. If Al had been beside her she'd have made a quip that would let Clare know her best pal still thought she was a whole lot smarter than she gave herself credit for. Piper, on the other hand, just sat there silently, which kind of put a damper on Clare's sense of accomplishment.

Once deciphered, the rest of Clare's message to herself was brief and to the point:

*milo took the diary*
*trying to save al himself*
*find it in his hotel room bedside table*
*get to top of tor before path complete*
*call maggie first tell her to bring blood*

*Blood? What?* Clare wished she'd been *slightly* less cryptic with herself ...

The last line in the code had only one word:

*hurry*

Clare finished the tail on the "y" on the word "hurry" and put the pencil down, a slight tremor in her hand. She glanced up at Piper, who'd been reading over her shoulder as she wrote. The two girls looked at each other, and then looked back down at the page for a brief, gobsmacked moment. Clare reached for her other shoe. Then she reached for her cell phone and made the excruciating call to Maggie.

And then, together, she and Piper bolted for the door.

## 19

Marcus hadn't even bothered to order her manacled this time. And, as Allie grudgingly admitted to herself, there was really no need. Even if she managed to escape from the camp again, where on earth would she go? She'd wind up bog bait inside of two days. Despite her furious, less-than-kind words to him before he'd left her at the tent, she had to hand it to young used-to-be Mark O'Donnell for having managed to survive as long as he had before Postumus found him. Allie doubted she could have done the same. Three weeks? Not a chance.

As the tent flap closed behind her sentry, she sank down on the neatly made camp cot in the corner. Feeling sorry for herself, sorry for what she'd said to Marcus, and sorry that she couldn't help the praefect out of what was surely to become a fairly dire situation, she curled up into a ball and drifted off into a fitful doze, emotionally exhausted to the point of numbness.

*Clare,* she thought as she nodded off, *I know you're trying. You have to be. I'll wait, okay? I'll wait right here. For as long as I can. Patience. Virtue.*

And in the back of her mind, she could almost hear Clare's voice answer back: "Patience. Shove it. I'm working on it, pal ..."

*Okay,* Allie thought, a half-smile forming on her lips, *she's working on it.*

She must have still been smiling when Marcus woke her up after what seemed a very short while later.

"Nice dream?" he asked, crouching down beside the bed where she lay.

Allie surreptitiously checked for drool before she pushed herself up onto her elbows, blinking blearily. "Um," she answered. "If it was, it wasn't about this place ..." She hadn't meant it as a personal insult, but the second she said it she saw Marcus's mouth flatten into a line and his brows come together in a frown.

*Gawd, not again. Rude much, McAllister?*

She sighed. "Look ... I'm sorry. I didn't—"

"No," he cut in before she could really apologize. "Don't. You're right." He stood and paced a few steps from the bed as she sat up. When he turned back, his expression was rueful. "I don't think ...I mean, I haven't been very polite to you."

*That's an understatement,* Allie thought. *Manacles? Not really up there in Miss Manners's Top Ten Polite Things.*

"What you said to me ... it made me think. Which is something the Legion tries to breed out of its soldiers." A kind of half-smile dimpled one cheek, and he looked away. "Allie, forgive me. Between the two of us, *I'm* the one who should be sorry, not you. I know who—or at least, what—you are. Any of the others, Junius or the praefect ... they'd be well within their rights to think wrongly of you. To think you were the enemy. You don't know what they've been through, these men. Half the tents in this camp are empty. We can't leave this place, we can't stay. They'll win in the end. But that's neither here nor there. When I first saw you ... and I *did* see you appear, just as Junius said, I knew with one glance that you were like me. And because of that if nothing else, I should have been kinder to you."

As Allie listened, her eyes traced his profile, and for an instant she could see the shadow of the boy he'd been—a ghost-image cast over the features of the young man he'd become.

"I guess part of it was just ... I thought *I* was the only one. I thought I'd always be the only one. I never expected to see anyone from my world ever again. You were right. In a lot of ways, I *have* made myself a life here and I was afraid that ..."

"That I'd blow your cover."

"For lack of any other way to put it." His mouth quirked in that half-smile again. "Yes. But I also remember what it felt like when I first got here. The fear. The bewilderment. Even just the lack of creature comforts."

"Well, I have to admit," Allie said, "I'd probably be willing to go one on one with a scathach for a hairbrush and a breath mint."

"That's ... why I'm here now." The other half of Marcus's mouth turned up, making it a full smile—if a still-wary one. "You get used to things like no showers and no shampoo after a while, but ... it's tough. At first. I thought you might appreciate an opportunity to ... um ... freshen up."

Allie blinked up at him. This really wasn't the conversation she'd been expecting.

"I'm not staying here," she said quietly. "I'm going to find a way home."

"I know." He raised one hand in a placating gesture. "I actually kind of don't doubt that you will. But ... in the meantime, I brought you this."

He turned and Allie saw that he had a lidded box with him, like a square, shallow wicker basket. He brought it over and set it down beside her on the cot. Allie opened the lid. Inside were several folded lengths of silky cloth, dyed a rich midnight blue with an exquisitely embroidered silver border. There was also a hair comb that looked as if it was carved out of ivory or bone, some silver bangles (that would, unfortunately, slide right off her wrists, just as the manacles had), and a pair of dainty, lace-up leather sandals. She could smell lavender and saw a small linen bag that looked as though it contained toiletries.

*Soap?* Oh dear god, how she longed for soap ...

There were also a few green twigs, and several sprigs of spiky green leaves. She raised them to her nose. "Mint!" she exclaimed.

"It grows wild around here. I can show you how to make a kind of toothbrush by chewing on the ends of the twigs. You strip the bark off first and the end gets all fibrous—works surprisingly well—especially using the mint. Not exactly up to hotel standards, but it's the best I could do in a pinch."

The best he could do? Allie almost started to cry at the kindness of the gesture. To distract herself, she reached out a hand to touch the fabric. It was smooth, almost slippery to the touch; it might even be actual silk. Allie marvelled at the skill that had gone into weaving such a thing, wondering for a moment where it had come from.

"It's beautiful," she said.

"It was made in a town in Crete famous for their cloth-making," Marcus said as if reading her mind. "It belonged to Postumus's wife. He kept a few of her things for the rare occasions when she'd visit him in the camps. He always travelled with a fresh stola and palla for her—that's the long wrap the goes over the tunic dress. He gave them to me to give to you."

Allie looked up at him warily. "Is this some kind of bribe?"

Marcus laughed. "More of a gift, with perhaps a touch of incentive tucked in. I mean, yes. He still thinks that maybe you can help him. And Postumus is an honourable man."

"Isn't his wife going to be a little miffed he's passing around her stuff?"

"She's dead."

"I ... oh."

"There was a raid on their villa to the south of here three years ago. A Durotrigan band of rebels attacked the place not long after he found me. I'd met her only the week before, when I'd accompanied the praefect on his leave. His wife was a gracious lady. I think she wouldn't mind at all."

Allie blinked away the sudden shine of tears on her lashes.

"His troops mean everything to him. Allie ... if you can help him break this curse—" Marcus stopped and rubbed a hand over the top of his head. "So, yeah. Maybe a bit of a bribe. But I also think he saw that *I* wanted to do something ... nice for you."

"You did? I mean ... you do?"

"I really do. Like I said—I should have been kinder to you. Maybe I'm just rusty at talking to girls." He ducked his head. "Hell ... who am I kidding? Girls never talked to me in the first place. I have nothing to be rusty about. For that matter, guys never talked to me either. I wasn't what you'd call one of the in crowd. I guess that was one of the reasons I was so excited about joining up with the Free Peoples. For the first time, I felt like I actually belonged. Sure—I mean, they were a bunch of other weirdos and misfits, but ... it was belonging of a sort."

"Is that why you're suddenly being nice to me now?" Allie could feel her left eyebrow creeping up her forehead along with the touch of frost creeping into her voice. "Help a fellow dork out?"

But Marcus blinked at her, a look of genuine confusion on his face. "Dork?"

She stared back defiantly and, after a prolonged moment, Marcus began to laugh.

"Allie ... you're coated in mud, your hair is a mess, you're out of your world and your time and totally out of your league." He put up a hand to forestall impending outrage. "And you're *still* the coolest girl I've ever met. If you're what dorks are like in the twenty-first century? Sign me up. Take me home."

Okay. The sudden about-face was ... confusing. But, also? *Whoa.* To cover her sudden flusteryness, she shrugged, her fingers toying with the hem of the silk wrap. "I wish I knew how."

"Well ... if you're stuck here—for the *moment*—don't you at least want to take a bath and change your clothes?"

She nodded, not looking at him.

"Come on. I'll take you down to the river."

She glanced up. Amusement glinted in his eyes at whatever look crossed her face just then.

"I'll turn my back, I'll stand guard. Just promise you won't try to escape again?"

"Like you said," Allie sighed, "where would I go?"

He was as good as his word.

His back was kept turned and he even kept her safe by shooing away a curious badger that came wombling by. When Allie came back up from the river and out from behind a hawthorn brake that had substituted for a dressing room, she felt clean, refreshed, and a little awkward. Clare could have pulled off the flowy, draped garment and looked like a goddess doing it. Allie, on the other hand, had never worn anything that girly in her life. She wasn't even sure she'd put the damn thing on right, but it seemed to be covering all the important bits while still leaving her arms free and not tangling around her legs when she walked ... hopefully she didn't look like a complete lameoid.

"Uh ..." Marcus was staring at her.

She glanced down, horrified to think she'd missed a fastening or something and that all the important bits *weren't* covered the way they should be.

"Allie ..."

"Not good?" She looked back at him, at the expression on his face.

"Not good," he agreed, shaking his head. "Magnificent."

*Mag* ...

No one had ever described her in that way before. Feeling a flush of hectic colour surge into her cheeks, she dropped her head forward so that tendrils of her dark, still-damp hair brushed the sides of her face. Without a blow dryer and flat iron to give her back her sleek, techno-ninja coif, she'd had to improvise. So she'd pulled a few sections of her hair back and plaited it as best she could in a couple of little tiny braids. At least it kept some of it out of her face and left her shoulders feeling bare and cool and ...

"You look like a goddess," Marcus murmured in a suddenly husky voice.

Her. Not Clare. *Her.* Allie McAllister, goddess.

Marcus glanced over his shoulder to where the sun was starting its slow descent. "You need a setting worthy of such a look," he said. "Come on. I just happen to know where we can get the best view."

"What about the scathach?"

"Like I told you, they don't ever appear unless it's after dark or we send out a patrol. Then they spring up like weeds." He looked down at her with a gleam in his eyes that made Allie's toes tingle in the delicate sandals. "But you're not likely to be mistaken for a patrol grunt looking like that, and it's still two hours before sunset. I wouldn't mind spending a few minutes of quality time with you while we're outside the camp. Try and make up for being such a jerk earlier. If, that is ... if you want to."

Well, did she? You bet she did. If Clare could get distracted by her blue-painted barbarian babe, Allie could certainly do the same with her manly-man legionnaire.

They took it slow so that Allie wouldn't trip over the hem of her stola. Marcus held her hand, steadying her as they climbed to the top of the hill.

"So ... you really think all those songs your mom listens to are crap?" he asked her when they'd almost reached the top where the hill plateaued. Allie noticed clumps of wind-stunted trees growing here and there. In her time, there was only grass at the top of the Tor.

"Not really ..." she said. "I mean, not all of them. Duran Duran, for example, has a couple of good songs ..." She heard him laugh a little at the Duran Duran recall. "And I like the Police and U2. And some of the New Wave stuff is, y'know, a little goofy and kind of earnest, but ... honestly? Most of it's better than a lot of the crap out there today. With the possible exception of Culture Club. Those guys drive me nuts."

"I'm glad to hear you say that," Marcus said, pulling her toward the centre of the plateau. There he shrugged off the military pack he'd been carrying and kneeled on the ground. Then he untied the leather lace that held the top flap closed, dug deep into the bottom of the thing, and hauled out a tightly rolled woollen cloak along with a variety of tools and weapons, all part of every legionnaire's travel gear. Finally he extracted a small, carefully wrapped package about the size of a chunky paperback novel and started to unfold the cloth. Allie's mouth dropped open as four AA batteries rolled out. Marcus looked up at her and grinned, a mischievous light dancing in his eyes. He drew the cloth to the side to reveal the canary-yellow plastic of an old-school portable cassette-tape player he held reverentially in his hand. An honest-to-god Walkman. She'd heard about those things. Marcus popped the back cover off and carefully inserted the batteries.

"These are the last," he said, a touch of regret in his voice. "I brought a whole multi-pack of them with me on that trip to Glastonbury, along with seven or eight mix tapes. The Walkman was brand new—I'd just bought it—but I was so excited about Stuart's promised spell-casting that I never got around to putting the batteries in the silly thing." He laughed a little and shook his head.

"That's probably why it survived the trip," Allie told him.

Marcus looked up at her.

"The time travel," she explained. "I told you about my friend Clare ... she's Maggie's niece, actually ..."

That got a raised eyebrow out of him, but at least he didn't go on another rant about Clare's aunt this time.

"Yeah," Allie shrugged. "Long story. Anyway, Clare's sort of an accidental expert at it. But we discovered that 'shimmering'—um, that's what we call the time-travelling even though I voted for 'zotting' because it sounds way more retro-cool but I totally got overruled—anyway, it tends to fry anything with an active electrical current running through it. If you can take the batteries out of something you're fine. But, like, my iPod? Forget it. If I'd been wearing that? It would have been a crispy critter."

"Your what?"

"My iPod ... um. It's, well, it's sort of like that." She pointed at the Walkman. "Only it's this big." She made a tiny square with her fingers and thumbs. "And it's digital—no tapes. But it holds, like, hundreds of songs."

Marcus blinked at her, his expression falling somewhere between awe, disbelief, and maybe a little disappointment. He looked back down at the contraption in his hands.

"But I think *that's* cool!" Allie said quickly. "Really. It's ... it's like steampunk. Sort of. Without the steam. And—hey—you said it still plays. Which my super-snazzy digital device wouldn't, given similar circumstances. Sometimes low-tech is totally the way to go ..." She was babbling.

While she was babbling, Marcus stood and took a step toward her; less than six inches separated them now. Then he reached out and gently lowered a set of foam-padded headphones over her ears. It felt a little weird—Allie was so used to cramming in a set of buds—but these were actually more comfortable. Her babbling drifted off to silence as Marcus pressed the play button on the side of the machine.

The music started off quietly, building slowly as a singer—his voice airy and ethereal—began to sing. Allie recognized the tune, a song by a band called Alphaville. "Forever Young." She'd heard it before—when her mom was having one of her karaoke parties with her other weird friends—and Allie had always thought it was a touch on the goofy side. Sort of emo, all heightened sentimentality and plaintive lyrics ...

Suddenly Marcus took her by the hand, pulling her even closer toward him. His other hand went around to the small of her back, exerting a gentle pressure. Allie blinked up at him, startled, not knowing quite what was going on. Marcus tilted his head down toward her and pressed his own ear against the outside of the headphone that covered Allie's left ear. Then he began to sway gently, in time with the music, moving in a slow circle and taking Allie with him.

*Dancing.*

For the first time in her life, Allie McAllister was dancing.

All of a sudden, she could scarcely breathe. She couldn't believe this was actually happening. She'd never once gone to any of the dances at her high school—no matter how much Clare had tried to cajole her—preferring to stay home and web-surf or read. She never figured she was missing out on anything special. And anyway, Clare would invariably tell her the next day that she'd probably made the right decision and the dance was lame and the boys were all stupid and grabby or too chicken to ask for dances and what kind of joke decoration was a glitterball anyway?

*Nothing special?*

Right. If *this* was what dancing was ... it was *the* most special thing in the world.

Marcus pulled her closer and Allie melted a little into his embrace. He smelled like leather and iron. And whatever herbs had been in the soap he'd used, bathing in the river that morning—

*Oh god, I think I'm blushing ...*

Thankfully, with Marcus's face pressed to the side of hers like that, he probably couldn't tell. Unless he could actually feel the heat radiating off her skin. Suddenly it occurred to Allie that she wasn't just dancing. She was slow-dancing with a handsome young soldier from not one but *two* other eras entirely, on top of a wildflower-carpeted Glastonbury Tor under a sky laced with cloud streamers of scarlet and mauve, the setting sun a fiery crimson orb sailing low in the sky—*who needs a glitterball?*—to the strains of a song she'd once thought cheesetastic but from that moment on would never hear as anything other than the most romantic song in the world.

Marcus's hand moved from around her waist up her arm, making her shiver at his touch. He lifted the headphones away from her ears, resting them around her neck so they could both hear the faint notes of the next song. Allie thought it might have been "Time After Time" by Cyndi Lauper. Which was, she thought, a fairly hilarious situational coincidence. But then she stopped thinking anything as Marcus cupped the sides of her face and gazed into her eyes. The blazing warmth returned to her cheeks in a rush. Maybe he wouldn't notice—

"You're blushing," he murmured. "Was it something I said?"

"I'm ... I'm just ... not a very good dancer," Allie stammered. "That's all."

"I'm going to disagree with you on that."

She managed to raise a sardonic eyebrow. "You disagree with me on everything."

"I do?"

"You do."

"Then let me ask you a question, Allie." A smile tugged at the corner of his mouth. "Do you think I should kiss you?"

Allie thought she could almost hear her heart skip a beat. "No," she said in a voice reduced to a bare whisper. "Definitely not."

She was really glad he disagreed with her on that, too.

*Maybe, just maybe, life in the first century wasn't all that bad,* she thought. *Maybe getting stranded here, just like Morholt, had an upside ... Damn.* The fleeting image of Stuart Morholt nudged Allie out of Marcus-kissing bliss. She'd avoided telling him that the man partly responsible for marooning him in the past was chained up in a tent in his very own camp, but now, when it seemed his feelings toward her had ... well, altered, or clarified, or something, Allie was feeling guilty for keeping that bit of information to herself. So finally, standing there wrapped in his arms, she bit the bullet.

"Marcus ..." she murmured, and looked up at him.

*Seriously,* she thought. *He's entirely too handsome.*

"What?" he asked when she hesitated. "What is it? Did I do something wrong?"

"No! No ..." She reached up and put a hand on his cheek. "It's just ... I don't want to wreck the moment ... but I do *really* want to kiss you again."

He smiled, pleased and bemused. "And?"

"And I can't do that if I'm not being completely honest with you."

So she told him. About Morholt. Marcus stared down at her, his face blank with disbelief. Allie worried that he'd get angry again, that he'd pull away from her, accuse her of keeping secrets.

Instead ... he just laughed.

Allie felt the tension melting from her limbs as Marcus hugged her, the rumble of his laugh reverberating through the wall of his chest.

"You're kidding me," he said finally. "The stupid jerk got himself stuck back here too? And then managed to get captured? By *me*? He must have been the one in the hood trying to hide in a thorn bush when we rounded them up after that fight. I can't believe I didn't recognize him."

"Well," Allie shrugged one shoulder, "it *has* been over twenty-five years for him, remember. He doesn't look quite so much like a Russell Brand–Johnny Depp love child as he did back in the eighties."

"Russell who?"

She grinned up at him. The yawning maw that separated their pop-culture references was a gap she was more than willing to bridge. Especially if he kept kissing her like that.

"Never mind," she said. "You're not mad at me for not telling you sooner?"

"No, Allie ..." Marcus shook his head. "Like I said, I didn't exactly give you much reason to confide in me before now."

"What are you going to do about Morholt?"

"I think we should have a little chat with him, you and I," he said, looking down at her. But then his expression shifted and the amused spark in his gaze turned smouldering. "*After* we're done here ..."

He leaned down and kissed her again and Allie closed her eyes and melted completely into the sensation of his mouth pressed against hers and his strong hands kneading the silken folds of the stola close around her skin. Her arms drifted up to wrap around his neck and she tilted her head back, coming up for air only after a very long time. She felt as if she was in a dream, staring up into his face, seeing the smile—the real, relaxed, full and happy smile—curving his lips.

"We should get going back soon ..." he murmured, not taking his eyes off her and seemingly unwilling to heed his own suggestion. "It'll be sundown in another half an hour ..."

Allie noticed that the sky behind his head was already shading swiftly toward a deep purplish colour. But then she looked straight up. It wasn't darkening because the sun was going down; rather, the sky was ... *Splitting at the seams* seemed to be the best description her brain could come up with. The Tor shuddered beneath their feet, lightning flashing overhead in shades of orange and blue. Marcus looked up too and made an astonished sound when everything—the Tor, the trees, the very air itself—began wavering like a mirage.

Allie clung to Marcus, who wrapped his arms around her as the whole world suddenly started to shimmer, dissolving before their very eyes.

## 20

The breath heaved in and out of Clare's lungs and she silently cursed last year's decision to drop track and field as an elective. She was woefully out of shape. By the time she and Piper had broken into Milo's hotel room (Piper's shop had, apparently, amassed a collection of handy antique-lock-jimmying kits over the years), found the diary, and started back toward the Tor, Clare was already a bit gaspy. And by the time they hit the first of the hill's terraces, her lungs were on fire.

So, it seemed, was the top of the Tor.

And Milo, just as she'd suspected, was already there.

As the two girls had approached the hill, they'd been amazed to see a faint, gleaming phosphorescence lighting up its terraces. Well, Piper had been amazed. Clare, who'd seen the same thing happen at Bartlow during the Shenanigans, mostly just felt queasy again. The gleaming trail was the visible remnant of the path Milo had walked to the top of the hill, unlocking the Tor's dimensional portal as he went.

It had, from the looks of it, taken him quite some time. Clare's crazy New Age landlady at the B&B had told her that walking the mazy, switchback path of Glastonbury Tor could take well over two and a half hours. Milo probably had a much better sense of the twists and turns—with all that Druid knowledge stuffed up his head, he could probably see the track as if it were laid out with runway-marker lights—but still, he must have been at it since shortly after he'd sent her that text.

Clare and Piper didn't have the luxury of time to follow the circuitous path. But because Milo had been opening up a gate to temporarily connect the past to the present, that wasn't a problem. So the girls took the most direct, and significantly steeper, route. When they reached the top, what they saw was ... incredible. Impossible.

*Really freaking cool ...*

The whole top of the Tor was awash in blinding-bright swaths of shimmering rainbow light. Piper gasped and yanked her goggles down over her eyes. Clare, squinting against the glare herself, had to grudgingly admit that Piper's eccentric eyewear fixation might, on occasion, have its advantages. Then she glanced back at the dark, peaceful valley below and felt an irony-tinged moment of sympathy for all the seekers, hippies, and shamanic wannabes who were tucked away in their beds or mellowing over a pint in the pub, oblivious to the staggering amount of mystic mojo currently on display atop their beloved overgrown molehill.

She knew perfectly well that they'd have severed a limb or two just for the experience. An experience that—rather less romantically inclined at that moment—Clare herself considered more of a large-scale paranormal nuisance than any kind of spiritual awakening.

The medieval St. Michael's Tower ruin was only a faint, filmy shadow standing at the heart of the plateau. The four pillars that made up its corners were vague, transparent shapes surrounding the figure of Milo McAllister, who stood at the very centre of the square, barefoot, bare-chested—

*Wait. What? Oh, hello ...*

—with his long arms flung out to the side and his face lifted to the sky. His deep blue eyes were wide and staring and his golden hair was blown back by a wind Clare couldn't feel. There were markings on his arms and torso: swirling knotted designs painted in blue. The patterns seemed to almost writhe like snakes on the surface of his skin. They also had the distracting side effect of emphasizing the muscles *beneath* his skin.

"Whoa," Piper said, her jaw hanging open slightly. "He's really kinda something, isn't he?"

Clare suppressed the urge to snark. Milo *was* ... really kinda something. Something incredibly, intensely precious to her in that moment. She knew why he was doing this. He was rescuing Al—so that Clare wouldn't have to. But as sweet and noble a gesture as that was, for all his brains he hadn't stopped to consider the fact that, if something went wrong and he got stuck in the past with Al and no way to get home, he would lose her anyway.

Well, not if Clare had anything to say about it.

Directly above Milo's head, large swaths of sky were midday blue while others were indigo and starlight or crimson with sunset. Still others shone with the pale wash of predawn clouds tinged with pink. Shimmering, glowing cracks—like frozen spears of lightning stabbing down from the sky—appeared between the fragments, splitting the air into fractured shards of different realities.

A rumbling, shuddering sensation vibrated up through the soles of her shoes—and Clare suddenly realized that she and Piper and Milo weren't the only ones on the Tor. Other figures were shimmering into view within the fragmented realities. On one side of the plateau Clare could clearly see Al, draped in some kind of long, flowing, toga-looking thing and wrapped in ... wait.

*Al is wrapped in the arms of a tall, muscly soldier-looking type?*
Clare made a small, surprised "Uh-*wha*?" sound.

She almost called out Al's name. But right then, off to the side, another rift opened up and more shadowy figures appeared just beyond its wavering threshold. She saw a woman with long curly hair, and it took Clare a moment to recognize her aunt Maggie—how could she have forgotten the spiral perm from the 1986 photograph? And behind Maggie came eighties Morholt, striding (as much as his leather pants would allow) up the hill with his long flowy hair and Chriss Angel Mindfreak wardrobe, a corseted, overly mascaraed eighties Ceciley Jenkins following in his wake.

Then eighties Mark O'Donnell, resplendent in hair pouf and tartan, brought up the rear, along with a handful of others from the photo whom Clare had no names for. *Almost* no names for.

"Hail, hail, the gang's all here," she muttered.

She nudged Piper and pointed to one of the Free Peoples. At least he *seemed* to be from that group. He was hanging back from the rest, lurking in the shadows of the stone tower ruins—a tall man with a big beard and long hair, his face hidden beneath a wide-brimmed leather hat ...

"Ashbourne," Piper whispered.

"In yet another whimsical facial-hair disguise."

"What did I tell you about that?" Piper said smugly.

"Hey. *You* trusted him more than I did—"

"Oh my god!" Piper pointed at one of the other rifts. "*That* looks like my gran!"

Clare peered at the shadowy figure whom Piper had described as "kookookajoob" crazy. She saw a slender, angular woman in a flowing paisley skirt and peasant blouse. Her long dark hair shot through with grey was hanging in a braid down her back, but she had the same heart-shaped face and dark eyes as the goggle-wearing girl standing beside Clare.

As Clare and Piper watched, mouths agape, they saw another figure appear in Crazy Granny's rift—a vague outline of a tall man that flickered and shimmied like a television set not properly tuned to the right channel. But before the girls could figure out what to make of it, the ground beneath them shuddered again. And this time it felt as if the hill was trying to buck them off.

Clare glanced back at where Milo stood and saw that his spine was arched with tension, his torso curving like a longbow. He seemed to be caught in some kind of energy wave, his entire body wrapped in a gauzy cocoon of flickering lights. He was so beautiful Clare wanted to weep. Or maybe jump him. But his jaw was clenched and the muscles of his neck were rigid with effort. The rifts began to move across the summit's plateau toward the single point where Milo stood. In another moment they would all come together.

"What are we going to do?" Piper asked tremulously. Faced with an *actual* spatio-temporal event of some fairly spectacular magnitude, she seemed to have lost some of her know-it-all-ness.

"Nothing else *to* do." Clare took a step forward. "Time to go—"

Piper grabbed her by the arm. "Wait! If we go ... how are we going to get back?"

Her voice sounded small and thin in the gathering chaos. All its musicality was gone, along with her prickly self-assurance. Piper Gimble was clearly terrified, from her goggles right down to her boots, and Clare felt a surge of sudden sympathy for her. Maybe she should suggest that Piper stay behind.

And then it hit her.

She couldn't just suggest it. She had to *insist* on it.

Piper had asked the single most obvious question. Clare knew that once they'd gone through the portal, the portal could close. And there was no guarantee that Milo, despite whatever Druid was left in him, could open it again.

Shimmering was one thing. Apparently. Portals? Something else entirely.

When Clare had time-travelled before, she'd done it alone. Her trips had been triggered by contact with an artifact that had been enchanted, spell-cast, whatever you wanted to call it, with Clare's blood. The artifacts themselves had stayed behind in the present, with Al, Clare's blood sister, who'd been there to call her home.

*Wait ...*

The other shoe dropped in Clare's mind. Blood left stains. Rust-brown, faded by time, almost undetectable ... She started to dig frantically through her bag. Finally her fingertips brushed cool metal and she pulled out the diary tin and the memorial letter opener she'd nicked from Piper's shop. Piper glowered at her briefly. She glowered even more when Clare popped open the tin, tucked the notebook under one arm, and said, "Hold out your hand."

Before Piper could react, Clare was jabbing the needle-sharp point of the little silver dagger into the fleshy part of her thumb.

"Sonova—!" Piper yelped as a single, deep red bead of blood welled. Through her ruby goggles her eyes practically shot lasers out at Clare. Then her mouth disappeared in a thin line. "Ow."

"Don't be a baby," Clare muttered, grabbing the diary from under her arm and flipping to the page at the back with the number code on it. She peered closely at the doodle on the bottom half of the page—the slightly elongated swirl she'd dismissed as her clumsy rendition of the spiral path circling the Tor. "Sure," she said, half to herself. "It could be that ... or it could be a badly drawn interpretation of a *thumbprint*."

And the barely discernible rusty stain at the centre of the whorl just might have been an old, faded bloodstain. Never mind "might have been." It *had* to be. The minute she formed the thought, Clare sensed the rightness of it. She'd probably run out of time trying to communicate with herself—the code took a bit of figuring out—so she'd drawn the remainder in a pictogram. Of course she had. Just to overcomplicate things as much as possible and leave the widest possible margin for error. What a clever girl.

*Gawd, I'm such an idiot sometimes.*

And yet it made a kind of twisty Clare-sense. To wit: Clare and Al had once, long ago, shared blood pricked from their thumbs with a safety pin. Al had been Clare's anchor during her shimmers. The diary had been enspelled by Llassar—Clare was sure of it. So sure of it, she was going to make him do exactly that when she wound up back in the past. He could—he *would*—use Clare's blood to magic the thing up, just like the shimmer triggers that had sent Clare back in time before.

With one crucial difference. This time, it wasn't meant to send Clare *back*. It was meant to bring her *forward*. She held out the page and told Piper to press her bleeding thumb to the very same spot on the doodle as she herself must have done—or, at least, would soon—and she could almost feel an electric tingling along her outstretched arms as Piper did as she was asked. It might have been Clare's imagination, but then again ... it might not. She closed the book gently and handed it to the other girl, who stood sucking her thumb and staring at Clare in wide-eyed confusion.

"Remember you said you thought you were *meant* to discover this book?"

Piper nodded.

"You *were*. This book ... it's a link. It's the thread that ties you and me together."

"You and ... *me?* What on earth—"

"Listen. My blood was already on that page. I put it there two thousand years ago. I mean, *will* put it there. Now yours is there, too. Here and now. So I'm going *there* and you're staying *here*. And it's going to be up to you to bring me back from there—from *then*—when I need you to."

"How do I do that?" Piper's voice was actually warbling with panic now. "How will I know?"

"I ... I can't tell you that." Clare shrugged helplessly. "I'm not really even sure how it works myself. If Al was here she could maybe explain it to you, but insofar as her lack of hereness is the actual crux of our difficulties, well ... all I can say is this: Al told me she just always kind of *knew* when the moment was right. Sensed it. Instinct, I guess. And when it was, she just sort of ... willed me back."

"Sure. That's great." Piper crossed her arms, a mutinous look on her face. Her pale ponytails lifted on the breeze like wide white wings and she glared fiercely at Clare through her ruby-lensed goggles. "You and your buddy Al have a bond of friendship stretching back years and years. You just met me. And I'm *reasonably* sure you can't bloody stand me."

"Oh, come on." Clare punched her encouragingly on the shoulder. Admittedly, there was a bit of mustard behind the blow. "You're the bloody descendant of a bloody arch-druidess and my bloody arch-nemesis. That's a lot of arch. And blood. Plus, you know what they say—there's a fine line between love and hate. If that's true? Then you and me are practically besties."

"I ..."

"You can *do* this, Goggles. I'm counting on you. We all are. Hell ... in a way, you're kind of counting on yourself."

Beneath them the Tor heaved again, this time feeling like it was about to crack asunder. Milo cried out in what sounded like excruciating pain, and Clare's head whipped back around to see him spread-eagled on the wind, limbs outstretched as though invisible giants were playing tug-o-war with him. She glanced wildly back at Piper, ready to plead with her. But then Piper nodded once. Decisively. With a flash of sudden steel in her gaze.

*Good enough.*

It would have to be. Without another word, Clare turned and launched herself in a sprint across the Tor's summit just as all the rifts were converging on Milo's position. She had to gauge it exactly right—and so, when she slammed into Milo in the centre of his back, between his shoulder blades, she made sure to shove him in the direction of the rift where Al was still hanging off the neck of the soldier guy. Milo stumbled forward with a grunt of pain, taken by surprise and knocked off balance. Clare wrapped her arms around his waist, and—just as she felt them falling through space and time—saw the bearded-'n'-hatted figure of Nicholas Ashbourne grab the poufed-'n'-tartanned figure of Mark O'Donnell by the shoulders and heave him toward the converging rifts.

So *that's* what had happened all those years ago.

Somehow Ashbourne/Postumus had known he'd have to send Mark O'Donnell from the eighties back into the first century in order for events to come to pass as they had. And Clare now knew, instinctively, just *how* that "somehow" had occurred. She made a mental note to add it to her list of things to tell Al to tell the Roman commander to remember to do when the moment came upon him ... in 1986. Even though Clare still wasn't sure how he ended up in that time period.

*Damn.*

Clare felt a sharp stab of guilt at the look of surprise and fear that flashed across the young man's face just before the darkness of the storm-ridden, gale-lashed time fracture swallowed him whole. Maggie's fellow student—a poor, unsuspecting *kid*—disappeared into the past without a trace, his parents and friends left to mourn his absence in the present, and it was all her fault. Or all Boudicca's fault, or all Morholt's fault ... or Mallora's, or Postumus's ... it didn't matter. It was done. And she had to make sure that it *got* done. Her gaze lingered on the space in the fragment of the time where he'd been standing only a moment before. Postumus/Ashbourne turned and locked eyes on her for an instant, and then there was nothing more for Clare to see. The fractured sky-rifts winked out, and with her arms wrapped tight around Milo, Clare squeezed her eyes shut as everything flashed fireworks-bright, blinding her utterly.

Next thing she knew, she and Milo were windmilling across the grassy surface of the Tor's plateau. Limbs tangled, rolling and bouncing, they came to a stop only after they'd taken the legs right out from under Allie ... and the dude in the leather skirt she was sucking face with.

Clare lay on her back, gasping painfully for air and making baby seal noises as she gazed up at a sky now uniformly early-evening blue. Half on top of her, Al struggled to push herself up onto her hands and knees.

*"Clare?"* Allie peered down at her through the tangle of her dark hair. "Oh. My. God!"

"Hey, pal," Clare wheezed. She waggled the fingers of one hand, barely able to contain the smile that split her face at the sight of her best friend. Up close and in person after way, *way* too long. In fact, she thought, she might just burst into actual tears of joy as Al sat back on her haunches, grinning sardonically.

Especially when Al laughed and said, "Damn. You have *crappy* timing."

## 21

"**I** thought we agreed," Clare panted. "No punning."

"What?" Allie blinked at her. "'Crappy timing'? That wasn't even wordplay."

"I just thought '*time*-ing' ..."

"It was really more just a statement of fact," Allie snorted, rolling an eye at her epically tardy best friend while trying to untangle herself from the folds of her borrowed silk palla. Then she threw herself at Clare and hugged her so hard she thought both their heads might pop off. When she stepped back, both girls were grinning from ear to ear. Clare glanced over to where Marcus and Milo were climbing to their feet, and Allie shook her head at the look on her face.

"Seriously," Allie murmured in a voice low enough that the boys wouldn't hear. "Did *I* interrupt *you* when you were getting all historically romantic back during the Shenanigan days? Did I?"

"Yes," Clare answered dryly, equally *sotto voce*. "Yes, you did."

"Oh. Right." Allie remembered now: she'd once called Clare back from a shimmer trip only to have her rematerialize with smears of blue paint on her cheek because Connal, the woad-painted Druid Prince of Hotness, had decided it might be fun to kiss a magical girl from the future. "Well .... I guess we're even now."

"Even?" Clare spluttered in a half-whisper. "*Even?* I've spent the last couple of days worried crazy-*sick* about you and here you are, flouncing around in red-carpet couture—*good* look, by the way—

and getting all cozy with a random Roman! I had flaming arrows! How is that *even*?"

"I'll see your flaming arrows and raise you a fiery spear," Allie said. "And he's not really random. He's ... um. You're not going to believe this, but he's Maggie's lost boy. From that night. His name is Marcus. Mark."

"Uh?" That knocked Clare right out of murmur mode. She'd known she was bound to encounter Mark O'Donnell in the past because of what Nicholas Ashbourne had told her. She just hadn't expected him to look like ... *This* guy? This guy is Mr. Poufy?"

"Clare!" Allie tried ineffectively to shush her.

"This is *that* guy? The skinny guy in the plaid pants?"

Marcus ambled over to where the girls stood, smoothing down the leather straps of his legionnaire's armoured skirt. "I had a late growth spurt," he said. "Cut my hair. Ditched the pants and started wearing these gnarly leather skirts. You know, the usual. Plus four years of strength training digging fortification ditches and marching with a fifty-pound rucksack on my back. Totally beats the hell out of Jazzercise."

Clare blinked and Allie laughed at her expression.

"He has a few weirdo eighties pop-culture references you kinda have to overlook," she explained. "Also a few first-century ones. You get used to it."

"Ohmigod," Clare snorted. "Did you tell him about your mom's karaoke nights?"

Allie felt herself on the verge of blushing again as she thought about dancing to Marcus's mix tape ... "It's been discussed. Yeah."

Marcus put out a hand. "Hi. You must be Clare."

"She really must," Allie agreed as Clare tentatively shook the handsome young legionnaire's hand. "She just can't help herself."

Milo stepped forward. "Nope. She can't. Not even a little bit." He raised a hand in a kind of modified Legion salute that looked only a *little* bit like a Vulcan greeting. "Hi. I'm Milo. That's my cousin you were making out with."

"Marcus Donatus." Marcus nodded. "*Here*, that is. Mark O'Donnell where you lot come from. And my intentions were strictly honourable."

"Nice to meet you. You're a terrible liar."

"Nice to meet you, too. Your cousin's a total babe."

Milo eyed Marcus's Roman tunic and leathers. "Wicked party dress."

Marcus took in Milo's spiral Druid markings. "Bitchin' body paint."

The two of them nodded, shook hands, and—just like that—seemed to have totally understood each other and already formed the basis for a deep and lifelong brotherhood. Clare and Allie shook their heads at the mysteries of the male of the species.

When that was all taken care of, Allie was surprised to see Clare suddenly round on Milo and smack him right in the middle of a squiggly blue swirl painted on his bare chest. Then Clare glared up at him wordlessly, seemingly on the verge of bursting into tears. Milo just bowed his head a little, opened his arms, and Clare walked into his embrace.

"Dumbass," she muttered, in the tenderest of tones.

Marcus glanced at Allie, who shrugged in response. After a moment she cleared her throat. "So ... uh ... now that you guys're here, how do we get the hell home? 'Cause I assume that's the plan, right?"

"That's the thing." Clare frowned, stepping reluctantly out of the embrace. "It *is* the plan. We're just not exactly sure how to implement it. Yet. I mean ... I'm sure we will be soon. But there's a couple of things we have to do first. So. Where's Morholt?"

Allie blinked, but didn't even bother to ask Clare how she knew Morholt was in the vicinity. She just sort of rolled with that stuff now. "He's down in a holding tent with a bunch of other Celts who are due to be shipped back to Rome to become slaves. Llassar's one of them."

Clare nodded. "I know. Did he have a book with him? Morholt, I mean—a diary kind of thing?"

"Yup. Scribbling in it like a maniac. Well, y'know ..." Allie shrugged. "Like the maniac he *is*."

"Good. I need to get my hands on it." Clare's eyes tracked back and forth and Allie could see she was thinking fast and furiously. Even Milo deferred to her in that moment. "So that means *you*," Clare turned to Marcus, "are going to have to find a way to sneak us into that prisoners' tent."

He grimaced. "Easier said than done—"

"Sure, fine, whatever," Clare said with a wave of her hand. "Don't worry. You'll make it happen."

"You have a great deal of confidence in me, considering we just met."

"Al is a keen judge of character and she deems you kissable. Therefore, you're now part of the club. Your super-secret decoder ring is in the mail and Al can give you directions to the tree house. Excelsior!" Clare grinned. "Also? I happen to know that you've *already* somehow managed to sneak me into the tent. It's a done deal."

Marcus blinked. "It is?"

Allie patted his arm. "It's a time-monkey thingy."

"Has slang changed an awful lot then, in my absence?" he murmured, bemused.

Allie stifled a laugh. "Trust me. Trust *her*." She nodded at Clare.

Suddenly, Marcus glanced at the sky and the shadow of a frown creased his brow. "Speaking of time, I seem to have lost track of it. Whatever we're going to do, we should hurry," he said. "There are sometimes demons about after full dark and I'd rather not take any chances."

"You mean the scathach?" Clare asked. "Those are the scary-monster warrior chicks, right?"

Allie nodded and explained, illustrating with the metaphor she'd already devised for herself: "Think of them like a whole buncha Boudiccas hopped up on mystical Red Bull and steroids, only lacking the politeness factor."

Clare got the picture immediately. So did Milo.

"Right. And the sun's already sett— Wait …" Clare held up both hands and pointed in opposite directions. "Doesn't the sun set in the west?"

"Last time I checked," Milo said.

"Isn't *that* west?" She pointed to her left.

"Yeah …" Allie turned to look in that direction. "And, lo, the sun."

"Okay. But then why does the horizon look like it's on fire over *there?*" Clare pointed to the right.

Marcus ran to the edge of the summit plateau and looked down.

"Because it is!" he shouted back. "Damn! The camp is under attack! The scathach must have seen the rift you caused. It's riled them up. I have to get back …"

The others ran to join him, and looking down, saw that the camp was indeed besieged by a fearsome horde of howling-mad scathach warrior women. And this time, they'd brought fire. Lots of fire.

"Those are *our* bloody catapults," Marcus snarled as another flaming projectile flew through the air and slammed into the camp's front embankment. "They captured a few of them weeks ago, but we didn't think they'd ever use them."

"There's a *Star Trek* 'Prime Directive' lesson to be learned here about letting advanced technology fall into the hands of a less advanced culture …" Allie muttered.

Beside her, Milo grunted in acknowledgment. "Yup. And that lesson is—sooner or later, the less advanced culture will kick your ass with your own gear." He grabbed Marcus by the arm and pointed to the shadowed area at the back of the camp. "Is that a rear-entry gate?"

"Yeah." Marcus nodded. "But the scathach only ever attack from the front. It's like a—a sort of rule of engagement. Their twisted sense of honour."

"Okay, how is a direct attack *not* honourable?" Clare asked, bristling.

Allie suspected it was the Legion gear that made Clare prickly about what Marcus had just said. After what she'd been through with the Romans and the Iceni, Allie couldn't necessarily blame her.

"When they use their magic against our muscle," Marcus answered. "The way they fight, it doesn't matter what direction they come from. They still win. See?"

He pointed at a tiny figure at the front of the marauding sca-thach—a woman cloaked in darkness, holding fiery spears in both fists and howling imprecations at the Romans. Her words seethed and thrummed with power. Even from that distance. And the darkness and fire seemed almost to leap and twist to obey her commands.

"Mallora?" Clare asked Marcus, who nodded grimly.

"She's the chick who tried to flambé me when I first got here." Allie glared at the distant figure. "She's also Stu's girlfriend."

"I know," Clare said.

The girls shuddered in tandem.

Allie shook her head, her lip curling in disgust. "I don't even—"

Clare held up a hand. "No. Don't."

"She's the one who cursed Postumus," Marcus said.

"She's also Boudicca's sister," Milo noted.

Allie thought about that for a second. "Ah. It all sort of makes an insane kind of sense now ..."

"So. Morholt. And Llassar," Clare said, frowning down at the rampant chaos as the Legion troops struggled to drive the sca-thach back from the embankment. "Marcus ... you say they're down there?"

"In that double tent," he answered, pointing. "Third from the back gate, southeast quadrant."

"Can you get us in there without being seen?"

"You already said I could," Marcus said. "So I'm going to say yes."

"Good," Clare said and directed his attention to where the sca-thach were hurling all manner of projectiles at the beleaguered legionnaires. "The battling biker babes might just prove to be the handy distraction we need to get down there. Your buddies look like they've got their hands way too full with what's going on *out-side* the camp to worry about what's going on *inside*. All we have to do is get through the rear gate."

Marcus nodded tersely. "Done." He stepped off the edge of the plateau, motioning the others to follow as he started down the hill. Milo was right behind him.

Allie and Clare exchanged a glance. Clare shrugged and Allie hitched up the edges of her stola, tucking the silky material into the belt around her waist to free up her legs. The Tor was dotted here and there with stands of trees, which the four of them used for cover on the way down its shadow-cast slope.

"Wow ..." Clare panted when they were about halfway to the bottom. She gestured toward Marcus as he smoothly negotiated a particularly steep bit of hill, his spine ramrod straight and the leather straps of his skirt slapping against his legs. "He really is just like one of *them*, isn't he? A Roman."

"For four years, he has been," Allie said, sensing the disapproval in Clare's voice. "I mean ... think about it. That's as long as our entire high school existence. And doesn't that seem like it's been a lifetime? He's kind of grown up here. The soldiers are his friends, his brothers-in-arms ... the commander is practically a father figure to him. He's the one who gave Marcus these clothes for me to wear ..." Allie stopped on the hillside when she saw Clare's frown. "What?"

"Um, right ... I don't know if you happened to notice this, but the commander of the camp—the one he said was cursed?—is actually—"

"Bloody Nicky Ashbourne?" Allie finished Clare's sentence. "Uh-huh. I know. Weird, right?"

"Yeah ... And soon to be bloodier than expected." Clare grimaced and motioned Allie to hang back a bit, out of Marcus's earshot. "Al, when we get into the camp, you have to find him. Ashbourne—I mean, Postumus. And ... you have to give him a message. A couple of messages, actually," she added, and made a weird guilty-feelings face that only someone who knew Clare as well as Allie did would ever recognize.

"I do?" Allie asked. "Why?"

"Because you already did."

"Oh. Sigh. Stupid time paradox. Okay." Allie nodded. "What's the message?"

Clare hesitated. Allie watched her hesitate. And got a really bad feeling about what she was about to say.

Which was: "Al ... you have to tell Quintus Postumus to order Marcus to cut off Postumus's head. And then you have to tell him that, in the future ... in 1986, when the Free Peoples of Prydain climb Glastonbury Tor, he has to be there waiting for them. And when everything starts to go haywire ... *he* has to be the one who shoves Mark O'Donnell into the time vortex on that night he disappeared."

"Oh ..." Allie felt all the blood drain from her face. "Damn."

## 22

Morholt was sitting in the darkness, scribbling away, when Clare burst through the flap of the prisoner's tent and snatched the diary from his hand before he'd even realized she was there.

"Gimme that!" Clare said, just as she'd imagined she had. *So there.*

And, just as she'd expected, there on the page was the last thing he'd written, a pronouncement made in all its egotastic glory:

*My master plan now—obviously—set in motion, I will commit this diary to safekeeping in the hands of Llassar, the Druid smi~~*

"Pen," she snapped at Morholt, and he was far too flustered to argue. He handed it over without a word of protest and only a tiny bit of spluttering, the manacles around his wrists clanking as he did.

"Milo?" Clare said over her shoulder. "Can you get the chains off these people? Start with Llassar, he's the big dude over there—Hi, Llassar! Long time no see!—and he can help you with the others." She waved at the big smith, assuming he could still understand her.

Milo nodded at Llassar and hefted a heavy, hammer-axe thing they'd picked up running past the horse stalls, just before they'd split off from Marcus and Al. The plan was for Clare and Milo to round up Llassar and Morholt—procuring Morholt's diary and having Llassar transform it into a shimmer trigger—and then meet back up, topside on the Tor, with Al and Marcus. Who—if everything went according to plan—would have convinced Postumus that the only way to break the curse of Mallora and her scathach and free the rest of the Second Augusta was to sacrifice himself and bare his neck to the edge of Marcus's blade.

*Dead easy.*

While Clare rifled through Morholt's notebook, Milo raised the hammer-axe, bringing it down on the chain links between Llassar's irons and setting him free. After thanking Milo politely, the smith took up the axe himself, making quick, bulgy-muscled work out of freeing the other Celts.

Then they all stood, silent and wraithlike, watching Clare.

First, she took from her pocket the piece of paper with the code key she'd written down back at the B&B with Piper. Then, since she'd already copied it, she was able to swiftly scribble her cryptic sentences to herself in Morholt's diary, the tip of her tongue stuck out one side of her mouth as she wrote. She'd trained herself not to actually *think* about things like the circular temporal loop she'd just closed in doing so. The whole "which came first, the copy of the code or the code itself" conundrum would just make her head hurt, and frankly, she didn't need the distraction. When she finished, she drew the curlicue scribble of the thumbprint on the bottom of the page and plucked the letter opener back out of her bag.

Squeezing her eyes shut, she jammed the tip of the opener into her thumb, barked a single-syllable swear word, and blotted a drop of her blood on the page, right in the middle of the squiggle-doodle.

"That's a limited-edition deluxe Moleskine!" Morholt squawked.

"Yup," Clare nodded, sucking on her thumb. "Worth every pound you spent on its acid-free pages."

He glared at her in suspicious confusion, which she blithely ignored.

"Gimme the emergency road tin you're carrying in your pocket." She held out her hand.

The suspicious glare deepened. "What emergency road—"

"*Did* you ..." Clare took a deep breath to defuse her temper and keep from rifling through his pockets herself. "Or did you *not* leave me that diary so that I could come back here and rescue your insanely sorry ass?"

"Er."

"Right. So if you want that book to survive long enough for this moment to come to pass, then hand it over. And don't argue with me, because we both know you already do."

He did. Clare opened the tin and turned it upside down, emptying out its contents: a couple of candles, some matches in a zipper baggie (she kept the baggie), and a little leather bag that jingled a bit. Clare hefted it in the palm of her hand and could feel coins inside.

"Heh." Morholt shrugged. "Just a bit of 'mad money,' you know. And before you harangue me, I didn't steal it from—"

"I don't care," Clare said and tossed the bag to Llassar.

Next, Clare gave the tin back to Morholt, told him the exact wording of the snotty sentence he was about to scratch on the surface of it, and handed over her purloined letter opener for the purpose. It galled her to have to recite the "meddlesome brat" part, but she'd probably done that as a way of convincing her future ... er, *past* self that the thing really had come from Morholt. The same logic must have been behind the whole coded "do not tell Milo you can read this" thing. She'd written *that* so that she wouldn't, so that ... well ... so that things would fall out the way they had. Because they had.

*Stupid time paradoxes ...*

While Morholt transcribed, Clare tore the black zippered shoulder pocket from his silly suit. It made a satisfying ripping noise.

After Stu finished sputtering in outrage, Clare packaged up the diary and showed it to Llassar.

"I want you to come to the top of the Tor with us," she told him. "But first, I need you to magic up this book so that it can get me and my friends back to our own time. Can you do that for me?"

The burly man nodded his enormous head.

"Awesome. I knew you'd come through, Llassar. You're one of the good guys. Me and my friends are going home now, and this time we're going to stay there for good. After we're gone, I want you to take the book back to what has got to be the only woman in all of history who was crazy enough to sleep with *that* guy"—she pointed at Morholt—"and she'll know what to do from there. Or so I gather. Apparently she can see the future or something and already knows this is coming down the pipe. Along with a bouncing Baby Morholt." Clare shuddered. "Oh—and while you're at it, tell Mallora she can also back the hell off with the temporal incursions and blood curses and raging against the Romans and all." When Llassar blinked at her, she added, "It's not like she should be out there lobbing flaming spears in her delicate condition anyway, but you tell her. Tell her that if she or her wild women ever manage to set one woad-painted digit in *my* century, they will have me and Al and Milo to deal with. And if that happens? They. Will. Lose."

Llassar's face broke into a wide, slow smile beneath the singed tangles of his beard.

"We square?" she asked.

He frowned down at her for a moment, probably parsing exactly what she meant by that, and then nodded solemnly. Clare gave him a long, fierce hug.

Then she turned to survey the occupants of the tent. In one corner, Llassar's Celtic pals stood in a loose group, waiting silently. In the other, Milo was taking the hammer to Morholt's chains. (There'd been some half-hearted talk of leaving Morholt to his own devices, but Clare's conscience just wouldn't let her.) In another moment they would all be free to go, thanks to her blood and Llassar's Druid magic. Clare glanced down at her thumb. It still stung, and when she applied a bit of pressure, a bright red bead welled up.

Then her gaze fell on the little bag of coins Llassar held in his meaty palm. Clare thought for a second. Tugging the Druid smith by the sleeve, she pulled him away from the others and murmured one more request, for him alone to hear. Then she turned back to see Morholt climbing awkwardly to his feet, freed from his shackles.

Stu drew himself up with all the unearned dignity he could muster, upper lip curled in his customary sneer. "Right. Well done then, Miss Reid," he proclaimed airily. "I see you've followed my instructions adequately. Mission accomplished."

Clare rolled her eyes and, without a word, stalked out of the tent before she plowed him one right in the kisser.

*Mission Accomplished.*

Sure. So far. And that part of the whole operation, from the time she'd entered the tent, had probably taken just under twenty minutes. What was it Al had once said to her—back before all the crazy Shenanigans, and, appropriately enough, in Latin? Right ...

*Tempus fugit.*

Time flies.

*When you're having fun ... it sure does.*

Or, alternatively, when you're surrounded by first-century hostiles and you kind of already know what you have to do to save your own delicate skin. Not to mention your best friend's newly freckled skin and the blue-painted epidermis of the boy who was determined to save yours no matter how dumb an idea that was.

*Speaking of which ...*

Once they were both outside the tent, just before they went to rendezvous with Al and Marcus, Clare pulled Milo aside. And by the light of the scathach's fires, she called him on that very thing.

"Milo ..." She looked up into his eyes—they were sapphire and sea-deep in the flame-lit gloom, and she'd much rather kiss him just then than chastise him. "No pun intended, but ... what *pos-*

*sessed* you to pull a crazy stunt like opening up the portal without me?"

He bit his lip and shrugged. "I didn't want you to risk going back again, Clare. So I figured out a way to change that scenario. At least I thought I had. I guess I should have known better." He shook his head and stared at his feet, his expression rueful. "You seem to be the only one who's any good at monkeying with the time stream. Piper was right. It's a gift."

Clare made him look at her again. "Why did you think I'd come back here in the first place? Without a shimmer trigger, I didn't even think it was *possible*. How did you know?"

He raised an eyebrow at her. "You think I didn't recognize your handwriting in the back of Morholt's diary?"

"Oh." She blinked. "You could tell that was me?"

Milo laughed. "Don't you remember the day I asked you to write down your cell number for me—and then I had to call Allie to figure out what it actually said? You have famously crappy handwriting, Clare de Lune. And even if I couldn't actually decipher that code, I knew that since your chicken scratch managed to show up in Morholt's book, you'd gone back again. I wanted to stop that from happening."

"But ... what about the whole 'let's not monkey with the time stream' thing?"

"You changed the past once. You brought Comorra back from the dead. I wanted to be able to bring Allie home myself. Without you having to put yourself in danger." Milo's voice dropped down to a throaty whisper as he said, "Because that's what you do when you love someone. You try, more than anything else, to keep them safe."

"Yeah but I—"

Clare's brain suddenly caught up with her ears and a spectacular sort of synaptic cascade failure took place in her cerebral cortex as she processed *exactly*—word for word—what Milo had just said. All of her higher cognitive functions winked out and she just stared up at him, mouth drifting open.

"Yeah ..." Milo said, a soft smile curving his lips and a gleam of apprehension in his sky-blue eyes. "I do."

A fireball slammed into the outer wall of the camp about thirty yards away—and Clare didn't even flinch at the roar and the shower of sparks that climbed into the night sky. Scathach apocalypse or no scathach apocalypse, she wasn't going to let that moment go by. She reached up, pulled Milo's head down to hers, and pressed a kiss onto his lips until she felt her own start to tingle. His eyes were closed when she looked back up at him again. She waited until he opened them before she said, "I do, too."

The look on his face melted her heart.

"Promise me, though," she whispered. "No more saving me."

"I promise. I'll leave the saving to the professional. You."

Clare was going to kiss him again, but just then a discreet throat-clearing sound came from over her shoulder. She glanced back and saw Llassar standing there.

"It is done. What you have asked of me." He held out the tin box containing the diary.

Clare breathed a sigh of relief. Now all they had to do was get back up to the top of the Tor—and hope that Allie had somehow managed to convince Postumus to convince Marcus to lop off his Legion boss's melon. Then, with Piper's help and Clare's ability and Morholt's now-magic-soaked diary, the whole lot of them could simply shimmer away and Bob's your uncle. No problemo.

"Speaking of problemos," Clare murmured to herself, "where is Stu?"

"The last I saw of him, he was heading over the embankment with the rest of the freed captives." The smith shrugged. "I do not think he is ... right in the head."

"Oh boy." Clare snorted. "You don't know the half of it. Well, fine. If he's decided he digs it here, then here he can stay."

She almost felt callous saying that. Cruel. But honestly, the dude was just insufferable. And old enough to be able to decide his own damn destiny. She should just leave well enough alone and let him go his own way. Right ...? Before Clare could decide whether to have another crisis of conscience, the Druid smith gestured to the markings on Milo's torso and arms, where the paint had smudged and some of the swirling lines had broken.

"He should repaint the lines before the travelling," Llassar suggested. "They will protect the Druiddyn magic he carries within him."

Clare didn't know if that was such a good idea—after all, the Druiddyn magic Milo carried around seemed to be part of the problem. But if it was a part of him now, then damn straight, he was going to protect it. She was going to protect *him*. She thanked the smith for his advice and he nodded, striding back in the direction of the tent to wait for them.

Clare turned and put a fingertip on one of the painted lines. "What ... what is this stuff?" she asked. "I didn't think woad had sparkles."

"I had to use this ..." Milo grimaced sheepishly as he dug in the pocket of his jeans, pulled out a little pot of blue cream eye shadow, and handed it to Clare. "I found it at the drugstore in Glastonbury. It's not the paint so much as the symbols, but you're right. I do feel a little like one of Katy Perry's backup dancers ..."

"Yeah ... one of the ones she fell onto with her face," Clare snorted.

Speaking of faces, she figured she should probably direct her eyes at Milo's. Her gaze skimmed over his shirtless chest on the way up. Sort of skimmed. Her gaze wanted to linger on the contours of his torso, but her brain told her eyes firmly to mind their manners.

*This is* business *shirtless, not* pleasure *shirtless.*

Nevertheless, Clare was still breathing a little quicker by the time she locked eyes with him again. She unscrewed the lid of the pot and dipped her fingertip into the blue cream.

"I wasn't even sure this part was really necessary." Milo shrugged. "I mean ... the markings are supposed to be protective, but Connal didn't need them."

Clare nodded. "Sure. Connal also wasn't sending his body along for the ride when he shimmered with me into the present to help us. Just his spirit. And, for the record, I'd like to do everything I possibly can to keep your body intact. I mean ... um."

Clare, feeling her cheeks blaze crimson, forced her eyes back down to Milo's chest as she started to retrace the designs there. "Forced" being a wholly inaccurate description of just how much (very little) effort that took. She started with a spiral that began just under his left collarbone.

"You know what I mean ..."

"Yeah ..." Milo agreed, and she could hear the smile in his voice. "Let's not take any chances."

"Exactly."

He flinched a little. "Sorry. Tickles."

Clare bit her lip. If they weren't on a mission at the moment, she could have a lot of fun with this.

"Let's face it," Milo continued. "Connal was an *actual* Druid. I'm just a mapmaking nerd with a head full of hazy details that somehow managed to get me this far."

Clare stopped drawing and blinked up at him. "And when does a mapmaking nerd find *this* much time to go to the gym?" She poked one of his pectoral muscles.

That made it Milo's turn to blush. "Just ... draw."

Clare grinned, feeling better now that they were both slightly pinkish shades, and dipped her finger in the pot of makeup again. Then, as she looked back at his chest, she couldn't help thinking she might have to appropriate part of Dr. Ashbourne's vocabulary.

*Marvellous.*

# 23

The moon shone like a curved silver blade, its white light in stark contrast to the fires of Mallora's scathach that painted the darkness with a sullen orange sheen far below. The northern rim of the Tor's plateau was fringed with a stand of silver birch trees that were long gone by the time Allie and Clare had first set foot on Glastonbury Tor, way in the future. Now Allie stood in the shadow of those trees, counting down the moments before the horrible instant when Quintus Postumus, praefect of the Second Augusta Legion, would finally manage to goad his young protégé into lopping off his head. Because it was a "necessary thing to do."

Because *that's* what she'd told him it was. She felt pretty shitty about that.

Still. Clare had explained it to her—because Ashbourne had explained it to Clare, because Allie had explained it to Ashbourne— that this was the way it went down. And the evidence that Allie herself had unearthed in a farmer's field (what seemed like a billion years ago) was pretty compelling. One big unending time-paradox circle. It made her head hurt. And her heart. Quintus Phoenius Postumus must die. So that, just like the Phoenix—the mythical, reincarnating bird his Roman name derived from—he could live.

*Huh,* Allie thought. *"Ashbourne"* ...

Ash-born. Well, at least he'd demonstrated a sense of humour in choosing his modern name. *Posthumously. Er ...*

That was probably just a coincidence ...

Allie shook her head before she completely disappeared into a word-game morass. Mentally shying away from grim realities was all well and good, but she needed to concentrate. *Imagine what Clare had to go through with that stupid blood-cursed torc,* she thought. She turned her attention back to where Postumus stood—tall, proud, and doing his damnedest to sacrifice himself and thus give his men a chance to make it off that cursed moor and away from that godforsaken hill.

Boudicca's torc fuelled the curse.

Postumus's spirit fuelled the torc.

The one had to be separated from the other.

And Allie's erstwhile dance partner, Marcus Donatus, was the only one available to perform that deed. Allie had briefly thought about tracking down the foul-tempered centurion Junius—the one who'd expressed such contempt for his commander—and asking him to do it instead. *He'd* have likely been more than happy to perform a little noggin-lopping where Postumus was concerned. But in the chaos of the camp, Allie and Marcus had only just managed to find the commander—who'd been on his way to the gate to rally the men—and convince him of the need to head in the other direction.

"Why?" he'd asked Marcus, glancing suspiciously at Allie where she stood in the Roman finery he'd provided for her. "What kind of sorcery is this?"

Of course, Allie's messy, cheese-grater-accented Latin (as Marcus had so delicately put it) was in no way sufficient to communicate with the praefect. So, sorcery to the rescue, she'd just lunged forward and grabbed Postumus's arm. The physical contact activated the blood-magic linguistic bond and, after an electrifying jolt that sent them both staggering, she could speak directly to the Roman commander in English and have him understand her. It was an impressive enough display that Allie had his full attention from that moment on. Which led, in fairly short order, to the three of them standing together on top of the hill.

Waiting for Marcus to execute his duties. In the gravest sense of the word.

Only, it seemed he couldn't bring himself to follow the order. The sensitive nerdo-linguist really *did* still hide beneath the hardened Roman exterior. Even though Allie had explained to him that somehow, through a kind of temporal sleight-of-hand that had yet to reveal itself, Postumus *still* wound up in the twenty-first century, rolling merrily along with a pith helmet perched at a jaunty angle on his still-attached head.

Her assurances hadn't made it any easier for him.

So Postumus decided to make it hard on him, in the hope that Marcus's Legion training would kick in and take over. Allie winced at the excruciating exchange.

"What kind of a soldier are you?" Postumus snarled through clenched teeth, his helmet lying on the ground and his neck bared for the blow from Marcus's sword.

Marcus blanched. "Don't make me do this, Quintus ..."

"Is this what I taught you?" the praefect snapped, the words spitting like bullets from a gun out of his mouth. "Cowardice? Weakness? Compassion instead of necessity?"

*He does the whole hard-ass act really well,* Allie thought.

"You shame me!" he goaded Marcus mercilessly. "Do what must be done."

Marcus shook his head in desperation. "No! There has to be another way ..."

There wasn't. They were running—quite literally—out of time. And options.

Allie knew it the second she saw Clare and Milo, with Llassar close behind, running for all they were worth as they crested the edge of the hill plateau off to her right. She knew it because Clare was wildly waving her arms. And screaming.

In another second, Allie saw just *why* Clare was running and waving and screaming. To her left, Stuart Morholt was stumbling and gasping his way across the plateau from the opposite direction. At his side, eyes blazing, face bone-white within the cowl of her raven-feathered cloak, stalked the Druid high priestess, Mallora. And she was chanting.

*Oh, like things aren't bad enough!* Allie thought as she spun around to see Postumus and Marcus still arguing, oblivious to the approaching Druid peril ...

And *then* things got even worse.

Because, not only was the sky beginning to do that weird, shattery thing again, but also (whether due to Mallora's Druiddyn imprecations, Clare's now-magic-fuelled diary, the torc around the praefect's neck, or some kind of overall mystical circuitry overload) the shattery bits were looking grim and angry. In one of them, Allie thought she could see a waiting horde of scathach.

She started to run for Marcus, shouting "Now or never!"

And it was. Because if he didn't break the curse in the next few seconds, they'd all have every never *after* that—for who knows how long—to contemplate the repercussions.

"Quintus—for the love of the gods—at least turn your back on me so I don't have to see your face!" Marcus hissed through clenched teeth.

Postumus nodded grimly and spun on his heel. Head high, spine arrow-straight, he closed his eyes and held his breath. Marcus drew back his sword. He glanced over at Allie, almost pleading for her to tell him there was something else to be done.

The thing was ... there wasn't.

Ribbons of temporal distortion were rippling across the hill now, whiplashing the air all around them. Postumus, in an act of supreme bravery that turned him almost blue in the face, screamed "DO IT! That is an *ORDER!*"

Allie turned away and covered her eyes. She heard the sword slice clean through the neck of the Roman commander—a sickening, meaty sound—and she heard the muted *thump-thump-thump* of Postumus's head as it bounced down the hillside ... where it would ultimately come to rest, buried in a field, waiting for her to find it in a couple of thousand years.

And then she heard an unfamiliar, ice-cold voice.

"*Never* defy the direct order of a superior officer, boy."

CLARE HAD SHOUTED A WARNING no one could hear over the chaos of the temporal rifts. A handful of Roman soldiers—led by a tall, harsh-featured man in an ornate, red-plumed helmet—had suddenly emerged out of the trees behind Al and Marcus and Postumus. The moment seemed to stretch out, twisting and distorting before her eyes, as the helmeted man drew his sword, stepped forward, and struck Quintus Postumus's head from his shoulders.

Clare flinched, throwing a hand up to hide her eyes. Then she heard what the man said to Marcus and knew instantly who it was.

*Gaius Suetonius Paulinus.*

Come from his bloody successes in the east to exact a vicious revenge on the man who'd dared to defy his horrible orders, refusing to follow him into battle against the Iceni rebel queen. When Clare was able to look again, her gaze fell on something ... impossible.

The praefect's headless body lay slumped at the feet of a horrified Marcus Donatus. And *another* Quintus Postumus stood frozen, suspended in a crackling, flickering temporal rift, head still firmly attached to neck, eyes wide in surprise.

Al's mouth was open wide in astonishment or a silent scream—Clare couldn't tell.

And further off in that same rift, Clare could see the paisley-skirted figure of Piper's grandmother, looking just as surprised as Postumus.

In the current slice of time Clare occupied, the great golden torc slipped from the stump of Postumus's neck and fell on its side in a widening pool of blood that looked black in the moonlight. A moment later, the time rifts wavered like mirages and disappeared, leaving behind only the fading screams of a pack of frustrated scathach. Screams echoed by the thwarted Druidess Mallora.

*Okaaay ...*

At least now Clare knew how Postumus managed to survive his beheading long enough to become Nicholas Ashbourne. He'd quite literally been in two places at once when Paulinus had struck his blow. And the coincidence of Piper's weirdo granny wandering around on the Tor at the exact same time struck Clare as not a coincidence at all. She too, after all, had been a descendant of the same Druidess who now stood screaming bloody murder, hurling all sorts of vile epithets in her ancient language.

*Speaking of Piper,* Clare thought, glancing up at the star-spattered sky, *now would be a good time, Goggles ...*

Clare and Milo jogged up beside Al. The two girls hugged briefly.

"That was weird," Al said, gesturing at where the spatio-temporal rift had vanished. "Weird*er.* Than usual."

"Yeah," Clare panted.

"Who was that woman I saw?"

"Grandmother of our helper birdie back in Glastonbury. A girl named Goggles." Clare scanned the sky again. "She's gonna call us home any second now."

Al blinked. "I've been replaced?"

"You can't *replace* her!" Marcus said, stepping forward. "She's amazing."

Clare glanced at him, startled by the fierceness of his tone.

"Al's not being replaced," she said.

"I'm not?" Al looked at Clare. "Wait." She looked at Marcus. "I'm *what*?"

"You're *amazing.*" He stared down at her as if they stood alone on top of the Tor. No Romans, no Druids, no corpses. "You barely know me. You don't have to do any of this for me. And yet? Here you are. Risking your own safety for the sake of a guy who was too dumb not to get caught in a time portal years before you were even born." He laughed, and it was a small, lost sound. "I never got the girl in school, Allie. I'd never have had a chance with someone like you."

Al blushed furiously and said in a strangled voice, "I'm pretty sure you must be mistaking me for someone else. Someone cool."

Clare suppressed a snort of amusement at Al's utter discombobulation. Milo elbowed her, but it looked like he was biting his own lip to keep from laughing, too.

Marcus didn't seem to notice. He just shook his head. "I already told you. You're the coolest person I've ever met." He raised her hand and kissed her knuckles. "You're magic, Allie."

Clare felt her heart swell at the expression on her best friend's face.

It was a lousy moment for the Roman governor with a bad attitude and a sword-happy swinging hand to interrupt. But he didn't seem big on manners. He'd made that pretty clear with the abruptness of Postumus's beheading.

"Legionnaire!" he barked.

Marcus turned, glared murder at the man, and executed a precise if desultory salute in his direction. "Governor Paulinus," he said in a low voice that was almost a growl. "Was that really necessary?" He gestured to the body of the praefect.

"*He* seemed to think it was." Paulinus grinned coldly—the smile of a predator. "I heard what he said. The man longed for death. No doubt bitterly ashamed of his dereliction of duty. But I confess, I do not fully understand. What just happened here, soldier?"

"*Magic* just happened here," Al said, stepping out from behind Marcus. "Magic and sacrifice and bravery. And it's going to keep happening and you're going to stand there and let it."

The governor frowned at her in confusion. Clare was about to remind her pal that he didn't speak English, not that Al seemed to care. But just then a wide-winged, snowy-white owl with huge ruby eyes swooped low out of the tumbled sky. A pale shadow on the wind, the owl drifted overhead, skreeling its haunting cry.

Clare, one fist clutching Morholt's diary, threw her arms triumphantly in the air and shouted, "Way to be, Goggles! Yes!" She pulled the tin out of her bag, swiftly bundled up the diary, stuffed it inside, shut the lid, and tossed the whole package to Llassar, who stood waiting for it. Then Clare lunged at Al, latching onto her wrist with one hand and grabbing Milo with the other.

"Grab Soldier Boy, Al!" she said as her signature shimmering began to build. "And whatever you do—don't let go!"

Al reached out ...

The owl screeched a second time ...

And Stuart Morholt suddenly called frantically to Paulinus, who stood there, agog, the sword in his fist still dripping blood onto the Tor.

"Stop them!" Morholt cried out in mangled, snotty-English-movie-villain-accented Latin, pointing back and forth at Marcus and the great Snettisham Torc. "That legionnaire! He knows where the rest of the gold is—*gold!*" He jabbed a finger wildly at the gleaming torc. "It was he who hid it on the way back from Mona! He's the only one who knows where it is! Don't let him get away!"

Paulinus's eyes narrowed and he sprang, cobra-fast, wrenching Marcus from Al's grasp just before the shimmering took hold. A scream tore from Al's throat and she thrashed in Clare's grip, desperate to grab on to Marcus again ... but it was too late. The white owl screeched for the third and last time, the night bloomed with fireworks ... and Clare, Milo, and Al shimmered away to stardust. Leaving Mark O'Donnell behind once more, in a time and place where he would remain Marcus Donatus.

Trapped in the past.

Trapped with Stuart Morholt.

That lousy, treacherous snake.

# ACKNOWLEDGMENTS

I'm so very thrilled to have been given the opportunity to continue Clare and Allie's story in these pages. These characters and their adventures are so much fun to write and I want to sincerely, enthusiastically, possibly with strange toothy facial expressions and flappy-hand gestures, thank all of the people who have made it possible for me to do so. First and foremost are the usual suspects: John and Jessica. John for his belief in, support of, and utterly indispensible creative contribution to both my life and the books. And Jessica for continuing to fiercely champion both me and my stories.

Massive thanks to Penguin Canada and the fantastic folks at Razorbill, especially Lynne Missen who took up the editorial reins on this go-around. I'm fairly certain that poking my manuscripts into shape feels like herding cats a lot of the time, but she does a fantastic job, asks all the right questions, and this story is stronger and smarter for it. Thanks to Mike Bryan for his enthusiasm and insight. And to Mary Ann Blair and Karen Alliston for time and talent and attention to the details. Thank you once again to the design department for making this book look just as good—if not better—than its predecessor. Thanks to Liza Morrison and Charidy Johnston, both of whom I've owed thanks for their unflagging support of me and my books for quite some time now. And thanks again to Vimala Jeevanandam, my wonderful publicist, for taking such good care of me.

Thanks to Matthew Skinner, Humberside Collegiate Institute, for doing my Latin homework!

Thank you, as always, to Jean Naggar and the staff of JVNLA. And "thank you," in this case, while grossly inadequate, also means that I promise I will not forget to bring another box of TimBits next time I drop by the office. You. Guys. Rock.

Thanks—also *grossly* inadequate in this case—to my family. I love you guys. Simple as that.

To all of my friends who continue—still!—to indulge me, help me, and put up with me: please continue. Also? Thank you!

To all of you out there who keep reading, and writing, and—this is a biggie, having met so many of you over the last year or two and been witness to your collective awesomeness—blogging, I don't even know what words to use to convey the depths of my gratitude and glee. So I'm just going to go with my stand-by and assure you that these two words are infused, soaked, positively stuffed with all of that:

THANK YOU.